Legal English

法學英文

| 增訂第三版 |

五南圖書出版公司 印行

邱彥琳／著

Introduction

Legal English is an essential skill for professional jurists working in an international setting. Notably in Taiwan, legal English is since 2011 a new professional subject, which is tested on national exams. In the light of these developments, the author hopes that this book might help students prepare for the national exams, but also promote their future legal careers in a globalized world.

This book introduces six legal topics focusing on contract law (Chapter 1), tort law (Chapter 2), company law and securities regulations (Chapter 3), constitutional law (Chapter 4), criminal law and criminal procedure (Chapter 5), as well as civil procedure law (Chapter 6). It thus offers a comprehensive and systematic overview that covers the broad scope of legal English as required by the national exams. In particular, the third edition of this book now also includes the legal English exam questions that have been tested on the national exams for judges, prosecutors and lawyers since 2011.[1]

Each chapter starts with a summary of Anglo-American law that explains some of the most significant rules and principles, including English-Chinese translations of basic words and phrases. The second part provides excerpts from respective laws in the Republic of China (Taiwan), which contain important key terms or are interesting from a comparative perspective. The third part encourages students to apply and practice their newly acquired knowledge by filling out certain exercises that will help them to

---

1 The exam questions and answers are available at the homepage of the Ministry of Examination R.O.C (Taiwan), https://wwwq.moex.gov.tw/exam/wFrmExamQandAS-earch.aspx (accessed 11.10.2019).

★ ★ ★

　　法學英文是法律人於國際上執業的必備能力。尤其在臺灣自民國100年起法學英文已被新增為國家考試的專業科目。就此趨勢發展而言，作者希望本書既可協助學生準備國考，並且也能促進學生將來在全球化的世界裡足以應付法律執業生涯。

　　本書介紹六個法學領域，集中於契約法（第一章），侵權法（第二章），公司法與證券交易法（第三章），憲法（第四章），刑法與刑事訴訟法（第四章），以及民事訴訟法（第六章）。因此本書提供整體性的概述，涵蓋國家考試所必要理解的法學英文範圍。本書的第三版本開始也包含自民國100年以來所有司法官和律師考試的法學英文試題。[2]

　　每一個章節首先解釋英美法中的核心規定與原則，包含基本單字及片語之英中翻譯。第二部分摘錄中華民國相關法律，特別是若有提到重要關鍵字或從比較法角度來看是有趣的條款。第三部分透過填寫練習，鼓勵並促進學生能應用新掌握到的知識，逐步讓學生熟練並記住專門術語。每章末附正確答案，既實用且有益於複習和自我能力檢視。

2　試題與答案公布在考選部網站，https://wwwq.moex.gov.tw/exam/wFrmExamQan-dASearch.aspx（11.10.2019）。

become familiar and remember special terminologies. The correct answers can be found in the last part of each chapter, thus offering a useful tool for review and self-check.

Hoping that this book may serve as a valuable contribution for legal English courses taught at universities, as well as for objectives of self-study, the author would like to express her deep gratitude for the support from Fu Jen Catholic University, School of Law, its faculty members, administrative staff, and student assistants!

　　希望本書對於法學英文教學課程及學生自主學習目標能有所幫助，作者在此謹向輔仁大學、法律學院之教師同仁以及行政人員和教學助理等對本書寫作的支持，致上最深切的感謝。

目錄 CONTENTS

Introduction
導讀

目錄 CONTENTS

目錄 CONTENTS

ANGLO-AMERICAN CONTRACT LAW
單元一 英美契約法

Definition 定義

A contract is an agreement that is enforceable by court.

- contract 契約
- agreement 合約、協議、協定
- enforceable 可執行
- court 法院

What is a contract?

Contract = agreement + enforceable by court

Contract = promise(s) + remedy

- promise 允諾、承諾、答應
- remedy 救濟

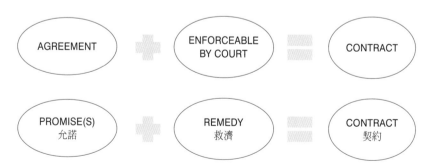

Governing law 管轄法律、適用法律、所依據法律、準據法

Contracts are generally governed by state laws (e.g. statutes, cases). A coherent overview of the most important rules and common law principles can be found in the Restatement of Contracts issued by the American Law Institute (ALI). First published in 1932 and revised in 1981, the Restatement (Second) of Contracts is an influential and frequently cited treatise in the fields of contract law.

- state law 州法
- statute 法規、成文法
- case 案例
- common law 普通法
- American Law Institute (ALI) 美國法律協會
- Restatement (Second) of Contracts 美國法律整編契約法(第二版)

Given the need to harmonize diverse state laws and thereby facilitate commercial transactions across borderlines, the American Law Institute (ALI) moreover drafted the Uniform Commercial Code (UCC) in collaboration with the National Conference of Commissioners on Uniform State Laws (NCCUSL). Article 2 UCC in particular applies to contracts for the sale of goods. Most states have adopted this model code based on its original version from 1952 or subsequent revisions.

- Uniform Commercial Code (UCC) 美國統一商法典
- National Conference of Commissioners on Uniform State Laws (NCCUSL) 統一州法律委員全國會議
- sale of goods 貨物買賣、貨物銷售
- model code 模範法典

If the parties to a sales contract are located in different countries, the United Nations Convention on Contracts for the International Sale of Goods (CISG) must be taken into account. This international treaty has the same binding force as federal law in the United States, thus taking precedence over state law, unless its application is expressly excluded in the contract.

▧ United Nations Convention on Contracts for the International Sale of Goods (CISG) 聯合國國際貨物銷售合同公約

▧ treaty 條約

Last but not least, contracts involving the U.S. government are subject to laws and regulations for public procurement.

▧ public procurement 政府採購

FIELD OF LAW	TYPE OF LAW	LAWMAKER	EXAMPLE
inter-national law	treaty	Countries "Contracting States"	CISG adopted 1980, effective 1988
federal law	statute	U.S. Congress	public procurement laws and regulations for government contracts
state law	statute	State Congress	Statute of Frauds
	model code	*ALI & NCCUSL*	*Article 2 UCC: Sale of Goods published 1952*
	case	judge	
	treatise	*ALI*	*Restatement of Contracts published 1932, revised 1981*
private law	private agree-ment	parties	contract including governing law clause

Types of contracts 契約種類

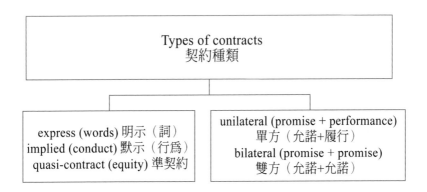

An express contract is formed by words. An implied contract is formed by conduct. A quasi-contract is not a contract in a legal sense. It applies equitable principles to prevent unjust enrichment.

- express contract 明示契約
- implied contract 默示契約
- quasi-contract 準契約
- equitable principles 衡平法原則
- unjust enrichment 不當得利

A unilateral contract is a promise in exchange for a performance (e.g. Anton offers to pay $1,000 to the person who brings back his lost dog; Anton does not want a promise, Anton wants action / performance). A bilateral contract is a promise in exchange for a promise (e.g. Anton offers to pay Berta $1,000 if Berta promises to bring back his lost dog; Anton is satisfied with a promise).

- unilateral / bilateral contract 單方 / 雙方契約
- promise 承諾、允諾、答應
- performance 履行

Contract formation 契約之成立

The essential elements of a contract are offer, acceptance and consideration.

- offer 要約
- acceptance 承諾、接受
- consideration 約因

How is a contract formed?

Contract = offer + acceptance + consideration

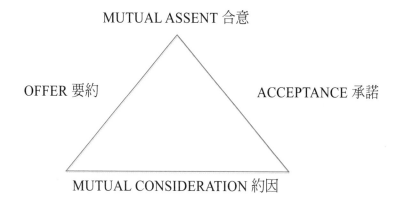

MUTUAL ASSENT 合意

OFFER 要約   ACCEPTANCE 承諾

MUTUAL CONSIDERATION 約因

Offer 要約

An offer is a manifestation of willingness to enter into a contract, which creates a power of acceptance. The person who makes an offer is called the offeror. The person to whom the offer is made is called the offeree.

- manifestation 表明、顯示
- willingness 意願
- power of acceptance 接受要約權、承諾能力

- offeror 要約人
- offeree 受要約人、要約相對人

A valid offer exists if:

1. The offeror makes a promise or commitment. Note that mere advertisements or preliminary negotiations are not offers.
   - commitment 諾言、承諾
   - advertisement 廣告
   - preliminary negotiations 初步談判、締約前商議

2. The offer must contain the essential terms, e.g. subject matter, offeree, time. But missing terms can be substituted by reasonable terms or subsequent performance.
   - essential terms 必要之點／條款
   - reasonable terms 合理條款

Second Restatement of Contracts	美國法律整編（第二版）契約法
§ 41. Lapse of Time (1) An offeree's **power of acceptance** is terminated at the **time specified** in the offer, or, if no time is specified, at the end of a **reasonable time**. (2) What is a **reasonable time** is a question of fact, depending on all the **circumstances** existing when the offer and attempted acceptance are made.	第41條　存續期間之經過 (1) 受要約人之**承諾能力**於要約所**指定之期間**終止之，或如未指定期間時於一**合理期間**終了時終止之。 (2) 何者為一**合理期間**係一事實問題，應依要約及意欲之承力作成時所存在之一切**情勢**決定之。

3. The offer must be communicated to the offeree, so that the offeree has knowledge of the offer.

▪ communicate 溝通、通知

▪ knowledge 知識、知道

4. The offer is not revoked. As a general rule, an offer can be revoked any time before acceptance, unless there is (i) an option (ii) a firm offer (= signed writing by a merchant to keep his offer valid for a maximum period of three months, see Article 2-205 UCC) or (iii) part performance / detrimental reliance.

▪ revoke 撤回、撤銷

▪ option 選擇權

▪ firm offer 穩固要約、確定要約、不可撤銷的要約

▪ part performance 部分履行

▪ detrimental reliance 不利信賴

UCC	美國統一商法典
§ 2-205: Firm Offers An offer by a **merchant** to buy or sell goods in a **signed writing** which by its terms gives assurance that it will be held open is not revocable, for lack of consideration, during the time stated or if no time is stated for a reasonable time, but in no event may such period of irrevocability exceed **three months**; but any such term of assurance on a form supplied by the offeree must be separately signed by the offeror.	第2-205條：穩固要約 由商人提出買入或賣出貨物之要約以書面作成，並經要約人簽名於其上，且該書面要約之條款明示保證其要約於約定期限內，或未定期限但定有以合理期間為期限且該期間不逾三個月內不可撤銷者，為穩固要約，要約人不得任意撤銷之。前項保證條款由受要約人提出者，應經要約人分別於條款上簽名，始生效力。

What is a valid offer?

Offer = promise + essential terms + communication

Acceptance 接受要約、（要約之）承諾

Acceptance is the offeree's manifestation of assent to the terms of the offer (mutual assent). The power of acceptance is terminated once the offeree rejects the offer or makes a counter-offer, the offer is revoked, or time has lapsed.

- assent 同意
- mutual assent 合意
- reject 拒絕
- counter-offer 反要約
- lapse of time 時間經過、期限已屆至

The requirements for valid acceptance are:

1. Unequivocal assent by offeree: The offeree must have knowledge of the offer and accept as specified in the offer (e.g. by registered mail); if the offer does not specify the method of acceptance, the offeree may use any reasonable method.
   - unequivocal assent 明確的同意
   - reasonable method 合理方法

2. Under common law, the terms of the acceptance must be the same as those of the offer ("mirror image rule"). In contrast, the UCC (see Article 2-207 UCC) provides a more flexible rule: If the acceptance includes additional terms and one of the parties is not a merchant, they become part of the contract if the offeror explicitly assents. If both parties are merchants, the additional terms automatically be-

come part of the contract, unless they materially alter the original offer or the offeror objects. If the acceptance includes conflicting terms, they do not become part of the contract ("knock out rule"), instead UCC gap fillers or common law applies.

- mirror image rule 鏡子形象規則
- additional terms 附加條款
- merchant 商人
- explicitly assent 清楚的 / 明確的同意
- materially alter 重要變更
- object, objection 反對、異議
- conflicting terms 衝突條款

UCC
§ 2-207: Additional Terms in Acceptance or Confirmation ("battle of forms")
(1) A definite and seasonable expression of acceptance or a written confirmation which is sent within a reasonable time operates as an **acceptance even though** it states **terms additional to or different** from those offered or agreed upon, unless acceptance is expressly made conditional on assent to the additional or different terms.
(2) The additional terms are to be construed as proposals for addition to the contract. **Between merchants such terms become part of the contract unless**: (a) the **offer expressly limits** acceptance to the terms of the offer; (b) they **materially alter** it; or (c) notification of **objection** to them has already been given or is given within a reasonable time after notice of them is received.

3. Communication of the acceptance: According to the "mailbox rule", the acceptance is effective upon dispatch, if not otherwise provided in the offer.
- ■ communication 溝通、通知
- ■ mailbox rule 發信原則

Examples:

Offeror sends offer > offer is valid when received by offeree.

Offeree sends acceptance. Contract is formed when offeree sends acceptance (mailbox rule).

Offeror revokes offer.

Offeree sends acceptance before receiving revocation.

Contract is formed when offeree sends acceptance (mailbox rule).

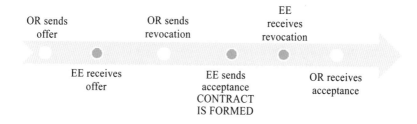

Offeree first sends acceptance, then rejection.

Contract is formed when offeree sends acceptance (mailbox rule).

Offeree first sends rejection, then acceptance (mailbox rule does not apply). Contract is formed or not, depending on what offeror receives first.

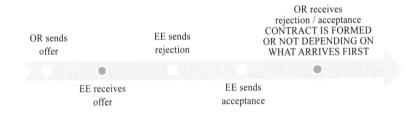

4. The power of acceptance terminates due to offeree's rejection, counter-offer (= rejection + new offer), or lapse of time (stated / reasonable time).

   ■ power of acceptance 接受要約權、承諾能力
   ■ terminate 終止

What is a valid acceptance?

Acceptance = assent + terms of offer + communication

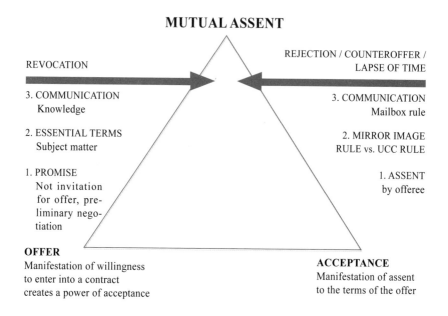

MUTUAL ASSENT

REVOCATION

REJECTION / COUNTEROFFER /
LAPSE OF TIME

3. COMMUNICATION
Knowledge

3. COMMUNICATION
Mailbox rule

2. ESSENTIAL TERMS
Subject matter

2. MIRROR IMAGE
RULE vs. UCC RULE

1. PROMISE
Not invitation
for offer, pre-
liminary nego-
tiation

1. ASSENT
by offeree

OFFER
Manifestation of willingness
to enter into a contract
creates a power of acceptance

ACCEPTANCE
Manifestation of assent
to the terms of the offer

Consideration 約因

In addition to mutual assent, Anglo-American law requires that a contract must be supported by mutual consideration in order to be enforceable. Consideration consists of two elements: Bargain and value. Bargain means that each party has a motive to induce the other party to pay a price for the mutual exchange. Value is given where there is a change of legal position (do / refrain) or legal detriment; economic benefit is not required. Thus, it was held in *Hamer v. Sidway*, 124 N.Y. 538 (1891), that "(r)efraining from the use of liquor and tobacco for a certain time at the request of another is a sufficient consideration for a promise by the latter to pay a sum of money." However, no value is given, where a party promises to do something he is already legally obliged to (pre-existing duty rule).

■ enforceable 可執行

■ bargain 談判、交易磋商

- value 價值
- motive 動機、目的
- induce 引誘
- price 價格
- mutual exchange 相互交易、交換
- legal position 法律上的地位
- legal detriment 法律上的損害
- economic benefit 經濟上的利益
- pre-existing duty rule 既有義務規則

What is valid consideration?

Consideration = bargain + value

MUTUAL ASSENT 合意

MUTUAL CONSIDERATION = BARGAIN + VALUE
約因　　　　談判　　價值

Exceptions: Certain promises are binding without consideration.

1. In particular, consideration can be substituted by detrimental reliance (promissory estoppel), where actual reliance is reasonably foreseeable.

- substitute 代替
- detrimental reliance 不利信賴
- promissory estoppel 允諾禁反言、允諾後不得否認
- actual reliance 實際信賴
- reasonably foreseeable 可合理預見

Second Restatement of Contracts	美國法律整編（第二版）契約法
§ 90. Promise Reasonably Inducing Action or Forbearance (1) A promise which the promisor **should reasonably expect to induce** action or forbearance on the part of the promisee or a third person and which **does induce** such action or forbearance is binding if **injustice can be avoided only by enforcement of the promise**. The remedy granted for breach may be limited as justice requires.	**第90條　合理引致作為或不作為之約定** (1) 約定人合理**期待**其之約定應會**誘引**相對人或第三人作為或不作為，且**實際會引致**此等作為或不作為者，其之約定於非**予以執行**不足以**避免**不公平之情況下有其拘束力。因違約而付與之賠償得限於公平之所需。

2. Contracts for the sale of goods can be modified in good faith without providing new consideration (Article 2-209 UCC).

   ■ modify in good faith 善意修改

UCC
§ 2-209 Modification, Rescission and Waiver (1) An agreement modifying a contract ... needs no consideration to be binding.

Defenses 抗辯、辯護

For a contract to be enforceable it is required that no defense exists. Following defenses can be raised:

1. Lack of legal capacity: A contract is voidable by a party who lacks legal capacity to enter into a contract (e.g. infant).
   - ▪ lack 缺乏
   - ▪ legal capacity 法律能力、權利能力、行為能力
   - ▪ voidable 可撤銷
   - ▪ infant 未成年人

2. Lack of mutual assent due to mistake: When both parties are mistaken (mutual mistake) about an existing fact, the contract is voidable by a party who does not bear the risk of the mistake, if the mistake concerns a basic assumption and has a material effect. Where only one party is mistaken (unilateral mistake), the contract is voidable, if in addition to the above mentioned requirements the other party had reason to know of the mistake or enforcement of the contract would be unconscionable.
   - ▪ mistake 錯誤

- mutual / unilateral mistake 雙方 / 單方錯誤
- bear the risk 承擔風險
- basic assumption 基本假設
- material effect 重大影響
- unconscionable 不公正的

3. Lack of mutual assent due to misrepresentation: A party who justifiably relied on the (intentional or negligent) misrepresentation of a material fact (not opinion) may use this defense to avoid a contract.
   - misrepresentation 不實說明、不實陳述
   - justifiable reliance 合理信賴
   - fact 事實
   - opinion 意見

4. Lack of mutual assent due to duress: If a party was compelled (e.g. by physical force, improper threat) to enter into a contract, there is no mutual assent.
   - duress 脅迫
   - compel 強迫
   - threat 威脅

5. Lack of consideration: In order for a contract to be enforceable, it must be supported by valid consideration. Under certain circumstances consideration can be substituted (e.g. by detrimental reliance).
   - consideration 約因

6. Public policy: A contract may be void due to public policy reasons (e.g. illegality of subject matter).

■ public policy 公共政策
■ illegality 非法、違法

7. Statute of Frauds: Under the Statute of Frauds, certain contracts must be in writing in order to be enforceable.

Marriage: Contract in consideration of marriage

Year: Contract cannot be performed within one year

Land: Contract for sale of interest in land

Executor: Contract of decedent's executor / administrator

Goods: Contract for sale of goods if price is $500 or more

Surety: Promise to pay the debt of another

■ Statute of Frauds 防止詐欺條例
■ writing 書面
■ contract in consideration of marriage 以婚姻為約因之契約
■ contract cannot be performed within one year 一年內不能履行完成之契約
■ land 土地
■ executor / administrator 遺產執行人 / 管理人
■ goods 貨物
■ surety 保證

Second Restatement of Contracts	美國法律整編（第二版）契約法
Chapter 5 The Statute of Frauds **§ 110. Classes of Contracts Covered**	第五章　防止詐欺條例 第110條　適用契約之種類
(1) The following classes of contracts are subject to a statute, commonly called the Statute of Frauds, forbidding enforcement unless there is a **written** memorandum or an applicable exception:	(1) 除有**書面**備忘文件或得適用例外之情形外，下列種類之契約適用這種為防止詐欺條例之制定法而不得執行：
(a) a contract of an **executor or administrator** to answer for a duty of his decedent (the executor-administrator provision);	(a) 一由**遺產執行人或管理人**允諾償還被繼承人義務之契約（遺產執行人或管理人規定）；
(b) a contract to answer for the duty of another (the **suretyship** provision);	(b) 一允諾對他人義務負責之契約（**保證**規定）；
(c) a contract made upon consideration of **marriage** (the marriage provision);	(c) 以**婚姻**為約因之契約（婚姻規定）；
(d) a contract for the sale of an interest in **land** (the land contract provision);	(d) 出售**土地**上利益之契約（土地契約規定）；
(e) a contract that is not to be performed within **one year** from the making thereof (the one-year provision).	(e) 自作成時起不能於**一年**內完成履行之契約（一年規定）。
(2) The following classes of contracts, which were traditionally subject to the Statute of Frauds, are now governed by Statute of Frauds provisions of the Uniform Commercial Code: (a) a contract for the sale of goods for the price of **$500** or more (Uniform Commercial Code § 2-201) …	(2) 下列之傳統上適用防止詐欺條例之契約種類，現今適用美國統一商法典防止詐欺之規定： (a) 商品買賣價金為**五百元**以上之契約（美國統一商法典第2-201條） …
(5) In many states other classes of contracts are subject to a requirement of a writing.	(5) 於許多州裡其他種類之契約亦受須以書面為之之限制。

8. Unconscionability: A court may refuse to enforce an unconscionable contract provision, especially to protect consumers against one-sided, unfair business practices.
   ▥ unconscionable 不公正的、不合理的、無理的、非自由意識
   ▥ consumer 消費者

Validity 效力

valid 有效

unenforceable 不可執行

voidable 可撤銷

invalid / void 無效

In the best case, a contract is fully valid and enforceable.
   ▥ valid 有效
   ▥ enforceable 可執行

On the other hand, a contract may be invalid or entirely void (e.g. due to public policy reasons such as illegality).
   ▥ invalid 無效
   ▥ void 無效

Sometimes a contract is not automatically void but only voidable. This means that a party (e.g. an infant) can choose to affirm or disaffirm the contract.
   ▥ voidable 可撤銷

■ choose 選擇

■ affirm; disaffirm 確認；否認

Even if the parties have reached an agreement, the contract may be unenforceable due to formal requirements (e.g. Statute of Frauds, lapse of time).

■ unenforceable 不可執行

Discharge 免除、解除

A contract is discharged due to impossibility of performance (e.g. destruction of unique subject matter), impracticability (e.g. unforeseeable and severe change of circumstances), or frustration of purpose. As a result, the parties are not liable for breach of contract but may recover in quasi-contract.

■ impossibility 不可能

■ impracticability 不能履行、行不通

■ frustration of purpose 目的之無法達成、締約目的挫敗

Warranty 擔保

An express warranty is a statement of fact (not opinion), which can be given by way of description or showing a sample. If the seller is a merchant, he gives an implied warranty of merchantability (= fit for ordinary purpose). A warranty of fitness for a particular purpose is given, where seller knows that buyer is purchasing goods for a particular purpose and is relying on seller's skill / judgment.

■ express / implied warranty 明示 / 默示擔保

■ warranty of merchantability 可銷售性擔保

■ warranty of fitness for a particular purpose 符合特定用途的擔保

Contract interpretation 契約解釋

According to the parol evidence rule, evidence of prior agreements may not be admitted to contradict a partial integration (= final writing) and may not be admitted to supplement a total integration.

- ■ parol evidence rule 口頭證據法則
- ■ contradict 牴觸、不一致、反駁
- ■ supplement 補充
- ■ integration 整合

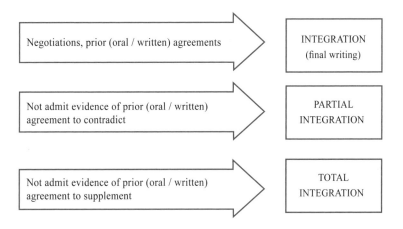

Exceptions to parol evidence rule:

1. A contemporaneous / ancillary document that is supported by separate consideration is not subject to the parol evidence rule.

- ■ contemporaneous / ancillary document 同時期的 / 輔助文件

2. A written agreement may be modified after its execution.
   ■ modify 修改
   ■ execution 完成、簽名蓋印使法律文件生效

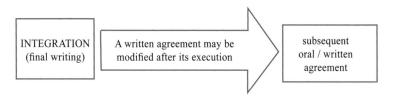

3. Admit evidence to show that the contract is void / voidable, e.g. illegality, fraud, duress, mistake.
   ■ contract is void / voidable 契約無效 / 可撤銷

4. Admit evidence to show existence of a condition (supplementing / consistent, not contradicting).
   ■ condition 條件

A variety of other factors are taken into account when interpreting the terms of a contract, such as the specific circumstances, the parties' primary purpose, usage of trade, the duty of good faith and fair dealing. Preference is given to meanings that are reasonable, lawful, and effective. In case of doubt, a contract will be construed against the draftsman.

- circumstances 情況、情形
- purpose 目的
- usage of trade 商業習慣
- duty of good faith and fair dealing 誠信及公平交易之義務
- reasonable, lawful, and effective 合理、合法且有效
- construed against the draftsman 對起草人不利之解釋

Breach of contract 違約、違反契約

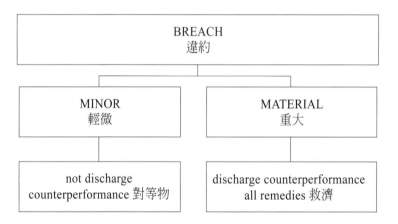

A contract is breached if a party fails to fulfill his contractual obligations when performance is due. A minor breach does not discharge counterperformance. A material breach discharges counterperformance and all contract remedies are available.

- contractual obligation 契約義務
- minor breach 輕微違約
- material breach 重大違約
- discharge 解除、免除

■counterperformance 對等物
■remedy 救濟

Remedies 救濟

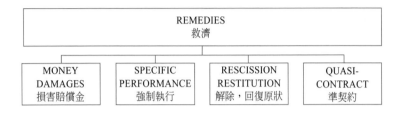

The typical remedy for breach of contract is money damages. The purpose of compensatory damages is to put a party in the position had the contract not been breached. For instance, expectation damages put a party in the position had the contract been performed (includes benefit / profit of the bargain). Reliance damages put a party in the position had there been no contract (replacing out-of-pocket fees). Consequential damages must have been reasonably foreseeable or the breaching party had actual notice when the contract was made. Where no actual loss has resulted from a contract breach, nominal damages might be awarded. Punitive damages are rarely awarded in contract cases. Where damages resulting from a contractual breach are uncertain or difficult to calculate, a liquidated damages clause stipulating a reasonable amount of damages is enforceable.

■remedy for breach of contract 違約之救濟
■money damages 損害賠償金
■compensatory damages 補償性損害賠償
■expectation damages 預期損害賠償
■reliance damages 信賴損害賠償

- consequential damages 間接損害賠償
- nominal damages 名義上損害賠償
- punitive damages 懲罰性損害賠償
- liquidated damages 預定損害賠償

When money damages are inadequate (e.g. because the subject matter of the contract is unique), a party may seek specific performance. If the non-breaching party wants to avoid the contract, he can instead sue for rescission (i.e. cancellation) and restitution (i.e. the other party must return the benefit / value received). To the extent that a legal contract does not exist, a court may award quasi-contractual or equitable relief to prevent unjust enrichment. When a breach occurs, the parties have a duty to mitigate damages.

- specific performance 強制執行
- rescission 解約
- cancellation 取消、解除
- restitution 返還原物、回復原狀
- equitable relief 衡平法救濟
- duty to mitigate damages 減少損害的義務

Third parties 第三人

As a general rule, only the parties are in privity of contract. This means only contractual parties (not third parties) have legal rights / duties and are entitled to sue each other for breach of contract.

- privity of contract 契約關係、合同當事人相互關係

However, there are certain exceptions.

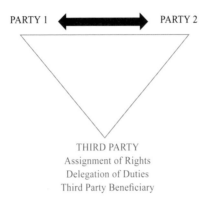

THIRD PARTY
Assignment of Rights
Delegation of Duties
Third Party Beneficiary

Assignment of rights: When a party (= assignor) assigns his existing contractual rights to a third party (= assignee), the assignor's rights are extinguished and only the assignee can enforce. The assignee stands in the shoes of his assignor.

- assignment of right 權利之讓與
- assignor 讓與人
- assignee 受讓人

Delegation of duties: When a party (delegator) delegates his contractual duties to a third person (delegatee), the delegator remains liable.

- delegation of duty 委託義務

Third party beneficiary: If at the time of contract formation, the promisee intends to confer a benefit to a third party (= intended third party beneficiary), that third party has a right to sue.

- third party beneficiary 受益第三人

Structure of contract 契約結構

PARTIES

This Agreement is made on ... [date] between ... [name / Company] whose registered office is at ... [address], (hereinafter referred to as "the Vendor") and ... [name / Company] whose registered office is at ... [address], (hereinafter referred to as "the Purchaser").

- party 當事人
- name 姓名
- address 地址
- vendor 賣方
- purchaser 買方

RECITAL (BACKGROUND, PURPOSE, OBJECTIVE)

Whereas ... [Company] is a private company limited by shares incorporated in ... The Vendor has agreed to sell all of the issued share capital of the Company to Purchaser for the consideration and upon the terms set out in this Agreement.

- recital 陳書
- background, purpose, objective 背景、目的、目標

IMPORTANT TERMS AND DEFINITIONS

"Execution date" shall mean 3 June 2012, the date of execution of this Agreement.

"Shares" shall have the meaning assigned to this term in section ... of this Agreement.

- important terms 重要名詞
- definition 定義

CONDITIONS

Completion of the sale and purchase of the Shares shall be conditional upon the following conditions (precedent, concurrent, subsequent) having been fulfilled: ...

- condition precedent 先決條件、契約生效之前置條件
- condition concurrent 並行條件、同時履行的條件
- condition subsequent 解除條件、契約生效之後置條件

AGREEMENTS

The rights and obligations of the parties concerning payment and delivery: The Vendor shall sell and the Purchaser shall purchase the Shares. The total price payable by the Purchaser to the Vendor for the Shares shall be the sum of $ ... Delivery shall be made on ... by means of ...

- agreement 協議
- rights and obligations of the parties 當事人之權利及義務
- payment 支付、付款、給付
- delivery 交付

REPRESENTATIONS AND WARRANTIES

The Vendor represents and warrants to the Purchaser that ... Representations are statements of facts. Warranties are contractual promises.

- representation 陳述、聲明
- warranty 擔保、保證、承諾

GOVERNING LAW

This Agreement is governed by and shall be construed in accordance with the laws of the State of New York, United States of America.

- governing law 管轄法律、適用法律、所依據法律、準據法

- construe 解釋
- in accordance with 根據

ARBITRATION

Any dispute arising out of this Agreement shall be finally settled by arbitration in accordance with the arbitration rules of ... [institution] in ... [place]. The arbitration tribunal shall consist of one arbitrator.

- arbitration 仲裁
- settle a dispute 結束糾紛／爭論
- tribunal 法庭

ENTIRE AGREEMENT

This Agreement is the entire agreement between the Parties and supersedes all prior written or oral agreements between the Parties.

- entire agreement 完整協議
- supersede 代替
- prior 在先的、在前的

SEVERANCE

The invalidity, in whole or in part, of any term of this Agreement does not affect the validity of the remainder of the Agreement.

- sever 切斷、分割
- invalidity; validity 無效；效力

PARTIES' SIGNATURES 當事人簽名：_____

SCHEDULES 列表

Detailed documents which are substantive part of contract.

APPENDIX 附錄、附件

Reference documents which are not substantive part of the contract.

References:

1. Steven L. Emanuel, Law Outlines: Contracts, Wolters Kluwer, 11th edition (2015).
2. Steven L. Emanuel, Crunch Time: Contracts, Wolters Kluwer, 6th edition (2016).
3. The American Law Institute, Restatements of the Law, https://www.ali.org/publications/#publication-type-restatements (accessed 8.7.2019).
4. Laws.Com, All You Need to Know About Restatement of Contracts, https://contract-law.laws.com/contract-law/restatement-of-contracts (accessed 6.7.2019).
5. 黃裕凱博士教研網站，Second Restatement of Contracts, http://merchantmarine.financelaw.fju.edu.tw/data/Teaching/English/US%20Restatement%202%20Contract.pdf (accessed 12.7.2019)。
6. Cornell Law School, Legal Information Institute, Uniform Commercial Code, https://www.law.cornell.edu/ucc/2/2-205 (accessed 13.7.2019).
7. USLegal, Uniform Commercial Code, https://uniformcommercial-code.uslegal.com/ (accessed 7.7.2019).
8. Law Study Systems, Basics of UCC 2-207, http://www.youtube.com/watch?v=s1I09IK7z0M (published 10.11.2008, accessed 18.7.2019).

9. Wikipedia, Uniform Commercial Code, https://en.wikipedia.org/wiki/Uniform_Commercial_Code (edited 8.6.2019, accessed 8.7.2019).

10. United Nations Commission on International Trade Law, United Nations Convention on Contracts for the International Sale of Goods (Vienna, 1980) (CISG), https://uncitral.un.org/en/texts/salegoods/conventions/sale_of_goods/cisg (accessed 6.7.2019).

11. Institute of International Commercial Law, Pace Law School, Guides for Business Managers and Counsel: Applying the CISG, https://www.iicl.law.pace.edu/cisg/page/guide-managers-and-counsel-applying-cisg (updated 27.3.2017, accessed 10.7.2019).

12. Wikipedia, United Nations Convention on Contracts for the International Sale of Goods, https://en.wikipedia.org/wiki/United_Nations_Convention_on_Contracts_for_the_International_Sale_of_Goods (edited 3.7.2019, accessed 6.7.2019).

13. Franco Ferrari, The Relationship between the UCC and the CISG and the Construction of Uniform Law, 29 Loy. L.A. L. Rev. 1021 (1996), https://digitalcommons.lmu.edu/llr/vol29/iss3/4 (accessed 6.7.2019).

14. Global Legal Group, International Comparative Legal Guides, USA Public Procurement 2019, https://iclg.com/practice-areas/public-procurement-laws-and-regulations/usa (published 28.1.2019, accessed 6.7.2019).

15. Richard O Duvall, Terry L Elling and Timothy J Taylor, Holland & Knight LLP, Public procurement in the United States: overview, Thomson Reuters, Practical Law, https://uk.practicallaw.thomsonreuters.com/3-521-7446?transitionType=Default&contextData=(sc.Default)&firstPage=true&bhcp=1 (1.3.2013, accessed 6.7.2019).

16. FindLaw, Federal Government Contract Overview, Thomson Reuters, https://corporate.findlaw.com/law-library/federal-government-contract-overview.html (accessed 6.7.2019).

17. USLegal, https://definitions.uslegal.com/p/preexisting-duty-rule/ (accessed 23.7.2019).

18. LexRoll.com, Inc., Pre-Existing Duty Rule, https://encyclopedia.lexroll.com/encyclopedia/pre-existing-duty-rule/ (accessed 23.7.2019).

19. Law Shelf Educational Media, National Paralegal College, Contract Consideration: The Pre-Existing Duty Rule, https://lawshelf.com/videos/entry/contract-law-the-pre-existing-duty-rule (accessed 23.7.2019).

20. wise GEEK, What is Privity of Contract, https://www.wisegeek.com/what-is-privity-of-contract.htm (accessed 6.7.2019).

21. Arthur Taylor von Mehren, Contract Law, Encyclopedia Britannica, Inc., https://www.britannica.com/topic/contract-law/The-rules-of-different-legal-systems (modified 24.5.2019, accessed 23.7.2019).

22. The Free Dictionary, Contracts, https://legal-dictionary.thefreedictionary.com/Contracts+for+the+Sale+of+Goods (accessed 23.7.2019).

23. Cambridge Dictionary, https://dictionary.cambridge.org/zht/詞典/英語-漢語-繁體/ (accessed 23.7.2019).

24. 維基百科，自由的百科全書，穩固要約，https://zh.wikipedia.org/wiki/穩固要約（19.7.2019，修訂於2017年7月16日）。

25. 線上翻譯，Web dictionary, https://tw.ichacha.net/unconscionable.html (accessed 23.7.2019)。

26. 高點法律網，http://lawyer.get.com.tw/Dic/DictionaryDetail.aspx?iDT=65430 (accessed 23.7.2019)。

27. Thomson Reuters, Westlaw.

TAIWAN CONTRACT LAW

Civil Code[1]

Part II Obligations
Chapter I General Provisions
Section 1 Sources of Obligations
Sub-section 1 Contracts

Article 153

When the parties have reciprocally declared their concordant intent, either expressly or impliedly, a contract shall be constituted.

If the parties agree on all the essential elements of the contract but have expressed no intent as to the non-essential elements, the contract shall be presumed to be constituted. In the absence of an agreement on the above-mentioned non-essential elements, the court shall decide them according to the nature of the affair.

Article 154

A person who offers to make a contract shall be bound by his offer except at the time of offer he has excluded this obligation or except it may be presumed from the circumstances or from the nature of the affair that he did not intend to be bound.

Exposing goods for sale with their selling price shall be deemed to be an offer. However, the sending of pricelists is not deemed to be an offer.

---

1 See Ministry of Justice, Laws & Regulations Database of The Republic of China, https://law.moj.gov.tw/Eng/LawClass/LawAll.aspx?PCode=B0000001 (amended on 19.6.2019, accessed 13.7.2019).

單元二　臺灣契約法

民法[2]

第二編　債
第一章　通則
第一節　債之發生
第一款　契約

第153條

當事人互相表示意思一致者，無論其爲明示或默示，契約即爲成立。

當事人對於必要之點，意思一致，而對於非必要之點，未經表示意思者，推定其契約爲成立，關於該非必要之點，當事人意思不一致時，法院應依其事件之性質定之。

第154條

契約之要約人，因要約而受拘束。但要約當時預先聲明不受拘束，或依其情形或事件之性質，可認當事人無受其拘束之意思者，不在此限。

貨物標定賣價陳列者，視爲要約。但價目表之寄送，不視爲要約。

2　法務部，全國法規資料庫，https://law.moj.gov.tw/LawClass/LawAll. aspx?pcode=B0000001（13.7.2019，修訂於2019年6月19日）。

Article 155
An offer ceases to be binding if it is refused.

Article 156
An offer made inter presentes ceases to be binding if it is not accepted at once.

Article 157
An offer made inter absentes ceases to be binding if it is not accepted by the other party within the time during which notice of acceptance may be expected to arrive under ordinary circumstances.

Article 158
If a period of time for the acceptance of the offer has been fixed, the offer ceases to be binding if it is not accepted within such period.

Article 159
If an acceptance arrives late though it should usually arrive within a reasonable time by its transmitting manner, and this might be known to the offeror, the offeror should immediately notify the acceptor of such delay.
If the offeror delays the notice specified in the preceding paragraph, the acceptance shall be deemed to have arrived without delay.

Article 160
An acceptance which arrives late, except under the circumstances in the preceding article, shall be deemed to be a new offer.
An acceptance with amplifications, limitations or other alterations shall be deemed to be a refusal of the original offer and the making of a new offer.

第155條
要約經拒絕者，失其拘束力。

第156條
對話為要約者，非立時承諾，即失其拘束力。

第157條
非對話為要約者，依通常情形可期待承諾之達到時期內，相對人
不為承諾時，其要約失其拘束力。

第158條
要約定有承諾期限者，非於其期限內為承諾，失其拘束力。

第159條
承諾之通知，按其傳達方法，通常在相當時期內可達到而遲到，其
情形為要約人可得而知者，應向相對人即發遲到之通知。
要約人怠於為前項通知者，其承諾視為未遲到。

第160條
遲到之承諾，除前條情形外，視為新要約。
將要約擴張、限制或為其他變更而承諾者，視為拒絕原要約而為
新要約。

Article 161

In cases where according to customs or owing to the nature of the affair, a notice of acceptance is not necessary, the contract shall be constituted when, within a reasonable time, there is a fact, which may be considered as an acceptance of the offer.

The provision of the preceding paragraph shall be mutatis mutandis applied when at the time of offer the offeror has waived notice of acceptance.

Article 162

If a notice of withdrawing an offer arrives after the arrival of the offer itself, though it should usually arrive before or simultaneously with the arrival of the offer within a reasonable time by its transmitting manner, and this might be known to the other party, the other party so notified should notify the offeror immediately of such delay. If such other party delays the notice specified in the preceding paragraph, the notice of withdrawing the offer shall be deemed to have arrived without delay.

Article 163

The provisions of the preceding article shall apply mutatis mutandis to the withdrawal of acceptance.

Article 164

When a public notice promises to reward the person for his performance of a particular act, it is a rewarding public notice. The promisor is bound to deliver the reward to the person who has performed the act.

第161條
依習慣或依其事件之性質，承諾無須通知者，在相當時期內，有可認為承諾之事實時，其契約為成立。

前項規定，於要約人要約當時預先聲明承諾無須通知者，準用之。

第162條
撤回要約之通知，其到達在要約到達之後，而按其傳達方法，通常在相當時期內應先時或同時到達，其情形為相對人可得而知者，相對人應向要約人即發遲到之通知。

相對人怠於為前項通知者，其要約撤回之通知，視為未遲到。

第163條
前條之規定，於承諾之撤回準用之。

第164條
以廣告聲明對完成一定行為之人給與報酬者，為懸賞廣告。廣告人對於完成該行為之人，負給付報酬之義務。

When the act specified in the preceding paragraph has been succes-sively performed by several persons, it is the person who has per-formed first acquires the claim for reward; when the act has been performed jointly by several persons or performed simultaneously by several persons respectively, it is these persons who acquire the claim for reward jointly.

In the preceding paragraph, if the promisor has delivered the reward in good faith to the person who has first notified his performance, the obligation of the promisor to deliver the reward shall be extinguished.

...

Article 165

When a promise of reward made by a public notice is withdrawn be-fore the act is performed, the promisor is bound to compensate the person performing the act in good faith for the injury arising there-from, unless the promisor can prove that the person could have never performed the act...

Article 166

If it is agreed between the parties that a contract shall be made in a certain definite form, the contract is presumed to be not constituted before the completion of such form.

Article 166-1

If a contract is made for the obligations of the transferring, creation, or altering of rights over the real property, it shall be made in the notarization made by the notary public.

數人先後分別完成前項行為時，由最先完成該行為之人，取得報酬請求權；數人共同或同時分別完成行為時，由行為人共同取得報酬請求權。

前項情形，廣告人善意給付報酬於最先通知之人時，其給付報酬之義務，即為消滅。……

第165條

預定報酬之廣告，如於行為完成前撤回時，除廣告人證明行為人不能完成其行為外，對於行為人因該廣告善意所受之損害，應負賠償之責。……

第166條

契約當事人約定其契約須用一定方式者，在該方式未完成前，推定其契約不成立。

第166-1條

契約以負擔不動產物權之移轉、設定或變更之義務為標的者，應由公證人作成公證書。

A contract not notarized according to the provision of the preceding paragraph could still be valid if the parties have agreed on the transferring, creation, or altering of rights over the real property and have completed the recordation.

Section 3 Effects of Obligations
Sub-section 1 Performance

Article 225
The debtor will be released from his obligation to perform if the performance becomes impossible by reason of a circumstance to which he is not imputed. ...

Article 226
If the performance becomes impossible by reason of a circumstance to which the debtor is imputed, the creditor may claim compensation for any injury arising therefrom. ...

Article 227-2
If there is change of circumstances which is not predictable then after the constitution of the contract, and if the performance of the original obligation arising therefrom will become obviously unfair, the party may apply to the court for increasing or reducing his payment, or altering the original obligation. ...

未依前項規定公證之契約，如當事人已合意為不動產物權之移轉、設定或變更而完成登記者，仍為有效。

第三節　債之效力
第一款　給付

第225條
因不可歸責於債務人之事由，致給付不能者，債務人免給付義務。⋯⋯

第226條
因可歸責於債務人之事由，致給付不能者，債權人得請求賠償損害。⋯⋯

第227-2條
契約成立後，情事變更，非當時所得預料，而依其原有效果顯失公平者，當事人得聲請法院增、減其給付或變更其他原有之效果。⋯⋯

Sub-section 4 Contracts

Article 255

If according to the nature of the contract or the expression of intent of the parties, the purpose of the contract can not be accomplished if not performed within the fixed period, and if one of the parties does not perform the contract within that period, the other party may rescind the contract without giving the notice specified in the preceding article.

第四款　契約

第255條
依契約之性質或當事人之意思表示，非於一定時期爲給付不能達
其契約之目的，而契約當事人之一方不按照時期給付者，他方當
事人得不爲前條之催告，解除其契約。

EXERCISES
單元三　練習

Fill in:

An ＿＿＿＿＿ is a person who makes an offer, an ＿＿＿＿＿ is a person to whom an offer is made. 的確

A ＿＿＿＿＿ is a person leasing out property, a ＿＿＿＿＿ is the person to whom the property is leased.

A ＿＿＿＿＿ is a person making a gift, a ＿＿＿＿＿ is a person to whom a gift is made.

A ＿＿＿＿＿ is a person who makes a promise, a ＿＿＿＿＿ is a person to whom a promise is made.

A ＿＿＿＿＿ is a person who sells something, a ＿＿＿＿＿ is a person to whom something is sold.

An ＿＿＿＿＿ is a person who makes an assignment, an ＿＿＿＿＿ is a person to whom an assignment is made.

An ＿＿＿＿＿ is a person who has to render an obligation, an ＿＿＿＿＿ is a person to whom an obligation must be rendered.

A ＿＿＿＿＿ is a person who makes a delegation, a ＿＿＿＿＿ is a person to whom a delegation is made.

Mark the odd word（選意義不同的字）：

ability – agree – assent – consent

to form – enter into – execute – sign – stop

to void – cancel – calculate – rescind – terminate

to cease – stop – end – select

to change – amend – modify – interpret – supplement

to reserve – revoke – withdraw – cancel

to prefer – opt for – like better – suggest

confidential – private – restricted – confirmation

enforceable – valid – enter into – in force

adult – child – minor – infant

perpetrator – punishment – penalties – additional fees

to obtain – omit – get – take

to communicate – inform – notify – neglect

to propose – suggest – offer – accept

void – value – invalid – not in force

Find the corresponding noun:

VERB	NOUN
accept	
agree	
alter	
anticipate	
apply	
arrive	
assent	
assume	
breach	
compensate	
confirm	
consider	
delay	
determine	
enforce	
intend	
limit	

mitigate	
notify	
perform	
propose	
reject	
refuse	
rely	
remedy	
rescind	
revoke	
withdraw	

Find the corresponding noun and person:

VERB	NOUN	PERSON
assign		
contract		
delegate		
draft		
execute		
interpret		
negotiate		
notarize		
oblige		
offer		
promise		
provide		
purchase		
sell		
transfer		
violate		

Find the corresponding adjective:

NOUN	ADJECTIVE
confidentiality	
consequence	
excess	
privacy	
punishment	
validity	

Choose the best answer:

1. A contract is an agreement that is _____ by court.

    (A) enforce   (B) void   (C) voidable   (D) enforceable

2. Anglo-American contracts are governed by Article 2 UCC and common law. Article 2 UCC is applicable to _____ of goods.

    (A) sell   (B) seller   (C) sale   (D) sold

3. John parks his car in the department store's garage. He is in a hurry to attend a lunch meeting on time. While talking to his secretary on the cell phone, he purchases a ticket from the automatic vending machine. John has entered into an _____ contract.

    (A) express   (B) implied   (C) oral   (D) invalid

4. An offer is a promise to enter into a contract. Thus an offer creates a power of _____.

    (A) bargain   (B) acceptance   (C) rejection   (D) affirmation

5. An offer ceases to be _____ if it is rejected.

   (A) binding (B) bound (C) benefit (D) beneficiary

6. An acceptance with additions, restrictions or other alterations shall be deemed to be a _____ of the original offer and the making of a new offer.

   (A) promise (B) rejection (C) renewal (D) remedy

7. If the acceptance does not match ("mirror") the terms of the offer, then it must be regarded as a _____.

   (A) counterclaim (B) condition (C) contract (D) counteroffer

8. A contract is legally binding if it is formalized or if it is supported by valid _____. It is often defined as a mutually bargained for exchange between the parties.

   (A) condition (B) compliment (C) cooperation (D) consideration

9. Anton posts a reward saying "I will give anyone who brings back my lost dog $ 1000." Since the offeror is bargaining for the act of bringing back the dog, not for a promise to bring back the dog, the contract is _____.

   (A) unilateral (B) bilateral (C) express (D) implied

10. Anton says to Berta: "I will sell you my car for $ 7000." Since the offeror does not expect the offeree to hand over the money immediately, but to accept the offer by promising to pay $ 7000, the contract is _____.

    (A) unilateral (B) bilateral (C) express (D) implied

11. A party is in _____ of contract when performance is due and the party fails to fulfill his contractual obligations.

    (A) defense   (B) mistake   (C) remedy   (D) breach

12. The typical _____ under the common law for breach of contract is money damages, but if the subject matter of the contract is unique, specific performance may be ordered.

    (A) right   (B) remedy   (C) obligation   (D) performance

13. A _____ clause is a clause concerning the treating of information as private and not for distribution beyond specifically identified purposes.

    (A) condition   (B) confidence   (C) confirmation

    (D) confidentiality

14. A severability clause is a clause providing that notwithstanding an unenforceable contract provision the remaining part of the agreement

    _____.

    (A) is null and void   (B) is unenforceable   (C) remains in force

    (D) is terminated

15. On his 16th birthday Anton decides to realize his dream of driving a BMW. Dressed up like an adult he enters a store and a few hours later signs a contract with the car dealer. Since Anton is still a minor the contract is _____.

    (A) unenforceable   (B) invalid   (C) void   (D) voidable

16. Anton sells his house to Berta for a price of $800,000. The contract must be in writing due to the _____.
(A) parol evidence rule (B) statute of frauds (C) principle of promissory estoppel (D) principle of good faith

17. When Anton _____ his existing contractual rights to a third party, Anton's rights are extinguished and only the third party can enforce.
(A) delegates (B) transfers (C) assigns (D) rescinds

18. Duane purchases counterfeit goods from Ken for NT$30,000. Duane fails to pay and Ken sues Duane for breach of contract. According to R.O.C. Civil Code, Duane may argue that the contract is invalid based on _____. (100年司法官)
(A) natural debt (B) incapacity (C) illegality (D) fraud

19. Kira contracts to sell and Lara to buy a Swiss watch for NT$100,000. Kira may sue Lara for breach of contract when Lara refuses the _____ of payment without a just cause. (100年司法官)
(A) tender (B) provide (C) offer (D) give

20. Emma contracts to sell and Elton to buy a machine for NT$100,000, delivery of the machine and payment of the price to be made at a stated place on July 7. On July 7 both parties are present at that place. Elton gives Emma a check payable to Emma in the amount of NT$100,000 but Emma refuses to deliver the machine. Elton may sue Emma for her _____. (100年律師)
(A) omission (B) non-performance (C) inaction (D) denial

21. Klingon contracts to sell and Kirk to buy 300 crates of Fuji apples, shipment to be from Japan on September 28. Klingon sends only 280 crates on September 28. By failing to ship the required number of crates, Klingon _____ the contract. (100年律師)

    (A) trespasses (B) infringes (C) breaches (D) breaks

22. Bert promises to sell to Elise a handbag for NT$8,000. Elise promises to pay in four _____ of NT$2,000 each, beginning one week after execution of the contract. (100年律師)

    (A) stages (B) phases (C) periods (D) installments

23. Curtis contracts to sell and Dale to buy ten bushels of oats. By very general _____, known to Curtis and Dale, 32 pounds constitute a bushel of oats. In the absence of contrary evidence, ten bushels in the contract mean 320 pounds. (101年司法官)

    (A) usage (B) practice (C) habit (D) custom

24. On May 1, Lucas contracts to sell and Bea to buy land, delivery of the deed and payment of the price to be on July 30. On June 1, Lucas tells Bea that he will not perform. Lucas's statement is a _____. (101年司法官)

    (A) submission (B) transmission (C) repudiation (D) pudiation

25. Ricky, while in a state of extreme intoxication, offers to sell his Rolex watch for a fair price to Andy, who knows of Ricky's intoxication. Andy accepts the offer. Ricky may avoid the contract when he becomes sober because Ricky lacks _____ when he makes the offer. (101年律師)

    (A) capability (B) capacity (C) awareness (D) ability

26. Blanche sells wine to Cora in barrels. Cora discovers that some of the barrels are leaky, in breach of warranty, but does not transfer the wine to good barrels that she has. Cora's damages for breach of contract do not include the loss of the wine that could have been saved by transferring the wine to the available barrels, because Cora fails to make efforts to _____ damages. (101年律師)

    (A) mitigate　　(B) deteriorate　　(C) alleviate　　(D) aggravate

27. Kate hires Mario, a famous chef, to cook for her wedding. The chef cannot _____ the duty to cook to someone else, because the party has specifically contracted for the experience and individual skill of this chef. (102年司法官)

    (A) transfer　　(B) pass　　(C) delegate　　(D) convey

28. On June 1, Todd agrees to sell and Wayne agrees to buy goods to be delivered in October at a designated port. The port is subsequently closed by quarantine regulations during the entire month of October; no commercially reasonable substitute performance is available, and Todd fails to deliver the goods. Todd is not liable to Wayne for breach of contract because Todd's performance is made _____ without his fault. (102年司法官)

    (A) unimaginable　　(B) impracticable　　(C) impossible

    (D) inconceivable

29. Kanawa, a noted opera singer, is induced by Justin's fraudulent misrepresentation to contract to sing the leading role in a new production designed for Kanawa at Justin's opera house in August. Kanawa soon discovers the misrepresentation. According to R.O.C. Civil Code, the contract between Kanawa and Justin is _____ . (102年律師)

(A) valid   (B) invalid   (C) avoidable   (D) avoid

30. Brian travels from Taipei to San Francisco. There is a statement on his electronic ticket which provides: "The Airline's liability to the passenger for any cause or combination of causes shall be, in the total amount, no more than the fees paid under this contract or NT$50,000, whichever is greater." This kind of clause is commonly referred to as a _____. (102年律師)

   (A) warranty clause   (B) limitation clause   (C) indemnification clause   (D) exclusion clause

31. A contract to sell someone a slave for NTD1,000,000 could not be enforced at law because the contract entered into was _____. (103年司法官律師)

   (A) against public policy   (B) out of mistake   (C) under duress   (D) short of meeting of the minds

32. Joanna, 21-year-old, orally promises to sell Ty, 30-year-old, a book in return of Ty's promise to pay NT$500. There is a valid contract, because there is _____ of legally capable parties. (104年司法官律師)

   (A) mutual assent   (B) mutual standing   (C) unanimous decision   (D) beating of two hearts

33. Miller rents an apartment from Tyler. Both parties do not specify the term of the lease. Under Article 450 of the Civil Code, Miller may _____ the lease at any time. (104年司法官律師)

   (A) breach   (B) enter into   (C) finish   (D) terminate

34. Vivian agrees to buy and Kenny agrees to sell a laptop at the price of

NT20,000. However, Kenny sells and delivers the laptop to Chris the next day. Vivian may refuse to pay the price because Kenny fails to _____ the contract. (105年司法官律師)

(A) revoke　(B) make　(C) carry　(D) perform

35. Abby walks into a restaurant and orders a tuna sandwich and a cup of soda. Edgar, the waiter, writes down the order. At this moment, Abby _____ a contract with the restaurant. (105年司法官律師)

　(A) takes into　(B) makes up　(C) gives up　(D) enters into

36. Oswald contracts to decorate a store for Winifred for NT$90,000 by a specified date or in the alternative to pay Winifred NT$500 a day during any period of delay. This type of provision is called _____ clause. (106年司法官律師)

(A) remunerated　(B) pre-calculated damages

(C) liquidated damages　(D) foreseeable damages

37. An acceptance which arrives late though usually it should have arrived earlier and within a reasonable time by its transmitting manner may nonetheless constitute a contract under R.O.C. Civil Code unless one of the following occurs: (106年司法官律師)

(A) The one making the offer has reason to know the facts and sends without delay a notice informing the offeree of the fact that "acceptance" being late.

(B) The one marking the offer does nothing to inform the offeree of the late acceptance while the former has reason to know the facts of its being late.

(C) The one marking the acceptance explains the reasons of its being late to the offeror.

(D) The one marking the acceptance apologizes to the offeror of its being late.

38. Under R.O.C. Civil Code, if an offeree responds to an offer by making a _____ - in effect, proposes terms other than those contained in the original offer - the law treats that response as the legal equivalent of a rejection. (107年司法官律師)

(A) rejection (B) acceptance (C) offer (D) counteroffer

39. In a contract of sale, which of the following warranty might not be honored by the seller? (107年司法官律師)

(A) Express warranty by the seller (B) Implied warranty of the superior quality of the goods (C) Implied warranty of merchantability (D) Implied warranty of fitness for particular purpose

40. Generally, a contract operates to confer rights and impose duties only on the parties to the contract and no other parties. This contractual relationship is summed up in the term _____. (107年司法官律師)

(A) novation (B) privity of contract (C) third-party beneficiary contract (D) privity in possession

Which of the following answers is NOT correct:

1. The essential elements of a contract are _____.

(A) offer (B) acceptance (C) defense (D) consideration

2. The power of acceptance is terminated if the offeree has _____.
   (A) rejected the offer   (B) made a counter-offer   (C) not responded within a reasonable period of time   (D) received a firm offer from a merchant

3. A contract can be discharged due to impossibility of performance, impracticability, or frustration of purpose. As a result, the parties _____.
   (A) are released from their contractual duties   (B) are not liable for breach of contract   (C) may sue for breach of contract
   (D) may recover in quasi-contract

4. When both parties are mistaken (mutual mistake) about an existing fact, the contract is voidable if _____.
   (A) the mistake concerns the price of the transaction   (B) the parties did not assume the risk of mistake   (C) the mistake concerns a basic assumption   (D) the mistake has a material effect

5. Compensatory damages may include _____.
   (A) expectation damages   (B) reliance damages   (C) consequential damages   (D) nominal damages

ANSWERS
單元四　答案

Fill in:

An offeror is a person who makes an offer, an offeree is a person to whom an offer is made.

A lessor is a person leasing out property, a lessee is the person to whom the property is leased.

A donor is a person making a gift, a donee is a person to whom a gift is made.

A promisor is a person who makes a promise, a promisee is a person to whom a promise is made.

A vendor is a person who sells something, a vendee is a person to whom something is sold.

An assignor is a person who makes an assignment, an assignee is a person to whom an assignment is made.

An obligor is a person who has to render an obligation, an obligee is a person to whom an obligation must be rendered.

A delegator is a person who makes a delegation, a delegatee is a person to whom a delegation is made.

Mark the odd word（選意義不同的字）：

ability – agree – assent – consent 能力

to form – enter into – execute – sign – stop 停止

to void – cancel – calculate – rescind – terminate 計算

to cease – stop – end – select 選擇

to change – amend – modify – interpret – supplement 解釋

to reserve – revoke – withdraw – cancel 保留

to prefer – opt for – like better – suggest 建議

confidential – private – restricted – confirmation 確認

enforceable – valid – enter into – in force 進入

adult – child – minor – infant 成年人

perpetrator – punishment – penalties – additional fees 犯罪者

to obtain – omit – get – take 遺漏

to communicate – inform – notify – neglect 疏忽

to propose – suggest – offer – accept 接受

void – value – invalid – not in force 價值

Find the corresponding noun:

VERB	NOUN
accept	acceptance 承諾
agree	agreement 協議、協定
alter	alteration 更改
anticipate	anticipation 預期
apply	application 適用、申請
arrive	arrival 到達
assent	assent 同意
assume	assumption 承擔
breach	breach 違反、違約
compensate	compensation 賠償
confirm	confirmation 確認
consider	consideration 約因、考慮
delay	delay 遲延、遲到
determine	determination 決定
enforce	enforcement 執行
intend	intent / intention 故意、意圖
limit	limit / limitation 限制

mitigate	mitigation 減輕
notify	notification 通知
perform	performance 履行
propose	proposal 提案、提議
reject	rejection 拒絕
refuse	refusal 拒絕
rely	reliance 信賴
remedy	remedy 救濟
rescind	rescission 解除
revoke	revocation 撤回
withdraw	withdrawal 撤回、撤銷

Find the corresponding noun and person:

VERB	NOUN	PERSON
assign 讓與	assignment	assignor / assignee
contract 契約、合同	contract	contractor
delegate 轉嫁、委託	delegation	delegator / delegate / delegatee
draft 起草	draft	drafter
execute 執行	execution	executor
interpret 解釋	interpretation	interpreter
negotiate 談判、協商	negotiation	negotiator
notarize 公證	notarization	notary
oblige 使成為必要	obligation	obligor / obligee
offer 提交要約	offer	offeror / offeree
promise 允諾	promise	promisor / promiser / promisee
provide 提供、規定	provision	provider
purchase 購買	purchase	purchaser
sell 賣	sale	seller
transfer 轉讓	transfer	transferor / transferee
violate 違反	violation	violator / violater

Find the corresponding adjective:

NOUN	ADJECTIVE
confidentiality 秘密	confidential
consequence 後果	consequential
excess 超過	excessive
privacy 隱私	private
punishment 懲罰	punitive
validity 效力	valid

Choose the best answer:

1. A contract is an agreement that is _____ by court.

   (A) enforce   (B) void   (C) voidable   (D) enforceable

2. Anglo-American contracts are governed by Article 2 UCC and common law. Article 2 UCC is applicable to _____ of goods.

   (A) sell   (B) seller   (C) sale   (D) sold

3. John parks his car in the department store s garage. He is in a hurry to attend a lunch meeting on time. While talking to his secretary on the cell phone, he purchases a ticket from the automatic vending machine. John has entered into an _____ contract.

   (A) express   (B) implied   (C) oral   (D) invalid

4. An offer is a promise to enter into a contract. Thus an offer creates a power of _____.

   (A) bargain   (B) acceptance   (C) rejection   (D) affirmation

5. An offer ceases to be _____ if it is rejected.

   (A) binding   (B) bound   (C) benefit   (D) beneficiary

6. An acceptance with additions, restrictions or other alterations shall be deemed to be a _____ of the original offer and the making of a new offer.

   (A) promise (B) rejection (C) renewal (D) remedy

7. If the acceptance does not match ("mirror") the terms of the offer, then it must be regarded as a _____.

   (A) counterclaim (B) condition (C) contract (D) counteroffer

8. A contract is legally binding if it is formalized or if it is supported by valid _____. It is often defined as a mutually bargained-for exchange between the parties.

   (A) condition (B) compliment (C) cooperation (D) consideration

9. Anton posts a reward saying "I will give anyone who brings back my lost dog $ 1000." Since the offeror is bargaining for the act of bringing back the dog, not for a promise to bring back the dog, the contract is _____.

   (A) unilateral (B) bilateral (C) express (D) implied

10. Anton says to Berta: "I will sell you my car for $ 7000." Since the offeror does not expect the offeree to hand over the money immediately, but to accept the offer by promising to pay $ 7000, the contract is _____.

    (A) unilateral (B) bilateral (C) express (D) implied

11. A party is in _____ of contract when performance is due and the party fails to fulfill his contractual obligations.

(A) defense (B) mistake (C) remedy (D) breach

12. The typical _____ under the common law for breach of contract is money damages, but if the subject matter of the contract is unique, specific performance may be ordered.

(A) right (B) remedy (C) obligation (D) performance

13. A _____ clause is a clause concerning the treating of information as private and not for distribution beyond specifically identified purposes.

(A) condition (B) confidence (C) confirmation

(D) confidentiality

14. A severability clause is a clause providing that notwithstanding an unenforceable contract provision the remaining part of the agreement _____.

(A) is null and void (B) is unenforceable (C) remains in force

(D) is terminated

15. On his 16th birthday Anton decides to realize his dream of driving a BMW. Dressed up like an adult he enters a store and a few hours later signs a contract with the car dealer. Since Anton is still a minor the contract is _____.

(A) unenforceable (B) invalid (C) void (D) voidable

16. Anton sells his house to Berta for a price of $800,000. The contract must be in writing due to the _____ .
   (A) parol evidence rule (B) statute of frauds (C) principle of promissory estoppel (D) principle of good faith

17. When Anton _____ his existing contractual rights to a third party, Anton s rights are extinguished and only the third party can enforce.
   (A) delegates (B) transfers (C) assigns (D) rescinds

18. Duane purchases counterfeit goods from Ken for NT$30,000. Duane fails to pay and Ken sues Duane for breach of contract. According to R.O.C. Civil Code, Duane may argue that the contract is invalid based on _____ . (100年年司法官)
   (A) natural debt (B) incapacity (C) illegality (D) fraud

19. Kira contracts to sell and Lara to buy a Swiss watch for NT$100,000. Kira may sue Lara for breach of contract when Lara refuses the _____ of payment without a just cause. (100年司法官)
   (A) tender (B) provide (C) offer (D) give

20. Emma contracts to sell and Elton to buy a machine for NT$100,000, delivery of the machine and payment of the price to be made at a stated place on July 7. On July 7 both parties are present at that place. Elton gives Emma a check payable to Emma in the amount of NT$100,000 but Emma refuses to deliver the machine. Elton may sue Emma for her _____ . (100年律師)
   (A) omission (B) non-performance (C) inaction (D) denial

21. Klingon contracts to sell and Kirk to buy 300 crates of Fuji apples, shipment to be from Japan on September 28. Klingon sends only 280 crates on September 28. By failing to ship the required number of crates, Klingon _____ the contract. (100年律師)

    (A) trespasses   (B) infringes   (C) breaches   (D) breaks

22. Bert promises to sell to Elise a handbag for NT$8,000. Elise promises to pay in four _____ of NT$2,000 each, beginning one week after execution of the contract. (100年律師)

    (A) stages   (B) phases   (C) periods   (D) installments

23. Curtis contracts to sell and Dale to buy ten bushels of oats. By very general _____, known to Curtis and Dale, 32 pounds constitute a bushel of oats. In the absence of contrary evidence, ten bushels in the contract mean 320 pounds. (101年司法官)

    (A) usage   (B) practice   (C) habit   (D) custom

24. On May 1, Lucas contracts to sell and Bea to buy land, delivery of the deed and payment of the price to be on July 30. On June 1, Lucas tells Bea that he will not perform. Lucas's statement is a _____. (101年司法官)

    (A) submission   (B) transmission   (C) repudiation   (D) pudiation

25. Ricky, while in a state of extreme intoxication, offers to sell his Rolex watch for a fair price to Andy, who knows of Ricky's intoxication. Andy accepts the offer. Ricky may avoid the contract when he becomes sober because Ricky lacks _____ when he makes the offer. (101年律師)

    (A) capability   (B) capacity   (C) awareness   (D) ability

26. Blanche sells wine to Cora in barrels. Cora discovers that some of the barrels are leaky, in breach of warranty, but does not transfer the wine to good barrels that she has. Cora's damages for breach of contract do not include the loss of the wine that could have been saved by transferring the wine to the available barrels, because Cora fails to make efforts to _____ damages. (101年律師)

    (A) mitigate (B) deteriorate (C) alleviate (D) aggravate

27. Kate hires Mario, a famous chef, to cook for her wedding. The chef cannot _____ the duty to cook to someone else, because the party has specifically contracted for the experience and individual skill of this chef. (102年司法官)

    (A) transfer (B) pass (C) delegate (D) convey

28. On June 1, Todd agrees to sell and Wayne agrees to buy goods to be delivered in October at a designated port. The port is subsequently closed by quarantine regulations during the entire month of October; no commercially reasonable substitute performance is available, and Todd fails to deliver the goods. Todd is not liable to Wayne for breach of contract because Todd's performance is made _____ without his fault. (102年司法官)

    (A) unimaginable (B) impracticable (C) impossible
    (D) inconceivable

29. Kanawa, a noted opera singer, is induced by Justin's fraudulent misrepresentation to contract to sing the leading role in a new production designed for Kanawa at Justin's opera house in August. Kanawa soon discovers the misrepresentation. According to R.O.C. Civil Code, the contract between Kanawa and Justin is _____. (102年律師)

(A) valid   (B) invalid   (C) avoidable   (D) avoid

30. Brian travels from Taipei to San Francisco. There is a statement on his electronic ticket which provides: "The Airline's liability to the passenger for any cause or combination of causes shall be, in the total amount, no more than the fees paid under this contract or NT$50,000, whichever is greater." This kind of clause is commonly referred to as a _____ . (102年律師)

(A) warranty clause   (B) limitation clause   (C) indemnification clause   (D) exclusion clause

31. A contract to sell someone a slave for NTD1,000,000 could not be enforced at law because the contract entered into was _____ . (103年司法官律師)

(A) against public policy   (B) out of mistake   (C) under duress   (D) short of meeting of the minds

32. Joanna, 21-year-old, orally promises to sell Ty, 30-year-old, a book in return of Ty's promise to pay NT$500. There is a valid contract, because there is _____ of legally capable parties. (104年司法官律師)

(A) mutual assent   (B) mutual standing   (C) unanimous decision (D) beating of two hearts

33. Miller rents an apartment from Tyler. Both parties do not specify the term of the lease. Under Article 450 of the Civil Code, Miller may _____ the lease at any time. (104年司法官律師)

(A) breach   (B) enter into   (C) finish   (D) terminate

34. Vivian agrees to buy and Kenny agrees to sell a laptop at the price of NT20,000. However, Kenny sells and delivers the laptop to Chris the next day. Vivian may refuse to pay the price because Kenny fails to _____ the contract. (105年司法官律師)

    (A) revoke　(B) make　(C) carry　(D) perform

35. Abby walks into a restaurant and orders a tuna sandwich and a cup of soda. Edgar, the waiter, writes down the order. At this moment, Abby _____ a contract with the restaurant. (105年司法官律師)

    (A) takes into　(B) makes up　(C) gives up　(D) enters into

36. Oswald contracts to decorate a store for Winifred for NT$90,000 by a specified date or in the alternative to pay Winifred NT$500 a day during any period of delay. This type of provision is called _____ clause. (106年司法官律師)

    (A) remunerated　(B) pre-calculated damages

    (C) liquidated damages　(D) foreseeable damages

37. An acceptance which arrives late though usually it should have arrived earlier and within a reasonable time by its transmitting manner may nonetheless constitute a contract under R.O.C. Civil Code unless one of the following occurs: (106年司法官律師)

    (A) The one making the offer has reason to know the facts and sends without delay a notice informing the offeree of the fact that "acceptance" being late.

    (B) The one marking the offer does nothing to inform the offeree of the late acceptance while the former has reason to know the facts of its being late.

    (C) The one marking the acceptance explains the reasons of its being late to the offeror.

(D) The one marking the acceptance apologizes to the offeror of its being late.

38. Under R.O.C. Civil Code, if an offeree responds to an offer by making a _____ - in effect, proposes terms other than those contained in the original offer - the law treats that response as the legal equivalent of a rejection. (107年司法官律師)

(A) rejection　(B) acceptance　(C) offer　(D) counteroffer

39. In a contract of sale, which of the following warranty might not be honored by the seller? (107年司法官律師)

(A) Express warranty by the seller　(B) Implied warranty of the superior quality of the goods　(C) Implied warranty of merchantability (D) Implied warranty of fitness for particular purpose

40. Generally, a contract operates to confer rights and impose duties only on the parties to the contract and no other parties. This contractual relationship is summed up in the term _____. (107年司法官律師)

(A) novation　(B) privity of contract　(C) third-party beneficiary contract　(D) privity in possession

Which of the following answers is NOT correct:

1. The essential elements of a contract are _____.

(A) offer　(B) acceptance　(C) defense　(D) consideration

2. The power of acceptance is terminated if the offeree has _____.

(A) rejected the offer　(B) made a counter-offer　(C) not responded within a reasonable period of time　(D) received a firm offer from a merchant

3. A contract can be discharged due to impossibility of performance, impracticability, or frustration of purpose. As a result, the parties _____.

(A) are released from their contractual duties　(B) are not liable for breach of contract　(C) may sue for breach of contract
(D) may recover in quasi-contract

4. When both parties are mistaken (mutual mistake) about an existing fact, the contract is voidable if _____.
(A) the mistake concerns the price of the transaction　(B) the parties did not assume the risk of mistake　(C) the mistake concerns a basic assumption　(D) the mistake has a material effect

5. Compensatory damages may include _____.
(A) expectation damages　(B) reliance damages　(C) consequential damages　(D) nominal damages

Chapter 2 第二章 | TORT LAW 侵權法

ANGLO-AMERICAN TORT LAW
單元一　英美侵權法

Definition 定義

A tort is a civil wrong not arising from a contract. The purpose of tort law is to serve justice, give compensation for unreasonable harm, and be a deterrence.

- civil wrong 民事不法行爲
- justice 正義、公平
- compensation 損害賠償
- deterrence 制止、妨礙物、威懾

Governing law 管轄法律、適用法律、所依據法律、準據法

Torts are governed by common law (e.g. court decisions) and statutory law. The Restatement of Torts published by the American Law Institute (ALI) is a highly influential treatise that summarizes and clarifies the general principles of tort law in the United States. First published in the 1930s, the original version was replaced by the Second Restatement of Torts during the period from 1965 to 1979. Ever since, the Third Restatement of Torts has been introduced in the fields of products liability (1998), apportionment of liability (2000) and liability for physical and emotional harm (2009 / 2012), with the remaining parts to be concluded in the near future.

- common law 普通法
- statutory law 成文法
- Restatement of Torts 美國法律整編侵權行為法
- American Law Institute (ALI) 美國法律協會

Types of torts 侵權種類

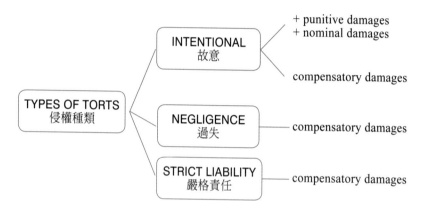

There are different types of torts depending on various standards of liability: Intent, negligence, strict liability.

- liability 責任
- intent 故意、意圖
- negligence 過失
- strict liability 嚴格責任

In addition to compensatory damages, also nominal and punitive damages are available in the event of intentional torts.

- compensatory damages 補償性損害賠償
- nominal damages 名義上的損害賠償
- punitive damages 懲罰性損害賠償

Case analysis 案件分析

1. Are the basic requirements for a prima facie case given?
   - ■ basic requirements 基本要求
   - ■ prima facie case 表面上證據確鑿的案件

2. Are there any defenses (e.g. consent, self-defense, contributory negligence, truth)?
   - ■ defenses 防衛、抗辯

3. What are the damages (e.g. medical expenses, lost income, pain)?
   - ■ damages 損害、賠償
   - ■ medical expenses 醫療費用
   - ■ lost income 收入損失
   - ■ pain 痛苦

Intentional torts 故意侵權

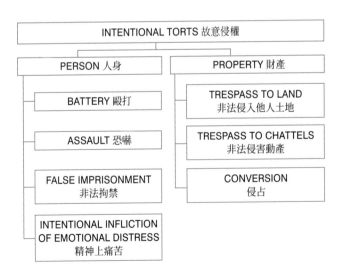

The basic elements of intentional torts are:

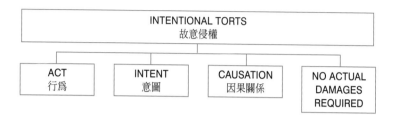

1. An act is a movement by the tortfeasor which is volitional or at least dictated by his mind.
   - act 行為
   - tortfeasor 侵權行為人
   - volitional 意志的
   - mind 精神、思想

2. The tortfeasor must act intentionally. His intent can be either specific or general, depending on whether it is his desired goal (specific intent) or whether he simply knows (general intent) the consequences of his conduct. If the tortfeasor misses his target and instead hits another person or commits a different tort, he is still liable. Thus, transferred intent suffices. However, the reason why a tortfeasor is doing this (i.e. his motivation) is irrelevant.
   - intent 故意、意圖
   - specific intent (goal) 特定／具體意圖（目標）
   - general intent (know) 一般意圖（知道）
   - transferred intent (different person/tort) 轉變意圖（不同的人／侵權）

3. The tortfeasor's act must be the direct or indirect cause (i.e. substantial factor) for plaintiff's harm.

■ cause 原因、起因
■ substantial factor 重大因素

4. Intentional torts do not require actual damage or harm.
■ actual damage / harm 實際損害 / 傷害

Intentional torts against the person 對人身的故意侵權

Battery 毆打

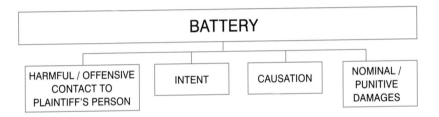

Battery is the intentional causation of harmful or offensive contact to plaintiff's person (including all that is connected, e.g. clothes, hand-bag).
■ harmful 傷害性
■ offensive (= no consent) 侵犯性、冒犯的（＝沒有同意）
■ contact 接觸、觸擊
■ person 人身

Assault 恐嚇、恫嚇、即時威脅、攻擊

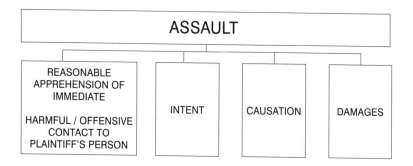

Assault is the intentional causation of a reasonable apprehension of immediate harmful or offensive contact to plaintiff's person.

- ■ reasonable (= apparent ability) 合理（＝表面／明顯的能力）
- ■ apprehension (= expectation/knowledge) 恐懼、憂慮（＝期待／知識）
- ■ immediate (= not future / distant) 立即（＝非未來／遠離的）

False imprisonment 非法拘禁

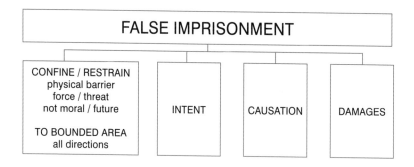

False imprisonment is the intentional causation of confinement or re-straint to a bounded area (i.e. there is no reasonable means of escape in all directions). Confinement or restraint can be exercised not only by physical barriers, but also by use of force or threat against the plaintiff, his family or his property (but the threat of moral or future consequences is not sufficient).

- confinement / restraint 限制
- bounded area (all directions) 界限區（向四面八方）
- physical barrier 實體限制
- force / threat 力量／威脅

Intentional infliction of emotional distress 使產生精神上痛苦之故意侵害行為、故意造成精神痛苦

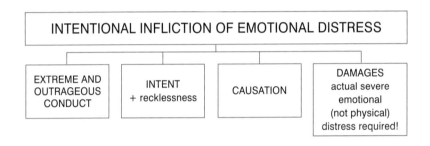

A person may be liable for intentional infliction of emotional distress where his conduct is extreme and outrageous (i.e. transcending all boundaries of decency, especially considering the existence of business, authority, or other special relationships). Transferred intent or even recklessness suffices. As a result, plaintiff must suffer from actual severe emotional (not physical) distress.

- extreme and outrageous conduct 極端粗暴行為
- recklessness 魯莽、輕率
- actual severe 實際上嚴重的
- emotional (not physical) distress 精神上（非身體上的）痛苦

Intentional torts against property 對財產的故意侵權

Trespass to land 非法侵入他人土地；非法侵犯土地

Trespass to land is the physical invasion of plaintiff's real property. Physical invasion can be exercised through a person (e.g. defendant enters plaintiff's house) or an object (e.g. defendant throws a stone in plaintiff's garden). Merely intangible matter (e.g. odor /noise) does not suffice (but defendant might be liable for nuisance or in accordance with strict liability standards). Note that the defendant must only have an intent to enter (i.e. mistake is no defense). *Example:* One night, defendant comes home very late after attending a party. It is dark and he has drunk a lot of alcohol. He staggers on his neighbour's land, mistakenly believing it to be the entrance to his house. Defendant is liable for trespass to land.

- physical 身體的、物質的
- invade, invasion 侵犯、侵入
- real property 房地產、不動產

Trespass to chattels 非法侵犯動產

Trespass to chattels is the intentional interference with plaintiff's right of possession (e.g. damaging). The tortfeasor must have an intent to do the act of interference (mistake is no defense). *Example:* On a rainy day defendant has a cup of coffee with a friend. When leaving the crowded cafe, he mistakenly takes someone else's umbrella. After walking in the rain with the umbrella for ten minutes, he notices the mistake and returns the umbrella.

- chattel (= movable personal property) 動產
- interfere, interference 干擾
- possession 占有、持有

Conversion 侵占、強占

Conversion is a substantial / serious interference with plaintiff's right of possession (e.g. serious damaging or destruction of property), which justifies that the defendant pay the full value of the property. Criteria for distinguishing conversion from trespass to chattels are e.g. duration, good / bad faith, resulting harm. Defendant must only have the intent to take possession (mistake as to ownership is no defense). *Example:* On a rainy day defendant has a cup of coffee with a friend. When leaving the crowded cafe, he mistakenly takes someone else's umbrella. Defendant never returns the umbrella.

- substantial / serious interference 嚴重干擾
- full value 全部價值

Defenses 防衛、抗辯

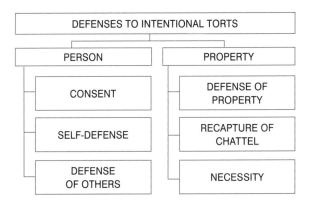

Where plaintiff sues for an intentional tort against the person, defendant may assert following defenses:

1. The defendant may claim that plaintiff gave his express consent. *Example*: Doctor asks patient to sign an express consent form before undergoing a surgery. Sometimes an implied consent is assumed, for instance due to conduct, custom, law, or an emergency (e.g. patient is unconscious). However, if defendant exceeds the boundaries of the consent, he may be liable.
   - consent 同意
   - express 明示
   - implied 默示
   - exceed 超過

2. The defendant may claim that he had a reasonable belief that there was a need for self-defense and that he did not use more force than necessary to prevent harm. Self-defense must not be used as retaliation and is generally not available to the aggressor. Retreat is not necessary, unless deadly force is used. Retreat is not necessary in one's own house.
   - self-defense 自衛
   - necessary 必要
   - to prevent harm 預防／防止損害
   - retaliation 報復
   - retreat 撤退

3. Likewise, a defendant may assert that he acted in defense of others, i.e. he had a reasonable belief that the aided person had a right of self-defense and he only used as much force as is permitted in the event of self-defense (necessary force).
   - defense of others 爲他人防衛
   - reasonable belief 合理相信

- use as much force as in event of self-defense 使用力量合於自衛所需（禁止防衛過當）

Where plaintiff sues for an intentional tort against property, the defendant may assert defense of property or recapture of chattel. However, defendant may only use reasonable force and not cause serious bodily harm (because bodily integrity is superior to protection of property).

- defense of property 對財產的防衛
- recapture of chattel 奪回動產
- reasonable force 正當的武力

Defense of property may be superseded by the privilege of necessity. Public necessity serves as an absolute defense (absolute privilege i.e. defendant must not pay for resulting harm), where it is necessary to protect public interests (e.g. public safety). *Example:* A large airplane makes an emergency landing on plaintiff's land. Even though this constitutes trespass to land, defendant may assert public necessity and is not liable. Private necessity serves as a qualified defense (qualified privilege i.e. defendant must pay for resulting harm), where it is necessary to protect a private interest (e.g. safety of an individual). *Example:* Defendant loses control over his car due to defective brakes. He drives on plaintiff's land to avoid a collision. If plaintiff claims trespass to land, defendant may assert the privilege of private necessity, but defendant must nevertheless pay for the harm done to plaintiff's land.

- public / private necessity 公共 / 私人必要行為
- absolute / qualified privilege 絕對 / 有限制的特權

Negligence 過失

The basic elements of negligence are:

1. The duty of care is generally owed to a foreseeable plaintiff (e.g. rescuer). An objective standard of care applies based on a reasonable person, who has the same physical traits as the defendant, as well as average mental capacity and average knowledge. However, if the defendant possesses higher knowledge or skills, he must use them (i.e. professionals are held to a higher standard of care). Note that children (usually above the age of four) can be capable of committing a tort (i.e. they are held to the standard of a reasonable child of similar age and education).

   - duty of care 注意義務
   - foreseeable plaintiff 可預見的原告
   - objective standard 客觀標準
   - reasonable person 合理的人
   - professionals 專家

2. The defendant must have breached his legal duty (i.e. breach of mere custom / usage is not sufficient). Negligence per se is found, where a statute is violated, which defines a clear standard and provides for a penalty, the statute is designed to prevent this type of harm and the plaintiff is within the protected class. Where direct evidence is not available, negligence can be established by circum-

stantial evidence if it can be inferred that in the absence of defendant's negligence the tort would not have occurred (theory of "res ipsa loquitur" = "the thing speaks for itself").

- breach of legal duty 違反法定義務
- negligence per se 當然過失
- circumstantial evidence 間接證據、情況證據
- res ipsa loquitur 事實本身即為說明、過失之推定

3. The defendant's negligence must have caused plaintiff's damage. In a first step, ask whether defendant was an actual cause (cause in fact). This question can be affirmed, if without defendant's negligence plaintiff's harm would not have occurred ("but for" test: CAUSE > RESULT. NO CAUSE > NO RESULT). Where concurrent causes exist, it suffices if defendant's negligence was a substantial factor in bringing about the harm ("substantial factor" test: CAUSE 1 + CAUSE 2 > RESULT). In the event of alternative causes, the burden of proof is on each defendant to show that his negligence was not a cause (CAUSE 1 / CAUSE 2 > RESULT). In a second step, limit the scope of defendant's liability by asking whether defendant was a proximate cause (cause in law). This question can be affirmed, if the consequences resulting from defendant's negligence were reasonably foreseeable.

- actual cause (cause in fact) 事實（上的）原因
- but for cause 若非有此原因，則無此結果
- concurrent / cumulative causes 共存原因 / 累積因果關係
- substantial factor 重大因素
- alternative causes 擇一原因
- proximate cause (cause in law) 近因、近接因果關係（法律原因）
- reasonably foreseeable consequences 可合理預見的結果

4. Following damages can be recovered: Personal damages (e.g. medical expenses, lost earnings, pain and suffering), property damages (e.g. reasonable cost of repair, fair market value). Note that punitive damages are only awarded under exceptional circumstancs (e.g. if defendant was reckless) and that nominal damages are not recoverable.

■ personal damages 人身損害賠償
■ property damages 財產損害賠償
■ punitive damages 懲罰性損害賠償
■ nominal damages 名義上的損害賠償

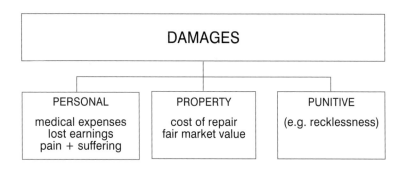

Defenses to negligence 過失侵權之抗辯

In jurisdictions where the doctrine of contributory negligence applies, plaintiff may generally not recover if he himself was at fault. In jurisdictions where the doctrine of comparative negligence applies, plaintiff may generally recover, but the amount of recoverable damages is reduced in accordance with his own fault.

■ contributory negligence 與有過失
■ comparative negligence 比較過失、過失比例分配

Furthermore, the defendant is not liable for negligence where plaintiff has (expressly / impliedly) assumed the risk. Assumption of risk requires that plaintiff knew of the risk and voluntarily consented to it.

■ assumption of risk 承擔風險

Strict liability 嚴格責任

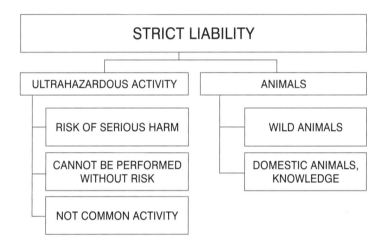

The basic elements of strict liability are:

1. absolute duty 絕對義務
2. breach 違反
3. causation 因果關係
4. damages 損害

Strict liability applies to operators of ultra-hazardous activities (e.g. storage of explosives). These are certain activities which are not common, entail a risk of serious harm and cannot be performed without risk of serious harm.

■ ultra-hazardous activity 極端危險行為、超常危險活動

Strict liability also applies to owners of wild animals (e.g. lion, snake). *Example:* Owner keeps a lion cub in his house. One day the lion cub escapes from the house and runs into neighbour's garden. Owner is strictly liable for any damages the lion cub causes in neighbour's garden. In comparison, owners of domestic or nondangerous animals (e.g. pig, cow, horse, rabbit) are liable only if they know of their animal's dangerous propensity. *Example:* Owner keeps a horse in his backyard. If owner knows that his horse has already once tried to bite the neighbour, owner is strictly liable even though a horse is not a wild animal.

■ wild / domestic animal 野生的 / 馴養的動物

Product liability 產品責任

The basic requirements for product liability are:

1. A product is defective, if it is unreasonably dangerous from the perspective of consumer expectation. A product may be defective due to

   - design (if it would have been possible to design a safer product without serious impact on the price = "reasonable alternative design"),

   - manufacturing (if a product departs from its design), or

   - inadequate warnings (where it is not apparent that a product is dangerous).

   ■ defective product 有瑕疵的產品

   ■ design defect 設計瑕疵

   ■ manufacturing defect 產品製造瑕疵

   ■ inadequate warning 不適當的警告

2. The defect existed when the product left defendant's control. Note that contractual privity between plaintiff and defendant (commercial supplier) is not required. *Example:* Manufacturer designs a defective product and sells it to wholesale company. Wholesale company sells the defective product to small retailer. Small retailer sells the defective product to consumer. Who is entitled to sue manufacturer? Wholesale company may sue manufacturer. But also small retailer and consumer may sue manufacturer, even though they are not in privity (i.e. they have no contractual relationship) with manufacturer.

▉control 控制

▉contractual privity 契約關係

3. The defect caused plaintiff's damage.

▉to cause 導致、使發生、引起

4. The plaintiff suffered damage.

▉damage 損害

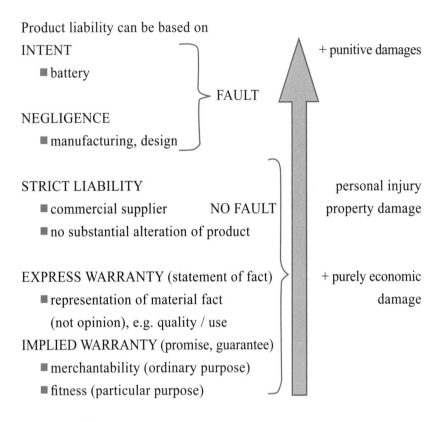

Product liability can be based on

INTENT
- battery

NEGLIGENCE
- manufacturing, design

FAULT

+ punitive damages

STRICT LIABILITY
- commercial supplier   NO FAULT
- no substantial alteration of product

personal injury
property damage

EXPRESS WARRANTY (statement of fact)
- representation of material fact
  (not opinion), e.g. quality / use
IMPLIED WARRANTY (promise, guarantee)
- merchantability (ordinary purpose)
- fitness (particular purpose)

+ purely economic
  damage

Warranty 擔保

An express warranty is a statement of fact (not opinion). Where the seller is a merchant, he gives an implied warranty of merchantability (= fit for ordinary purpose). An implied warranty of fitness for a particular purpose is given, where the seller knows that the buyer needs the goods for a particular purpose and is relying on his judgment. An implied warranty of merchantability can be disclaimed explicitly (must mention the word "merchantability") or impliedly ("as is"). A disclaimer of warranty of fitness for a particular purpose must be in writing and conspicuous.

- express / implied warranty 明示 / 默示擔保

- warranty of merchantability 可銷售擔保
- warranty of fitness for a particular purpose 符合特定用途的擔保
- disclaimer 免責條款、承諾之拒絕
- conspicuous 明顯的

Nuisance 非法妨害

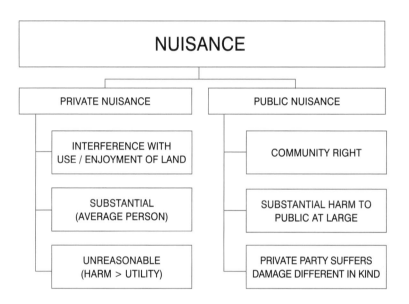

Nuisance is a special type of harm.

Private nuisance exists where defendant interferes with plaintiff's use / enjoyment of his land. (Compare: If defendant interferes with plaintiff's right to exclusive possession by way of physical invasion, this might constitute trespass to land!) The interference must be substantial for an average person and unreasonable (i.e. the harm resulting from the nuisance is greater than the utility). Possible remedies against private nuisance are compensatory damages, injunction, self-help / abatement.

- private nuisance 私人妨害
- interference with use / enjoyment 使用／享受之干擾
- substantial 重大
- unreasonable 不合理
- injunction 強制令、禁止令
- self-help 自助、自立
- abatement 消除、排除

Public nuisance exists where defendant interferes with a community right (e.g. health, safety, property) and thereby causes a substantial harm to the public at large. A private party is entitled to sue, if it can prove a particular damage that is different in kind.

- public nuisance 公共非法妨害
- community 社會、公眾、共有
- substantial harm 重大損害
- particular damage 特別之損害
- damage different in kind 損害種類不同

References:

1. Steven L. Emanuel, Law Outlines: Torts, Wolters Kluwer, 10th edition (2015).

2. Steven L. Emanuel, Law Outlines: Torts, Keyed to Prosser/Wade/Schwartz, Wolters Kluwer, 13th edition (2016).

3. Cornell Law School, Legal Information Institute, Tort, https://www.law.cornell.edu/wex/tort (accessed 9.8.2019).

4. American Law Institute, Restatement of the Law Second, Torts (1965, 1977, 1979), https://ali.org/publications/show/torts/#_tab-volumes (accessed 9.8.2019).

5. 黃裕凱博士教研網站，Second Restatement of Torts, http://merchantmarine.financelaw.fju.edu.tw/data/Teaching/English/ US%20 Restatement%202%20Torts.pdf (accessed 9.8.2019)。

6. ALI Director Richard L. Revesz, Completing the Restatement Third of Torts, Quarterly Newsletter (April 4, 2019), https://www.ali.org/news/articles/completing-restatement-third-torts/ (accessed 10.8.2019).

7. Law shelf Educational Media, National Paralegal College, Torts and Personal Injury, https://lawshelf.com/videocourses/topic/torts-and-personal-injury (accessed 9.8.2019).

8. The Free Dictionary, Tort Law, https://legal-dictionary.thefreedictionary.com/Tort+Law (accessed 9.8.2019).

9. Legal Dictionary, Tort Law, https://legaldictionary.net/tort-law/ (updated 19.8.2015, accessed 9.8.2019).

10. Legalcareerpath.com, What is Tort Law? https://legalcareerpath.com/tort-law/ (accessed 9.8.2019).

11. Wikipedia, United States tort law, https://en.wikipedia.org/wiki/United_States_tort_law (edited 5.4.2019, accessed 9.8.2019).

TAIWAN TORT LAW

Civil Code[1]

Part II Obligations
Sub-section 5 Torts

Article 184

A person who, intentionally or negligently, has wrongfully damaged the rights of another is bound to compensate him for any injury arising therefrom. The same rule shall be applied when the injury is done intentionally in a manner against the rules of morals.

A person, who violates a statutory provision enacted for the protection of others and therefore prejudice to others, is bound to compensate for the injury, except no negligence in his act can be proved.

Article 185

If several persons have wrongfully damaged the rights of another jointly, they are jointly liable for the injury arising therefrom. The same rule shall be applied even if which one has actually caused the injury cannot be sure.

Instigators and accomplices are deemed to be joint tortfeasors.

Article 187

A person of no capacity or limited in capacity to make juridical acts, who has wrongfully damaged the rights of another, shall be jointly

---

1   See Ministry of Justice, Laws & Regulations Database of The Republic of China, https://law.moj.gov.tw/Eng/LawClass/LawAll.aspx?PCode=B0000001 (amended on 19.6.2019, accessed 9.8.2019).

單元二　臺灣侵權行為法

民法[2]

第二編　債
第五款　侵權行為

第184條
因故意或過失，不法侵害他人之權利者，負損害賠償責任。故意以背於善良風俗之方法，加損害於他人者亦同。
違反保護他人之法律，致生損害於他人者，負賠償責任。但能證明其行為無過失者，不在此限。

第185條
數人共同不法侵害他人之權利者，連帶負損害賠償責任。不能知其中孰為加害人者，亦同。
造意人及幫助人，視為共同行為人。

第187條
無行為能力人或限制行為能力人，不法侵害他人之權利者，以行

---

2 法務部，全國法規資料庫，https://law.moj.gov.tw/LawClass/LawAll. aspx?pcode=B0000001（9.8.2019，修訂於2019年6月19日）。

liable with his guardian for any injury arising therefrom if he is capable of discernment at the time of committing such an act. If he is incapable of discernment at the time of committing the act, his guardian alone shall be liable for such injury.

In the case of the preceding paragraph, the guardian is not liable if there is no negligence in his duty of supervision, or if the injury would have been occasioned notwithstanding the exercise of reasonable supervision. ...

Article 188

The employer shall be jointly liable to make compensation for any injury which the employee has wrongfully caused to the rights of another in the performance of his duties. However, the employer is not liable for the injury if he has exercised reasonable care in the selection of the employee, and in the supervision of the performance of his duties, or if the injury would have been occasioned notwithstanding the exercise of such reasonable care.

... The employer who has made compensation as specified in the preceding paragraph may claim for reimbursement against the employee [who] committed the wrongful act.

Article 189

The proprietor is not liable for the injury wrongfully caused by an undertaker to the rights of another in the course of his work, unless the proprietor was negligent in regard to the work ordered or his instructions.

為時有識別能力為限，與其法定代理人連帶負損害賠償責任。行為時無識別能力者，由其法定代理人負損害賠償責任。

前項情形，法定代理人如其監督並未疏懈，或縱加以相當之監督，而仍不免發生損害者，不負賠償責任。……

第188條
受僱人因執行職務，不法侵害他人之權利者，由僱用人與行為人連帶負損害賠償責任。但選任受僱人及監督其職務之執行，已盡相當之注意或縱加以相當之注意而仍不免發生損害者，僱用人不負賠償責任。

……僱用人賠償損害時，對於為侵權行為之受僱人，有求償權。

第189條
承攬人因執行承攬事項，不法侵害他人之權利者，定作人不負損害賠償責任。但定作人於定作或指示有過失者，不在此限。

Article 190

If injury is caused by an animal, the possessor is bound to compensate the injured person for any injury arising therefrom, unless reasonable care in keeping according to the species and nature of the animal has been exercised, or unless the injury would have been occasioned notwithstanding the exercise of such reasonable care.

The possessor may claim for reimbursement against the third party, who has excited or provoked the animal, or against the possessor of another animal which has caused the excitement or provocation.

Article 191-1

The manufacturer is liable for the injury to another arising from the common use or consumption of his merchandise, unless there is no defectiveness in the production, manufacture, process, or design of the merchandise, or the injury is not caused by the defectiveness, or the manufacturer has exercised reasonable care to prevent the injury.

The manufacturer mentioned in the preceding paragraph is the person who produces, manufactures, or processes the merchandise. Those, who attach the merchandise with the service mark, or other characters, signs to the extent enough to show it was produced, manufactured, or processed by them, shall be deemed to be the manufacturer.

If the production, manufacture, process, or design of the merchandise is inconsistent with the contents of its manual or advertisement, it is deemed to be defective.

The importer shall be as liable for the injury as the manufacturer.

第190條

動物加損害於他人者，由其占有人負損害賠償責任。但依動物之
種類及性質已爲相當注意之管束，或縱爲相當注意之管束而仍不
免發生損害者，不在此限。

動物係由第三人或他動物之挑動，致加損害於他人者，其占有人
對於該第三人或該他動物之占有人，有求償權。

第191-1條

商品製造人因其商品之通常使用或消費所致他人之損害，負賠償
責任。但其對於商品之生產、製造或加工、設計並無欠缺或其損
害非因該項欠缺所致或於防止損害之發生，已盡相當之注意者，
不在此限。

前項所稱商品製造人，謂商品之生產、製造、加工業者。其在商
品上附加標章或其他文字、符號，足以表彰係其自己所生產、製
造、加工者，視爲商品製造人。

商品之生產、製造或加工、設計，與其說明書或廣告內容不符
者，視爲有欠缺。

商品輸入業者，應與商品製造人負同一之責任。

Article 191-3

The person, who runs a particular business or does other work or activity, shall be liable for the injury to another if the nature of the work or activity, or the implement or manner used might damage to another. ...

Article 192

A person who has wrongfully caused the death of another shall also be bound to make compensation for the injury to any person incurring the medical expenses, increasing the need in living, or incurring the funeral expenses. ...

Article 197

The claim for the injury arising from a wrongful act shall be extinguished by prescription, if not exercised within two years from the date when the injury and the person bound to make compensation became known to the injured person. The same rule shall be applied if ten years have elapsed from the date when the wrongful act was committed.

A person bound to make compensation shall, even after the completion of prescription under the preceding paragraph, return to the injured person in accordance with the provisions concerning Unjust Enrichment whatever he has acquired through a wrongful act and therefore prejudiced to the injured person.

第191-3條

經營一定事業或從事其他工作或活動之人，其工作或活動之性質或其使用之工具或方法有生損害於他人之危險者，對他人之損害應負賠償責任。……

第192條

不法侵害他人致死者，對於支出醫療及增加生活上需要之費用或殯葬費之人，亦應負損害賠償責任。……

第197條

因侵權行為所生之損害賠償請求權，自請求人知有損害及賠償義務人時起，二年間不行使而消滅。自有侵權行為時起，逾十年者亦同。

損害賠償之義務人，因侵權行為受利益，致被害人受損害者，於前項時效完成後，仍應依關於不當得利之規定，返還其所受之利益於被害人。

EXERCISES
單元三　練習

Mark the odd word（選意義不同的字）：

liability – obligation – duty – property

apprehension – anticipation – fear – mortgage

attack – aggression – invasion – negligence

privilege – beating – pounding – battery

bystander – tortfeasor – passerby – observer

deceit – fraud – misrepresentation – felony

conceal – hide – nondisclosure – collateral

deprive – take away – permanent – withhold

dignity – dismiss – respect – esteem

discretionary – free will – choice – loss

emotional distress – humiliation – mental suffering – malice

expert – specialist – professional – pecuniary

inherent – inseparable – intrinsic – immunity

physical – by itself – by operation of statute – per se

privilege – right – proceeding – advantage

volitional – willing – choosing – civil

Fill in: assault, battery, conversion, emotional distress, false imprisonment, trespass to chattels, trespass to land

	恫嚇	threatening immediate offensive physical contact or bodily harm
	毆擊，毆打，暴行	intentionally causing offensive physical contact or bodily harm
	精神痛苦	mental suffering, humiliation

	非法拘禁，人身拘禁	intentionally restraining / confining another by physical force or the threat of physical force without privilege or authority
	非法侵入他人土地	unlawful entry onto another's real property
	非法侵犯動產	intentional interference with possession of personal property
	侵占，強占	unauthorized dealing with or the assumption of rights of ownership to another's personal property

Fill in: comparative negligence, contributory negligence, negligence, negligence per se

	過失	breach of legal duty of care to another which results in loss or injury to the claimant
	當然過失	negligence that consists of a violation of a statute esp. designed to protect the public safety
	與有過失	plaintiff's negligence who contributed to the injury will bar recovery from defendant
	比較過失，過失比例分配	doctrine of apportioning liability and damages; negligence and damages are determined according to proportionate fault of plaintiff and defendant

Fill in: nuisance, product liability, strict liability, ultra-hazardous activity, vicarious liability

	嚴格責任	liability that is imposed without a finding of fault (as negligence or intent)
	極端危險行為，超常危險活動	abnormally dangerous activity

	產品責任	liability of a manufacturer or trader for selling a faulty product
	非法妨害	interfering with another's rights or interests (in particular the use or enjoyment of property) by being offensive, annoying, dangerous, obstructive, or unhealthful
	替代責任	liability that is imposed for another's acts because of imputed or constructive fault

Fill in: absolute privilege, deceit/fraud, defamation, libel, privilege, qualified privilege, slander

	欺騙，詐欺	misrepresentation of a material fact that is made with knowledge of its falsity and the intent to deceive another
	誹謗	injury of the good reputation of another
	文字誹謗	publication of defamatory matter in permanent form, as by a written or printed statement
	口頭誹謗	spoken / oral defamation
	特殊權利，特權	a right, license, or exemption from duty or liability granted as a special benefit, advantage, or favor
	絕對特權	a privilege that exempts a person from liability regardless of intent or motive
	受制約特權	a privilege that may be defeated, e.g. by a showing of actual malice; conditional privilege

Fill in: causation, cause in fact, proximate cause, superseding cause

	因果關係	producing an effect
	事實原因	a cause without which the result would not have occurred; actual cause; but-for cause
	近因	legal cause
	替代原因	an unforeseeable intervening cause that interrupts the chain of causation and becomes the proximate cause of the effect, also called intervening cause

Fill in: burden of proof, clear and convincing evidence, preponderance of evidence

	舉證責任	responsibility of producing sufficient evidence in support of a fact or issue
	清楚且令人信服的證據	evidence showing a high probability of truth of the factual matter at issue
	優勢證據	more likely than not

Fill in: expert witness, circumstantial evidence, res ipsa loquitur

	間接證據，情況證據	indirect evidence; proof of facts offered as evidence from which other facts are to be inferred; opposite of direct evidence
	事實本身即為說明，過失之推定	inference or presumption that a defendant was negligent on the basis of circumstantial evidence if the accident was of a kind that does not ordinarily occur in the absence of negligence
	專家證人	witness (as a medical specialist) who by virtue of special knowledge, skill, training, or experience is qualified to provide testimony to aid the factfinder in matters that exceed the common knowledge of ordinary people

Fill in: due process, good faith, injunction, statute of limitations

	正當程序	course of formal proceedings (as judicial proceedings) carried out regularly, fairly, and in accordance with established rules and principles
	誠信，善意	in accordance with standards of honesty, trust, sincerity, etc; vs. bad faith
	訴訟時效法規	statute defining the period within which legal action may be taken
	強制令、禁止令	court order compelling a party to do or refrain from doing a specified act

Fill in: force majeure, per se, prima facie case, respondeat superior

	不可抗力	an event (as war, labor strike, or extreme weather) or effect that cannot be reasonably anticipated or controlled
	本身，當然	inherently, strictly, or by operation of statute, constitutional provision or doctrine
	表面上證據確鑿的案件	a case established by evidence that is sufficient to raise a presumption of fact or establish the fact in question unless rebutted
	雇主責任	making an employer or principal liable for the wrong of an employee or agent if it was committed within the scope of employment

Find the corresponding noun:

VERB	NOUN
assume	
abuse	
cause	
conceal	

consent	
convert	
disclose	
dismiss	
interfere	
intrude	
invade	
invite	
prosecute	
represent	

Find the corresponding adjective:

NOUN	ADJECTIVE
defect	
liability	
malice	
necessity	
privacy	
recklessness	

Find the corresponding noun and adjective:

VERB	NOUN	ADJECTIVE
care		
compare		
contribute		
defame		
foresee		
inform		
intend		
neglect		

Find the opposite:

express warranty	
good faith	
public necessity	

Choose the best answer:

1. If the production, manufacture, process, or design of the merchandise is inconsistent with the contents of its manual or advertisement, it is deemed to be _____ .

    (A) default (B) defective (C) delegated (D) deliberate

2. The _____ is the person who produces, manufactures, or processes the merchandise.

    (A) merchant (B) manufacturer (C) minor (D) mortgagor

3. The employer shall be jointly liable to make compensation for any injury which the employee has wrongfully caused to the rights of another in the performance of his duties. However, the employer is not liable for the injury if he has exercised reasonable care in the selection of the employee, and in the _____ of the performance of his duties.

    (A) satisfaction (B) scienter (C) superior (D) supervision

4. Jae sees Lion about to strike Jae's son Jude. Jae may use reasonable force to prevent Lion from striking Jude based on _____ . (100年司法官)

    (A) self-defense (B) justifiable defense (C) emergent avoidance
    (D) defense of others

5. Pursuant to Article 10 of R.O.C. Consumer Protection Act, where there are sufficient facts to prove that the products will endanger the safety and health of the consumers, business operators shall immediately _____ such goods. (100年司法官)

   (A) recover　(B) reproduce　(C) recall　(D) renew

6. Without the consent of Veronica, a famous actress, Rene uses Veronica's picture on her cosmetic products. Rene is tortiously liable to Veronica for _____. (100年司法官)

   (A) misrecommendation　(B) misindorsement　(C) misexploitation
   (D) misappropriation

7. The complaint asserts that Nelnet, Chase, and Citigroup are acting in concert and therefore _____ liable to the plaintiffs for their injuries. (100年律師)

   (A) jointly and severally　(B) collectively　(C) aggregatedly
   (D) accumulatedly

8. A Taipei district court judge awarded NT$500,000 in _____ yesterday to a resident of Kaohsiung who sued a hospital for malpractice in plastic surgery. Please find the best answer to fill in the blank. (100年律師)

   (A) penalty　(B) charge　(C) fine　(D) damages

9. Cathy, a used car dealer, turns the odometer of the car back from 60,000 to 18,000 kilometers. Bill, relying on the odometer reading, purchases the car from Cathy. Cathy is liable to Bill for the fraudulent _____. (101年司法官)

   (A) omission　(B) quotation　(C) misrepresentation
   (D) disposition

10. Homer intentionally pulls the ears of Bo's large dog and injures Bo's dog. Homer is liable to Bo for trespass to chattels. Which of the following choices is the best meaning for "chattels"? (101年司法官)

    (A) Real estate   (B) Personal property   (C) Livestock   (D) Dogs

11. Lee posts a sign on the window of his coffee shop stating that Jimmy is a member of the gangsters, which is untrue. Lee is liable to Jimmy for _____ . (101年律師)

    (A) assault   (B) disgrace   (C) discredit   (D) defamation

12. Ken operates a fireworks factory in a highly populated city. Without any negligence, the factory explodes and damages Emma's apartment nearby. Since Ken is engaging in abnormally dangerous activity, Ken is _____ liable for Emma's loss. (101年律師)

    (A) strictly   (B) strict   (C) no-fault   (D) absolute

13. "The information contained in this report has been obtained from sources which we consider to be reliable. However, we do not guarantee its accuracy and, as such, the information may be incomplete or condensed. ..." This type of clause is usually referred to as _____ . (101年律師)

    (A) waiver clause   (B) pardon clause   (C) excuse clause   (D) disclaimer clause

14. Ally has a wart on her arm. Her physician, Eldon, anesthetizes Ally and removes the wart against Ally's will. The removal in no way affects Ally's health, and is in fact beneficial. Nevertheless, Ally still has suffered _____ and therefore can sue for damages. (102年司法官)

    (A) mental distress   (B) financial injury   (C) economic loss

(D) bodily harm

15. Pursuant to Article 187 of R.O.C. Civil Code, the guardian is not liable if there is no negligence in his duty of supervision. Which of the following is the best description of "Negligence"? (102年司法官)
    (A) Forgetfulness to the third party   (B) Continuing misconduct
    (C) Intention of the wrongful act   (D) Breach of a duty that proximately causes injury

16. Pursuant to Article 195 of R.O.C. Civil Code, Paragraph 1, if it is one's _____ that has been infringed, the injured person may also seek appropriate measures to restore it. (102年司法官)
    (A) body   (B) liberty   (C) privacy   (D) reputation

17. Pursuant to Article 184 of R.O.C. Civil Code, "A person who, _____, has wrongfully damaged the rights of another is bound to compensate him for any injury arising therefrom." (102年律師)
    (A) directly or indirectly   (B) legally or morally
    (C) intentionally or negligently   (D) potentially or immediately

18. Based on the evidence presented at trial, the judge (or jury) finds that the defendant breached a variety of duties to the plaintiff. The judge (or jury) also concludes that these breaches were the _____ cause of the portion of the plaintiff's damages. (102年律師)
    (A) proximate   (B) near   (C) fair   (D) approximate

19. E filed suit against G and H, and the judge found the defendants jointly and severally liable for E's injuries in the amount of NT$90,000. Pursuant to Article 185 of R.O.C. Civil Code, which of

the following is the correct description of the defendant's tort liability? (102年律師)

(A) E could recover NT$90,000 from each defendant.

(B) G and H would be liable for damages based upon their relative fault.

(C) Each defendant would be liable for NT$45,000.

(D) Both G and H would be liable for NT$90,000.

20. Alvin is a truck driver employed by Tasty Drink Inc. When Alvin delivers goods to a customer, he falls asleep and hits a pedestrian, Linda. Under Article 188 of R.O.C. Civil Code, Tasty Drink Inc. is _____ liable for Linda's injuries. (103年司法官律師)

(A) individually　(B) jointly and severally　(C) mutually

(D) separately

21. John, driving his truck on the street, was attracted by a burning car on his left side, then hit Mary, causing her personal injury. John felt sorry for Mary, but did not offer anything to compensate Mary. Which of the following is INCORRECT at law? (105年司法官律師)

(A) Mary may sue John on negligence to recover damages for her personal injury.

(B) John is not held criminally liable for his negligence unless Mary places criminal charge against John within six months after the incident.

(C) John is not legally liable for this incident at all for it is no more than an accident.

(D) The fact that Mary is covered by accident insurance is not a defense for John not to compensate Mary.

22. Under the Article 189 of the Civil Code, the proprietor is liable for third party's injury caused by the contractor's negligence ONLY if: (105年司法官律師)

    (A) The proprietor wrongfully selected the contractor.

    (B) The proprietor wrongfully supervised the contractor.

    (C) The work which caused injury was under the negligent instruction of the proprietor.

    (D) The work which caused injury was under the negligent instruction of the contractor.

23. Vincent has a 10-minute quarrel with Dan before he goes to work. On Vincent's way to work, a drunk driver hits him. Vincent sues Dan for his injuries and claims that Dan negligently delays his schedule. Dan may argue that there is no _____ between Vincent's injuries and Dan's acts. (105年司法官律師)

    (A) causation (B) casualty (C) link (D) collision

24. Mark's father is murdered by Hamlet. Under Article 194 of R.O.C. Civil Code, Mark may request Hamlet to compensate his _____ loss. (106年司法官律師)

    (A) monetary (B) economic (C) non-pecuniary (D) consequential

25. Jonathan negligently breaks two valuable vases of Evelyn in front of her. Three years later, Evelyn asks Jonathan to compensate her for her loss for the first time. Under Article 197 of R.O.C. Civil Code, Jonathan may assert _____ defense and refuse to pay. (106年司法官律師)

    (A) statute of limitations (B) statute of expiration (C) expiration of effectiveness (D) expiration of time

26. In recent decades, in the U.S., cases involving many people injured by the same conduct, known as _____ , have become more important than before. (107年司法官律師)

    (A) mass torts (B) mass asset (C) mass defect (D) mass spectrometry

27. Which of the following is not used to describe a defendant in any tort case? (107年司法官律師)

    (A) claimant (B) tortfeasor (C) trespasser (D) wrongdoer

28. Pursuant to Article 188 of R.O.C. Civil Code, Paragraph one, an employer shall be jointly and severally liable for any injury which the employee has wrongfully caused to the rights of another in the performance of his duties. In other words, an employer is _____ liable for the negligent acts by his employees. (107年司法官律師)

    (A) variously (B) venomously (C) vicariously (D) vexatiously

ANSWERS
單元四　答案

Mark the odd word（選意義不同的字）：

liability – obligation – duty – property 財產

apprehension – anticipation – fear – mortgage 抵押

attack – aggression – invasion – negligence 過失

privilege – beating – pounding – battery 特權

bystander – tortfeasor – passerby – observer 侵權行為人

deceit – fraud – misrepresentation – felony 重罪

conceal – hide – nondisclosure – collateral 附帶的

deprive – take away – permanent – withhold 永久的

dignity – dismiss – respect – esteem 駁回

discretionary – free will – choice – loss 損失

emotional distress – humiliation – mental suffering – malice 惡意

expert – specialist – professional – pecuniary 金錢的

inherent – inseparable – intrinsic – immunity 豁免

physical – by itself – by operation of statute – per se 身體的

privilege – right – proceeding – advantage 訴訟程序

volitional – willing – choosing – civil 公民的

Fill in:

assault	恫嚇	threatening immediate offensive physical contact or bodily harm
battery	毆擊，毆打，暴行	intentionally causing offensive physical contact or bodily harm
emotional distress	精神痛苦	mental suffering, humiliation
false imprisonment	非法拘禁，人身拘禁	intentionally restraining/confining another by physical force or the threat of physical force without privilege or authority

trespass to land	非法侵入他人土地	unlawful entry onto another's real property
trespass to chattels	非法侵犯動產	intentional interference with possession of personal property
conversion	侵占，強占	unauthorized dealing with or the assumption of rights of ownership to another's personal property

Fill in:

negligence	過失	breach of legal duty of care to another which results in loss or injury to the claimant
negligence per se	當然過失	negligence that consists of a violation of a statute esp. designed to protect the public safety
contributory negligence	與有過失	plaintiff's negligence who contributed to the injury will bar recovery from defendant
comparative negligence	比較過失，過失比例分配	doctrine of apportioning liability and damages: negligence and damages are determined according to proportionate fault of plaintiff and defendant

Fill in:

strict liability	嚴格責任	liability that is imposed without a finding of fault (as negligence or intent)
ultra-hazardous activity	極端危險行為，超常危險活動	abnormally dangerous activity
product liability	產品責任	liability of a manufacturer or trader for selling a faulty product
nuisance	非法妨害	interfering with another's rights or interests (in particular the use or enjoyment of property) by being offensive, annoying, dangerous, obstructive, or unhealthful
vicarious liability	替代責任	liability that is imposed for another's acts because of imputed or constructive fault

Fill in:

deceit, fraud	欺騙，詐欺	misrepresentation of a material fact that is made with knowledge of its falsity and the intent to deceive another
defamation	誹謗	injury of the good reputation of another
libel	文字誹謗	publication of defamatory matter in permanent form, as by a written or printed statement
slander	口頭誹謗	spoken / oral defamation
privilege	特殊權利，特權	a right, license, or exemption from duty or liability granted as a special benefit, advantage, or favor
absolute privilege	絕對特權	a privilege that exempts a person from liability regardless of intent or motive
qualified privilege	受制約特權	a privilege that may be defeated, e.g. by a showing of actual malice; conditional privilege

Fill in:

causation	因果關係	producing an effect
cause in fact	事實原因	a cause without which the result would not have occurred; actual cause; but-for cause
proximate cause	近因	legal cause
superseding cause	替代原因	an unforeseeable intervening cause that interrupts the chain of causation and becomes the proximate cause of the effect, also called intervening cause

法學英文

Fill in:

burden of proof	舉證責任	responsibility of producing sufficient evidence in support of a fact or issue
clear and convincing evidence	清楚且令人信服的證據	evidence showing a high probability of truth of the factual matter at issue
preponderance of evidence	優勢證據	more likely than not

Fill in:

circumstantial evidence	間接證據，情況證據	indirect evidence; proof of facts offered as evidence from which other facts are to be inferred; opposite of direct evidence
res ipsa loquitur	事實本身即為說明，過失之推定	inference or presumption that a defendant was negligent on the basis of circumstantial evidence if the accident was of a kind that does not ordinarily occur in the absence of negligence
expert witness	專家證人	witness (as a medical specialist) who by virtue of special knowledge, skill, training, or experience is qualified to provide testimony to aid the factfinder in matters that exceed the common knowledge of ordinary people

Fill in:

due process	正當程序	course of formal proceedings (as judicial proceedings) carried out regularly, fairly, and in accordance with established rules and principles
good faith	誠信，善意	in accordance with standards of honesty, trust, sincerity, etc; vs. bad faith
statute of limitations	訴訟時效法規	statute defining the period within which legal action may be taken

injunction	強制令、禁止令	court order compelling a party to do or refrain from doing a specified act

Fill in:

force majeure	不可抗力	an event (as war, labor strike, or extreme weather) or effect that cannot be reasonably anticipated or controlled
per se	本身，當然	inherently, strictly, or by operation of statute, constitutional provision or doctrine
prima facie case	表面上證據確鑿的案件	a case established by evidence that is sufficient to raise a presumption of fact or establish the fact in question unless rebutted
respondeat superior	雇主責任	making an employer or principal liable for the wrong of an employee or agent if it was committed within the scope of employment

Find the corresponding noun:

VERB	NOUN
assume	assumption 承擔
abuse	abuse 濫用
cause	cause 起因
conceal	concealment 隱匿
consent	consent 同意
convert	conversion 侵占
disclose	disclosure 公開
dismiss	dismissal 駁回
interfere	interference 干涉
intrude	intrusion 非法侵入
invade	invasion 侵害
invite	invitation 邀請
prosecute	prosecution 起訴
represent	representation 代表

Find the corresponding adjective:

NOUN	ADJECTIVE
defect	defective 有瑕疵
liability	liable 有責任的
malice	malicious 惡意的
necessity	necessary 必需的
privacy	private 私人的
recklessness	reckless 魯莽的

Find the corresponding noun and adjective:

VERB	NOUN	ADJECTIVE
care	care 注意	careful 小心的
compare	comparison 比較	comparative 比較的
contribute	contribution 貢獻	contributory 共同分擔的
defame	defamation 誹謗	defamatory 誹謗的
foresee	foreseeability 可預見性	foreseeable 可預見的
inform	information 資訊	informative 提供資訊的
intend	intent, intention 意圖	intentional 故意的
neglect	negligence 過失	negligent 過失的

Find the opposite:

express warranty	implied warranty 默示擔保
good faith	bad faith 惡意
public necessity	private necessity 私人必要行為

Choose the best answer:

1. If the production, manufacture, process, or design of the merchandise is inconsistent with the contents of its manual or advertisement, it is deemed to be _____ .
(A) default (B) defective (C) delegated (D) deliberate

2. The _____ is the person who produces, manufactures, or processes the merchandise.
(A) merchant (B) manufacturer (C) minor (D) mortgagor

3. The employer shall be jointly liable to make compensation for any injury which the employee has wrongfully caused to the rights of another in the performance of his duties. However, the employer is not liable for the injury if he has exercised reasonable care in the selection of the employee, and in the _____ of the performance of his duties.
(A) satisfaction (B) scienter (C) superior (D) supervision

4. Jae sees Lion about to strike Jae's son Jude. Jae may use reasonable force to prevent Lion from striking Jude based on _____. (100年司法官)
(A) self-defense (B) justifiable defense (C) emergent avoidance (D) defense of others

5. Pursuant to Article 10 of R.O.C. Consumer Protection Act, where there are sufficient facts to prove that the products will endanger the safety and health of the consumers, business operators shall immediately _____ such goods. (100年司法官)
(A) recover (B) reproduce (C) recall (D) renew

6. Without the consent of Veronica, a famous actress, Rene uses Veronica's picture on her cosmetic products. Rene is tortiously liable to Veronica for ＿＿＿＿. (100年司法官)

    (A) misrecommendation　(B) misindorsement　(C) misexploitation
    (D) misappropriation

7. The complaint asserts that Nelnet, Chase, and Citigroup are acting in concert and therefore ＿＿＿＿ liable to the plaintiffs for their injuries. (100年律師)

    (A) jointly and severally　(B) collectively　(C) aggregatedly
    (D) accumulatedly

8. A Taipei district court judge awarded NT$500,000 in ＿＿＿＿ yesterday to a resident of Kaohsiung who sued a hospital for malpractice in plastic surgery. Please find the best answer to fill in the blank. (100年律師)

    (A) penalty　(B) charge　(C) fine　(D) damages

9. Cathy, a used car dealer, turns the odometer of the car back from 60,000 to 18,000 kilometers. Bill, relying on the odometer reading, purchases the car from Cathy. Cathy is liable to Bill for the fraudulent ＿＿＿＿. (101年司法官)

    (A) omission　(B) quotation　(C) misrepresentation
    (D) disposition

10. Homer intentionally pulls the ears of Bo's large dog and injures Bo's dog. Homer is liable to Bo for trespass to chattels. Which of the following choices is the best meaning for "chattels"? (101年司法官)

    (A) Real estate　(B) Personal property　(C) Livestock　(D) Dogs

11. Lee posts a sign on the window of his coffee shop stating that Jimmy is a member of the gangsters, which is untrue. Lee is liable to Jimmy for _____ . (101年律師)

    (A) assault (B) disgrace (C) discredit (D) defamation

12. Ken operates a fireworks factory in a highly populated city. Without any negligence, the factory explodes and damages Emma's apartment nearby. Since Ken is engaging in abnormally dangerous activity, Ken is _____ liable for Emma's loss. (101年律師)

    (A) strictly (B) strict (C) no-fault (D) absolute

13. "The information contained in this report has been obtained from sources which we consider to be reliable. However, we do not guarantee its accuracy and, as such, the information may be incomplete or condensed. ..." This type of clause is usually referred to as _____ . (101年律師)

    (A) waiver clause (B) pardon clause (C) excuse clause (D) disclaimer clause

14. Ally has a wart on her arm. Her physician, Eldon, anesthetizes Ally and removes the wart against Ally's will. The removal in no way affects Ally's health, and is in fact beneficial. Nevertheless, Ally still has suffered _____ and therefore can sue for damages. (102年司法官)

    (A) mental distress (B) financial injury (C) economic loss (D) bodily harm

15. Pursuant to Article 187 of R.O.C. Civil Code, the guardian is not liable if there is no negligence in his duty of supervision. Which of the

following is the best description of "Negligence"? (102年司法官)

(A) Forgetfulness to the third party   (B) Continuing misconduct

(C) Intention of the wrongful act   (D) Breach of a duty that proximately causes injury

16. Pursuant to Article 195 of R.O.C. Civil Code, Paragraph 1, if it is one's _____ that has been infringed, the injured person may also seek appropriate measures to restore it. (102年司法官)

(A) body   (B) liberty   (C) privacy   (D) reputation

17. Pursuant to Article 184 of R.O.C. Civil Code, "A person who, _____, has wrongfully damaged the rights of another is bound to compensate him for any injury arising therefrom." (102年律師)

(A) directly or indirectly   (B) legally or morally   (C) intentionally or negligently   (D) potentially or immediately

18. Based on the evidence presented at trial, the judge (or jury) finds that the defendant breached a variety of duties to the plaintiff. The judge (or jury) also concludes that these breaches were the _____ cause of the portion of the plaintiff's damages. (102年律師)

(A) proximate   (B) near   (C) fair   (D) approximate

19. E filed suit against G and H, and the judge found the defendants jointly and severally liable for E's injuries in the amount of NT$90,000. Pursuant to Article 185 of R.O.C. Civil Code, which of the following is the correct description of the defendant's tort liability? (102年律師)

(A) E could recover NT$90,000 from each defendant.

(B) G and H would be liable for damages based upon their relative fault.

(C) Each defendant would be liable for NT$45,000.

(D) Both G and H would be liable for NT$90,000.

20. Alvin is a truck driver employed by Tasty Drink Inc. When Alvin delivers goods to a customer, he falls asleep and hits a pedestrian, Linda. Under Article 188 of R.O.C. Civil Code, Tasty Drink Inc. is _____ liable for Linda's injuries. (103年司法官律師)

(A) individually (B) jointly and severally (C) mutually

(D) separately

21. John, driving his truck on the street, was attracted by a burning car on his left side, then hit Mary, causing her personal injury. John felt sorry for Mary, but did not offer anything to compensate Mary. Which of the following is INCORRECT at law? (105年司法官律師)

(A) Mary may sue John on negligence to recover damages for her personal injury.

(B) John is not held criminally liable for his negligence unless Mary places criminal charge against John within six months after the incident.

(C) John is not legally liable for this incident at all for it is no more than an accident.

(D) The fact that Mary is covered by accident insurance is not a defense for John not to compensate Mary.

22. Under the Article 189 of the Civil Code, the proprietor is liable for third party's injury caused by the contractor's negligence ONLY if: (105年司法官律師)

(A) The proprietor wrongfully selected the contractor.

(B) The proprietor wrongfully supervised the contractor.

(C) The work which caused injury was under the negligent instruction of the proprietor.

(D) The work which caused injury was under the negligent instruction of the contractor.

23. Vincent has a 10-minute quarrel with Dan before he goes to work. On Vincent's way to work, a drunk driver hits him. Vincent sues Dan for his injuries and claims that Dan negligently delays his schedule. Dan may argue that there is no _____ between Vincent's injuries and Dan's acts. (105年司法官律師)

(A) causation　(B) casualty　(C) link　(D) collision

24. Mark's father is murdered by Hamlet. Under Article 194 of R.O.C. Civil Code, Mark may request Hamlet to compensate his _____ loss. (106年司法官律師)

(A) monetary　(B) economic　(C) non-pecuniary　(D) consequential

25. Jonathan negligently breaks two valuable vases of Evelyn in front of her. Three years later, Evelyn asks Jonathan to compensate her for her loss for the first time. Under Article 197 of R.O.C. Civil Code, Jonathan may assert _____ defense and refuse to pay. (106年司法官律師)

(A) statute of limitations　(B) statute of expiration　(C) expiration of effectiveness　(D) expiration of time

26. In recent decades, in the U.S., cases involving many people injured by the same conduct, known as _____, have become more important than before. (107年司法官律師)

(A) mass torts (B) mass asset (C) mass defect (D) mass spectrometry

27. Which of the following is not used to describe a defendant in any tort case? (107年司法官律師)

    (A) claimant (B) tortfeasor (C) trespasser (D) wrongdoer

28. Pursuant to Article 188 of R.O.C. Civil Code, Paragraph one, an employer shall be jointly and severally liable for any injury which the employee has wrongfully caused to the rights of another in the performance of his duties. In other words, an employer is _____ liable for the negligent acts by his employees. (107年司法官律師)

    (A) variously (B) venomously (C) vicariously (D) vexatiously

Chapter 3

COMPANY LAW & SECURITIES REGULATIONS
公司法、證券交易法

U.S. CORPORATE LAW
單元一　美國公司法

Definition 定義

A corporation is formed by one or more persons for a business purpose. It is a legal entity with legal rights and obligations that are distinct from its shareholders. For example, a corporation can own property or be sued under its own name. As a result, incorporation serves as away to protect its owners from personal liability. Only under exceptional circumstances (e.g. to prevent abuse or fraud) will the corporate veil be pierced and the shareholders remain liable.

- corporation 公司
- legal entity 法人
- legal rights and obligations 法律權利和義務
- distinct from 有區別的、與其他不同的
- shareholder 股東
- personal liability 個人責任
- piercing the corporate veil 揭開公司面紗

Compared with other business forms (e.g. partnerships), corporations offer certain benefits that might attract a large number of investors:

First, shareholders enjoy limited liability. Second, they can easily transfer their share ownership without affecting the continuous existence of the corporation. Third, shareholders do not have to possess professional skills, since a corporation is centrally managed by the board of directors. On the other hand, formal incorporation requirements may be associated with higher formation costs. The biggest disadvantage is the fact that corporations qualify as separate tax entities, thus resulting in double taxation of corporate profits (corporate income tax) and shareholders' dividends (personal income tax).

- business forms 企業種類
- partnership 合夥企業
- limited liability 有限責任
- transfer ownership 轉讓所有權
- continuous existence 不斷的生存
- centrally managed 集中管理
- board of directors 董事會
- formal requirements 正式必要條件
- separate tax entities 獨立納稅實體
- double taxation 雙重課稅
- corporate profits 公司利潤
- corporate income tax 公司所得稅
- dividends 股息
- personal income tax 個人所得稅

	CORPORATION	(GENERAL) PARTNERSHIP
LIABILITY	limited liability	unlimited liability
MANAGE-MENT	centralized board of directors	not centralized partners have equal voice
EXISTENCE	continuous perpetual	dissolved by death/withdrawal
TRANSFER-ABILITY	ownership transferable	consent required
FEDERAL INCOME TAX	separate tax entity double taxation	flow-through entity avoid double taxation
FORMATION COSTS	formal requirements	informal

Governing law 管轄法律、適用法律、所依據法律、準據法

In the United States, corporations are governed by state law. Many states have enacted their corporate law statutes with reference to the Model Business Corporation Act (MBCA) proposed by the American Bar Association (ABA) in 1950 and revised in 2016. Where no statutory provisions are applicable, recourse must be taken to common law (e.g. judicial decisions, general principles).

- state law 州法
- Model Business Corporation Act (MBCA) 模範公司法
- American Bar Association (ABA) 美國律師協會
- statutory provisions 法定條文
- common law 普通法

Although corporations are creatures of state law, federal laws are often relevant for their external relations. For instance, with the rise of large conglomerates in the late 19th century, Congress began introducing federal antitrust legislation to restrain monopolies and ensure fair competition on a nationwide basis (e.g. Sherman Act of 1890, Clayton Antitrust Act of 1914, Federal Trade Commission Act of 1914, Hart-Scott-Rodino Act 1976).

- federal law 聯邦法
- conglomerate 企業集團、聯合大企業
- antitrust 反托拉斯
- monopoly 壟斷
- fair competition 公平競爭、公平交易

Likewise, securities were originally regulated by the states in so called "blue sky" laws. But the stock market crash of 1929 made it clear that investors needed to be protected across state borders. The Securities Act of 1933 therefore enshrined the principle of "full and fair disclosure" for the primary market. Initial public offerings thus require a registration statement and prospectus containing all material information. A year later, the Securities Exchange Act of 1934 was passed to regulate the secondary market (i.e. trading of securities which are already on the open market). Not only did it impose periodic reporting obligations (e.g. quarterly and annual reports), but it also established the Securities and Exchange Commission (SEC) with the authority to prescribe detailed rules and broad enforcement powers.

- securities 證券
- blue sky laws 藍天法
- stock market 股票市場、股票交易

- Securities Act of 1933 1933年證券法
- disclosure 公開、披露
- primary / secondary market 初級 / 二級市場
- initial public offering 首次公開募股、首次公開發行股票
- registration statement 登記聲明、註冊書
- prospectus 公開說明書、招股說明書
- material information 重大訊息
- Securities Exchange Act of 1934 1934年證券交易法
- periodic reports (e.g. quarterly and annual reports) 定期報告
  （例如：季度與年度報告）
- Securities and Exchange Commission (SEC) 證券交易委員會

A wave of corporate scandals involving fraudulent reporting induced the Congress in 2002 to proclaim the Sarbanes-Oxley Act, thereby requiring financial statements of public companies to be audited by independent accounting firms and certified by their chief executive officers (CEOs) and chief financial officers (CFOs).

- financial statements 財務報表
- public company 股票上市公司、公開招股公司、公開發行公司
- audit 審計
- independent accounting firms 獨立會計師事務所
- certify 核實
- chief executive officers (CEOs) 執行長
- chief financial officers (CFOs) 財務長

Transparency and accountability in corporate governance and more generally in the financial system continue to be major concerns, as last but not least reflected in the Dodd-Frank Wall Street Reform and Consumer Protection Act of 2010. Drawing lessons from the subprime mortgage crisis, this federal legislation proposed a comprehensive set of measures, among others subjecting executive compensation in public companies to shareholder approval ("say on pay") and enhancing the protection of whistleblowers.

- transparency 透明度
- accountability 負有責任
- corporate governance 公司治理
- compensation 薪水
- shareholder approval 股東批准
- whistleblower protection 告密者保護

FEDERAL LAW	Sarbanes-Oxley Dodd-Frank Act	1933 Act 1934 Act	antitrust law
STATE LAW	corporate law *MBCA* common law	blue sky law	antitrust law

Incorporation 公司設立

To form a corporation, at least one person ("incorporator" or "promoter") has to sign and file the founding documents with a public register in the selected state of incorporation (e.g. Delaware). The most important document is called the "articles of incorporation" or "corporate charter". Like a constitution, it stipulates certain essential information that must be disclosed to the public (MBCA § 2.02. Articles of incorporation): "(a) The articles of incorporation must set forth: (1) a corporate name ... (2) the number of shares the corporation is authorized to issue; (3) ... mailing addresses of the ... registered office and ... agent at that office; and (4) the name and address of each incorporator."

- incorporator, promoter 發起人
- file 申報、呈報、提出（申請等）、把……歸檔
- public register 公共註冊處
- articles of incorporation, corporate charter 公司章程
- essential 必要的、不可缺的
- corporate name 公司名稱
- number of authorized shares 核定股數
- address 地址

The name must be distinguishable and contain one of the following words or abbreviations: company / co., corporation / corp., incorporated / inc., limited / ltd. Not distinguishable names are e.g. ABC Corporation = ABC Inc. = ABC Co. = ABC Corp., 2 = Two, d = D (MBCA § 4.01. Corporate name).

- distinguishable 可區別的
- abbreviation 縮寫

In addition, the articles of incorporation may contain optional provisions, e.g. regarding its purpose, powers and duration, limitation of directors' liability, removal of directors only with cause, different classes of shares, special voting rights for shareholders (see MBCA § 2.02. Articles of incorporation). Not only may a corporation engage "in any lawful business" (MBCA §3.01. Purposes), it also "has the same powers as an individual to do all things necessary or convenient to carry out its business and affairs" and has "perpetual duration" unless the articles of incorporation provide otherwise (MBCA §3.02. General powers).

- ■ optional 非必須的
- ■ purpose 目的
- ■ powers 權力
- ■ (perpetual) duration （永久的）期間
- ■ limitation of directors' liability 限制董事責任
- ■ removal of directors only with cause 解任董事須附理由
- ■ different classes of shares 不同股票種類
- ■ special voting rights 特殊投票權
- ■ engage in any lawful business 從事任何合法事務

ARTICLES OF INCORPORATION	
REQUIRED (MBCA § 2.02.a)	OPTIONAL (MBCA § 2.02.b)
corporate name	purpose, power, duration
registered office / agent incorporator	directors limitation of liability removal with cause
authorized shares	classes of shares special voting rights

Once the articles of incorporation have been approved and filed, the corporation starts to exist (MBCA § 2.03. Incorporation): "(a) Unless a delayed effective date is specified, the corporate existence begins when the articles of incorporation are filed. (b) The secretary of state's filing of the articles of incorporation is conclusive proof that the incorporators satisfied all conditions precedent to incorporation".

- ■ secretary of state 州務卿
- ■ conclusive proof 確鑿證據、確實的證據、決定性證明、確證

The initial directors named in the articles of incorporation or the incorporator(s) will then convene an organizational meeting to appoint officers and adopt detailed bylaws for the corporation's internal governance (MBCA § 2.05. Organization of corporation).

- appoint officers 任命高級職員
- bylaws 內部章程、辦事細則
- internal governance 內部治理

Capital and shares 資本與股份

A corporation's nominal capital is divided into shares, each representing a part of equity or ownership interest. The articles of incorporation must specify the total number of authorized shares and may also designate different classes of shares. For instance, preferred shares promise higher dividends albeit with no or only limited voting rights, whereas common shares confer full voting rights and the power to receive the corporation's net assets upon dissolution (MBCA § 6.01. Authorized shares).

- nominal capital 名義資本
- equity 產權
- ownership 所有權
- authorized shares 核定股份
- preferred shares 優先股
- common shares 普通股

A part or all of the authorized shares are then issued and sold to subscribers (MBCA § 6.21. Issuance of shares): "(b) The board of directors may authorize shares to be issued for consideration consisting of any tangible or intangible property or benefit to the corporation, including cash, ... services."

- issue 發行
- subscriber 認股人

Shares that have been issued and sold are outstanding until they are reacquired, redeemed, converted, or cancelled by the corporation (MBCA § 6.03. Issued and outstanding shares). Once a corporation acquires its own shares, such shares again qualify as authorized but unissued shares (MBCA § 6.31. Corporation's acquisition of its own shares): "(a) A corporation may acquire its own shares, and shares so acquired constitute authorized but unissued shares."

- outstanding shares 在外股票、流通股票
- reacquired shares 重取得股份、重獲股份
- redeemed shares 被贖回股份
- converted shares 轉換股份
- cancelled shares 註銷股份
- authorized but unissued shares 核定但非發行股份

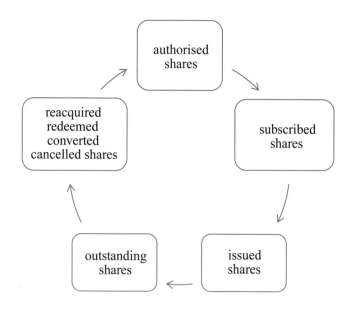

Restrictions on share transfers may be imposed in various ways (MBCA § 6.27. Restriction on transfer of shares): "(a) The articles of incorporation, the bylaws, an agreement among shareholders, or an agreement between shareholders and the corporation may impose restrictions on the transfer ... of shares ... (d) A restriction on the transfer ... of shares may: (1) obligate the shareholder first to offer the corporation ... an opportunity to acquire the restricted shares [right of first offer]; (2) obligate the corporation ... to acquire the restricted shares [buy-sell agreement]; (3) require the corporation ... to approve the transfer of the restricted shares [consent requirement]; or (4) prohibit the transfer of the restricted shares to designated persons [absolute prohibition]."

■ restriction 限制
■ share transfer 股份轉讓

Moreover, the articles of incorporation may grant shareholders a pre-emptive right to acquire shares that will be issued at a later time. This can prevent a dilution of the shareholders' voting power and maintain their overall equity participation in the corporation (MBCA § 6.30. Shareholders' preemptive rights): "The shareholders of a corporation do not have a preemptive right to acquire the corporation's unissued shares except to the extent the articles of incorporation so provide ... The shareholders of the corporation have a preemptive right ... to acquire proportional amounts of the corporation's unisssued shares upon the decision of the board of directors to issue them."

■ preemptive right 優先購買權

Shareholders 股東

Shareholders are persons who have acquired company shares. Depending on the types of shares they possess, shareholders are entitled to receive distributions, notably in form of cash or property dividends: "(a) A board of directors may authorize and the corporation may make distributions to its shareholders ... (c) No distribution may be made if, after giving it effect: (1) the corporation would not be able to pay its debts ... or (2) the corporation's total assets would be less than the sum of its total liabilities" (MBCA § 6.40. Distributions to shareholders).

- ■ entitled to receive distributions 有權獲得分配
- ■ dividends 股息

As investors or owners of a company, shareholders exercise indirect control over management through their power to elect and remove corporate directors. On top of that, all fundamental changes (e.g. sale of corporate assets exceeding certain thresholds, amendments to the articles of incorporation, merger, dissolution) require shareholder approval.

- ■ investor 投資者
- ■ owner 所有人
- ■ control 控制
- ■ elect and remove 選任與解任
- ■ fundamental change 基礎性變更
- ■ require shareholder approval 需要股東批准

Shareholders cast their votes in a shareholders' meeting, which shall be held at least once every year (MBCA § 7.01. Annual meeting):

"(a) Unless directors are elected by written consent ..., a corporation shall hold a meeting of shareholders annually at a time stated in ... the bylaws at which directors shall be elected."

- cast vote 投票
- shareholders' meeting 股東會
- annual meeting 年會

A shareholder can authorize a proxy to vote on his behalf (MBCA § 7.22. Proxies): "(a) A shareholder may vote ... in person or by proxy. (b) A shareholder ... may appoint a proxy to vote or otherwise act for the shareholder by signing an appointment form".

- authorize 授權
- proxy 代理人、代理委託書
- on behalf 代表

For proposed actions to be approved, not only must a minimum number of shareholders be present ("quorum"), but the number of votes in favour of such actions must reach a certain threshold ("voting requirement", e.g. majority /supermajority / unanimity).

- quorum 法定最低人數
- in favour of 贊成、支持、有利於
- must reach a certain threshold 必須達到特定門檻
- majority / supermajority / unanimity 多數 / 超級多數 / 全體一致

Instead of convening an oral meeting, shareholder actions can be taken by unanimous written consent (MBCA § 7.04. Action without meeting): "Action ... to be taken at a shareholders' meeting may be taken without a meeting if the action is taken by all the shareholders entitled to vote on the action. The action must be evidenced by ...

written consents bearing the date of signature and describing the action taken, signed by all the shareholders entitled to vote on the action and delivered to the corporation for filing by the corporation with the minutes or corporate records."

- oral meeting 口頭會議
- unanimous written consent 一致書面同意
- minutes 會議記錄

Last but not least, shareholders can seek judicial remedies to protect their rights. They can do so by filing a direct lawsuit in their own name (e.g. to enforce voting rights, payment of dividends) or by bringing a derivative suit on behalf of the corporation (e.g. against a director for breach of fiduciary duty).

- judicial remedy 司法救濟
- file a direct lawsuit 提起直接訴訟
- derivative suit 股東代表訴訟、代位訴訟、派生訴訟、衍生訴訟
- breach of fiduciary duty 違反受託義務

Board of Directors 董事會

Corporations are characterized by a separation of ownership and control: Although shareholders qualify as owners, they do not directly control a corporation. Instead, shareholders elect directors who – in their role as fiduciaries – are entrusted with the overall management and oversight of a corporation (MBCA § 8.01. Requirement for and functions of board of directors): "(A)ll corporate powers shall be exercised by or under the authority of the board of directors, and the business and affairs of the corporation shall be managed by or under the direction, and subject to the oversight, of the board of directors."

- separation of ownership and control 所有權與控制分離
- director 董事
- fiduciary 受託人
- management 管理、經營
- oversight 監督

Above all, directors have the power to adopt corporate policies and to appoint, supervise or remove corporate officers. Respective resolutions can be passed at board meetings or by unanimous written consent (MBCA § 8.21. Action without meeting): "Except to the extent that the articles of incorporation or bylaws require that action by the board of directors be taken at a meeting, action ... to be taken by the board of directors may be taken without a meeting if each director signs a consent describing the action to be taken and delivers it to the corporation."

- adopt policies 採取政策
- appoint, supervise, remove 任命、監督、解任
- resolution 決議

The corporate governance structure in the United States can be described as a one-tier system: A single, unified board is composed of directors exercising managerial functions within the corporation (inside directors) as well as independent supervisors (outside directors not employed by the corporation). In comparison, some countries (e.g. Germany) follow a two-tier system that clearly distinguishes between a management board and a separate supervisory board.

- one-tier / two-tier 一元制 / 二元制
- inside / outside directors 內部 / 外部董事
- independent supervisors 獨立監察人

■ management board 董事會
■ supervisory board 監事會

When carrying out their fiduciary duties, directors must comply with two basic standards of conduct: The duty of loyalty and the duty of care.

■ fiduciary duty 受託義務
■ comply with 遵守
■ standard of conduct 行為準則
■ duty of loyalty 忠實義務
■ duty of care 注意義務

According to the general duty of loyalty, directors must act in good faith and in the best interest of the corporation (MBCA § 8.30. Standards of conduct for directors): "(a) Each member of the board of directors, when discharging the duties of a director, shall act: (i) in good faith, and (ii) in a manner the director reasonably believes to be in the best interests of the corporation."

■ good faith 善意
■ in the best interest of the corporation 為公司最佳利益
■ discharge duties 履行義務
■ reasonably believe 合理相信

This duty involves an obligation for directors to avoid self-dealing transactions, conflicts of interest or acting in competition with the corporation. In these cases, disclosure of all material facts should be made to obtain the approval of the board or the ratification of the shareholders.

■ avoid self-dealing transactions 避免自我交易

▦ conflict of interest 利益衝突
▦ competition with the corporation 與公司競爭
▦ disclosure of all material facts 揭露所有重要事實
▦ approval 批准、認可、贊成、同意
▦ ratification 批准、正式簽署

Furthermore, directors have a duty of care to act like a reasonably prudent person under similar circumstances (MBCA § 8.30. Standards of conduct for directors): "(b) The members of the board of directors or a board committee, when becoming informed in connection with their decision-making function or devoting attention to their oversight function, shall discharge their duties with the care that a person in a like position would reasonably believe appropriate under similar circumstances."

▦ reasonably prudent person 合理謹慎之人
▦ in a like position 在同樣的職位
▦ under similar circumstances 在相類似的情形下

It can be presumed that a director has met the duty of care, if he has acted in good faith, with a reasonable belief to serve the corporation's best interest, on the basis of an informed decision. Hence, the critical question is not whether a director's decision turns out to be right or wrong, but whether the decision-making process was based on sufficiently reliable information (e.g. facts, research data, scientific studies, expert advice). This principle known as "business judgment rule" provides a "safe harbor" for inevitably risky business decisions and shields a director's conduct from liability.

▦ presume 假定、認為、相信
▦ informed decision 知情決定、在充分資訊下決策

- decision-making process 決策過程
- business judgment rule 商業經營判斷法則
- safe harbor 安全港、避風港

Only in rather extreme cases have courts found that the duty of care was breached and imposed money damages. For instance, in *Francis v. United Jersey Bank*, 87 N.J. 15 (1981), a director was held personally liable for the corporation's bankruptcy and losses suffered by its clients as a result of the director's ignorance of corporate affairs (e.g. absence from board meetings, lack of familiarity with financial and legal matters, failure to obtain professional advice). The decision made it clear that "directors are bound to exercise ordinary care ... Directors may not shut their eyes to corporate misconduct and then claim that because they did not see the misconduct, they did not have a duty to look. ... A director is not an ornament ... a director cannot protect himself behind a paper shield bearing the motto, 'dummy director.' ... With power comes responsibility."

- money damages 賠償金
- bankruptcy 破產
- ordinary care 一般注意、普通注意力

In practice, most states allow corporate charters to include an exculpatory clause stating that directors will not be personally liable for lack of due care (MBCA § 2.02. Articles of incorporation): "(b) The articles of incorporation may set forth: ... (4) a provision eliminating or limiting the liability of a director to the corporation or its shareholders for money damages ... except liability for ... (ii) an intentional infliction of harm on the corporation or the shareholders ... or (iv) an intentional violation of criminal law."

■ exculpatory clause 免責條款
■ intentional 故意的

Regardless of a director's performance, he / she can be removed by the shareholders even without cause, unless otherwise provided in the articles of incorporation (MBCA § 8.08. Removal of directors by shareholders): "The shareholders may remove one or more directors with or without cause unless the articles of incorporation provide that directors may be removed only for cause."

■ remove 解任
■ without cause 無須理由

Officers 高級職員

Officers are appointed by the directors to carry out the daily operations of a corporation. Important executives are, for instance, the president, vice-president, chief executive officer (CEO), chief financial officer (CFO), treasurer and secretary. Like directors, officers have a fiduciary duty to act in good faith and with due care (MBCA § 8.42. Standards of conduct for directors): "(a) An officer, when performing in such capacity, has the duty to act: (1) in good faith; (2) with the care that a person in a like position would reasonably exercise under similar circumstances; and (3) in a manner the officer reasonably believes to be in the best interests of the corporation."

■ carry out daily operations 執行日常業務
■ executive 經營者、執行官
■ president 公司總裁
■ vice-president 副總裁
■ chief executive officer (CEO) 執行長

■ chief financial officer (CFO) 財務長
■ treasurer 司庫
■ secretary 秘書

Termination 終止

A company is terminated in two stages: Dissolution and liquidation. The initial stage of dissolution can be commenced voluntarily by the board of directors with the approval of the shareholders. Apart from that, corporations can be dissolved involuntarily due to enforcement proceedings by the secretary of state (administrative dissolution) for failure to comply with legal obligations (e.g. pay fees and taxes), or ultimately by court decree (judicial dissolution) at the request of certain parties (e.g. state attorney general, shareholders, unsatisfied creditors). During the latter stage of liquidation, a corporation sells all its remaining assets and distributes the cash among creditors and shareholders.

■ stage 階段
■ dissolution 解散
■ liquidation 清算
■ administrative dissolution 行政解散
■ judicial dissolution 司法解散
■ creditor 債權人

Mergers and takeovers 合併與收購

A merger is the combination of two or more corporations. As a result, the corporation being acquired ceases to exist and the survivor (i.e. the acquiring corporation or a newly created entity) automatically assumes all assets and liabilities (MBCA § 11.07. Effect of merger or share exchange). The specific terms and conditions of the merger are adopted by the board of directors and require the approval of the shareholders, whereby dissenting shareholders have an appraisal right (i.e. they can sell their shares to the corporation for a cash amount that a court has determined to be the fair value). To take effect, the merger agreement must be signed and delivered to the secretary of state for public filing. If the transaction exceeds certain thresholds, the U.S. Department of Justice and the Federal Trade Commission (FTC) must be notified in advance to ensure compliance with federal antitrust laws.

- combination 結合
- corporation being acquired 被收購合併公司
- cease to exist 終止存在
- survivor 倖存者、生還者、殘存物
- acquiring corporation 合併公司、存續公司
- assume 承擔、就任、取得
- all assets and liabilities 所有資產與責任
- dissenting shareholder 異議股東
- appraisal right 股份收買請求權、股份評估權
- fair value 公允價值
- merger agreement 合併契約
- U.S. Department of Justice 美國司法部
- Federal Trade Commission (FTC) 聯邦貿易委員會

| ACQUIRING ENTITY | + | ACQUIRED ENTITY |

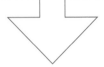

1. plan of merger
   adopted by board of directors
   approved by shareholders

2. articles of merger
   public filing

3. result: the acquired entity ceases to exist

SURVIVOR
only the acquiring entity survives A + B = A
or a new corporation is created A + B = C

A takeover is the acquisition of control over a publicly traded corporation either with the board of directors' consent (friendly takeover) or without such consent (hostile takeover). It is initiated by a bidder, who makes a public tender offer directly to the shareholders of the target corporation to purchase a substantial percentage of stocks at a premium price. For the protection of shareholders, tender offers are subject to certain disclosure requirements. In particular, the Securities and Exchange Commission (SEC) must be notified when the beneficial ownership exceeds a 5% threshold (Securities Exchange Act 1934 Section 14d): "It shall be unlawful for any person ... to make a tender offer for ... equity security ... if, after consummation thereof, such person would, directly or indirectly, be the beneficial owner of more than 5 per centum of such class, unless ... such person has filed with the Commission a statement."

- acquisition of control 取得控制
- publicly traded corporation 上市公司
- friendly takeover 善意收購
- hostile takeover 惡意收購、敵意收購、強制收購
- bidder 投標人
- public tender offer 公開收購
- target corporation 目標公司、被收購的公司
- substantial percentage of stocks 股票相當之比例
- premium price 溢價
- disclosure requirements 披露要求、公開要求
- beneficial ownership 實益擁有權、實際所有權

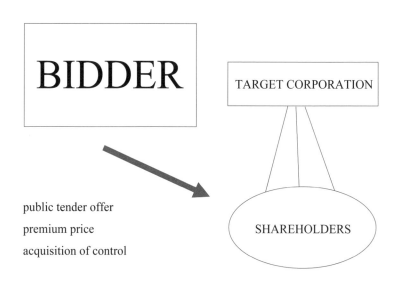

A comparison between mergers and takeovers thus shows following differences: First, a merger is generally based on a mutual decision between equals, whereas a takeover typically takes place between a larger corporation and a smaller corporation. Second, a merger is adopted with the consent of the board of directors, whereas a hostile takeover lacks such consent. Third, mergers are generally subject to the collective approval of a shareholders' meeting. Dissenting shareholders, who are overruled by a majority in favour of the transaction, have a right to appraisal. In contrast, formal shareholder voting does not take place in the course of a takeover, since each individual shareholder can simply decide whether or not to accept the tender offer. Hence, even if a tender offer succeeds, some remaining shareholders often continue to have a minority stake in the target corporation. Fourth, a merger must be filed with the secretary of state in order to take effect. Moreover, large-scale transactions that exceed certain thresholds trigger an obligation to notify the Securities and Exchange Commission (SEC), the U.S. Department of Justice and the Federal Trade Commission (FTC) respectively. Finally, a merger has the result that the acquired entity ceases to exist and is replaced by the surviving entity, which automatically assumes all assets and liabilities. In a takeover, however, the target corporation continues to exist and becomes a subsidiary of the acquirer.

	MERGER	**TAKEOVER**
PARTIES	equal (mutual decision)	unequal (large corporation buys small corporation)
BOARD OF DIRECTORS	consent (adopt merger plan)	consent not required (friendly / hostile takeover)

SHARE-HOLDERS	collective approval formal shareholder vote dissenting shareholders can be overruled	individual approval no formal shareholder vote minority shareholders remain
FILING	Department of Justice, Fair Trade Commission (FTC) (if transaction exceeds certain thresholds)	
	Secretary of State	SEC (5% beneficial ownership)
RESULT	acquired entity ceases to exist replaced by survivor	target corporation continues to exist becomes a subsidiary

References:

1. American Bar Association, Model Business Corporation Act (2016 Revision), https://www.americanbar.org/groups/business_law/committees/corplaws/ (accessed 14.10.2019).

2. William Klein/John Coffee/Frank Partnoy, Business Organization and Finance, 11th edition (2010).

3. Steven Emanuel, Corporations and other business entities, 7th edition (2013).

4. Angela Schneeman, The Law of Corporations and Other Business Organizations, 6th edition (2013).

5. Frank Cross/Roger Miller, The Legal Environment of Business, 10th edition (2017).

6. Arthur Pinto/Douglas Branson, Understanding Corporate Law, 5th edition (2018).

7. U.S. Securities and Exchange Commission, www.sec.gov (accessed 18.6.2019).

8. U.S. Securities and Exchange Commission, Fast Answers, The Laws That Govern the Securities Industry, https://www.sec.gov/

answers/about-lawsshtml.html (modified 1.10.2013, accessed 18.6.2019).

9. Cornell Law School, Legal Information Institute, Duty of Care, https://www.law.cornell.edu/wex/duty_of_care (accessed 13.6.2019).

10. Wikipedia, Directors and officers liability insurance, https://en.wikipedia.org/wiki/Directors_and_officers_liability_insurance (edited 19.9.2018, accessed 13.6.2019).

11. Wikipedia, United States antitrust law, https://en.wikipedia.org/wiki/United_States_antitrust_law (edited 4.6.2019, accessed 19.6.2019).

12. Investopedia, Dodd-Frank Wall Street Reform and Consumer Protection Act, https://www.investopedia.com/terms/d/dodd-frank-financial-regulatory-reform-bill.asp (updated 10.5.2019, accessed 17.6.2019).

13. Investopedia, Merger vs. Takeover: What's the Difference?, https://www.investopedia.com/ask/answers/05/mergervstakeover.asp (updated 13.4.2019, accessed 18.6.2019).

14. 國家教育研究院，National Academy for Educational Research，http://terms.naer.edu.tw/detail/958455/ (accessed 2.6.2019)。

15. 線上翻譯，Web dictionary，https://tw.ichacha.net/model%20business%20corporation%20act.html (accessed 3.6.2019)。

16. 行政院金融監督管理委員會保險局，行政院金管會保險局雙語詞彙，http://terms.naer.edu.tw/terms/manager_admin/File/LIST339.TXT (accessed 5.6.2019)。

17. Thomson Reuters, Westlaw.

TAIWAN COMPANY LAW

Company Act[1]

Article 1

The term "company" as used in this Act denotes a corporate juristic person organized and incorporated in accordance with this Act for the purpose of profit making.

When conducting its business, every company shall comply with the laws and regulations as well as business ethics and may take actions which will promote public interests in order to fulfill its social responsibilities.

Article 2

Companies are of four classes as set forth in the following:

1. Unlimited Company: which term denotes a company organized by two or more shareholders who bear unlimited joint and several liabilities for discharge of the obligations of the company.

2. Limited Company: which term denotes a company organized by one or more shareholders, with each shareholder being liable for the company in an amount limited to the amount contributed by him.

---

1 See Ministry of Justice, Laws & Regulations Database of The Republic of China, https://law.moj.gov.tw/Eng/LawClass/LawAll.aspx?PCode=J0080001 (amended on 1.8.2018, accessed 6.6.2019).

單元二　臺灣公司法

公司法[1]

第1條

本法所稱公司，謂以營利爲目的，依照本法組織、登記、成立之社團法人。

公司經營業務，應遵守法令及商業倫理規範，得採行增進公共利益之行爲，以善盡其社會責任。

第2條

公司分爲左列四種：

一、無限公司：指二人以上股東所組織，對公司債務負連帶無限清償責任之公司。

二、有限公司：由一人以上股東所組織，就其出資額爲限，對公司負其責任之公司。

1　法務部，全國法規資料庫，http://law.moj.gov.tw/LawClass/LawAll. aspx?PCode=J0080001（6.6.2019，修訂於2018年8月1日）。

3. Unlimited Company with Limited Liability Shareholders: which term denotes a company organized by one or more shareholders of unlimited liability and one or more shareholders of limited liability; among them the shareholder(s) with unlimited liability shall bear unlimited joint liability for the obligations of the company, while each of the shareholders with limited liability shall be held liable for the obligations of the company only in respect of the amount of capital contributed by him.

4. Company Limited by Shares: which term denotes a company organized by two or more or one government or corporate shareholder, with the total capital of the company being divided into shares and each shareholder being liable for the company in an amount equal to the total value of shares subscribed by him.

The name of a company shall indicate the class to which it belongs.

Article 4

The term "foreign company" as used in this Act denotes a company, for the purpose of profit making, organized and incorporated in accordance with the laws of a foreign country, and authorized by the R.O.C. Government to transact business within the territory of the Republic of China.

A foreign company, within the limits prescribed by laws and regulations, is entitled with the same legal capacity as a R.O.C. company.

Article 6

No company may be incorporated unless it has registered with the central competent authority.

三、兩合公司：指一人以上無限責任股東，與一人以上有限責任股東所組織，其無限責任股東對公司債務負連帶無限清償責任；有限責任股東就其出資額爲限，對公司負其責任之公司。

四、股份有限公司：指二人以上股東或政府、法人股東一人所組織，全部資本分爲股份；股東就其所認股份，對公司負其責任之公司。

公司名稱，應標明公司之種類。

第4條

本法所稱外國公司，謂以營利爲目的，依照外國法律組織登記之公司。

外國公司，於法令限制內，與中華民國公司有同一之權利能力。

第6條

公司非在中央主管機關登記後，不得成立。

Article 8

The term "responsible persons" of a company as used in this Act denotes shareholders conducting the business or representing the company in case of an unlimited company or unlimited company with limited liability shareholders; directors of the company in case of a limited company or a company limited by shares.

The managerial officer, liquidator or temporary manager of a company, the promoter, supervisor, inspector, reorganizer or reorganization supervisor of a company limited by shares acting within the scope of their duties, are also responsible persons of a company.

A non-director of a company who de facto conducts business of a director or de facto controls over the management of the personnel, financial or business operation of the company and de facto instructs a director to conduct business shall be liable for the civil, criminal and administrative liabilities as a director in this Act ...

Article 10

Under either of the following circumstances, the competent authority may, ex officio or upon an application filed by an interested party, order the dissolution of a company:

1. Where the company fails to commence its business operation after elapse of six months from the date of its company incorporation registration, unless it has made an extension registration; or

2. Where, after commencing its business operation, the company has discontinued, at its own discretion, its business operation for a period over six months, unless it has made the business discontinuation registration.

第8條

本法所稱公司負責人：在無限公司、兩合公司爲執行業務或代表公司之股東；在有限公司、股份有限公司爲董事。

公司之經理人、清算人或臨時管理人，股份有限公司之發起人、監察人、檢查人、重整人或重整監督人，在執行職務範圍內，亦爲公司負責人。

公司之非董事，而實質上執行董事業務或實質控制公司之人事、財務或業務經營而實質指揮董事執行業務者，與本法董事同負民事、刑事及行政罰之責任。……

第10條

公司有下列情事之一者，主管機關得依職權或利害關係人之申請，命令解散之：

一、公司設立登記後六個月尙未開始營業。但已辦妥延展登記者，不在此限。

二、開始營業後自行停止營業六個月以上。但已辦妥停業登記者，不在此限。

3. Where a final judgment has adjudicated to prohibit the company from using its company name, the company fails to make a name change registration after elapse of six months from the final judgment, and fails to make a name change registration after the competent authority has ordered the company to do so within a given time limit.

4. Where the company fails to attach the auditing certificate from an independent certified public accountant within the time period prescribed in Paragraph 1 of Article 7. ...

Article 11

In the event of an apparent difficulty in the operation of a company or serious damage thereto, the court may, upon an application from its shareholders and after having solicited the opinions of the competent authority and the central authority in charge of the relevant end enterprises and having received a defence from the company, make a ruling for the dissolution of the comany.

The dissolution application to be filed by the company under the preceding Paragraph shall be filed by shareholders who have been continuously holding more than 10% of the total number of outstanding shares issued by the company for a period over six months.

Article 12

If a company, after its incorporation, fails to register any particular that should have been registered or fails to register any changes in particulars already registered, such particulars or changes in particulars can not be set up as a defence against any third party.

三、公司名稱經法院判決確定不得使用，公司於判決確定後六個月內尚未辦妥名稱變更登記，並經主管機關令其限期辦理仍未辦妥。

四、未於第七條第一項所定期限內，檢送經會計師查核簽證之文件者。……

第11條

公司之經營，有顯著困難或重大損害時，法院得據股東之聲請，於徵詢主管機關及目的事業中央主管機關意見，並通知公司提出答辯後，裁定解散。

前項聲請，在股份有限公司，應有繼續六個月以上持有已發行股份總數百分之十以上股份之股東提出之。

第12條

公司設立登記後，有應登記之事項而不登記，或已登記之事項有變更而不為變更之登記者，不得以其事項對抗第三人。

Article 18

A corporate name shall be in Chinese Character. No company may use a corporate name which is identical with that of another company or limited partnership. Where the corporate names of two companies or a company and limited partnership contain any marks or identifying words respectively that may distinguish the different categories of business of the two companies, such corporate names shall not be considered identical with each other.

A company may conduct any business that is not prohibited or restricted by the laws and regulations, except for those requiring special approvals which shall be explicitly described in the Articles of Incorporation of the company. ...

Article 19

A company may not conduct its business operations or commit any juristic act in the name of its company, unless it has completed the procedure for company incorporation registration.

The person who has violated the provision set out in the preceding Paragraph shall be punished with imprisonment for a period of not more than one year, detention, or in lieu thereof or in addition thereto a fine of not more than NT$ 150,000 and shall assume on his own the civil liabilities arising there-from, or shall be jointly and severally liable therefore, in case there are two or more violators. In addition, the company shall be enjoined from using its corporate name for doing its business.

第18條

公司名稱，應使用我國文字，且不得與他公司或有限合夥名稱相同。二公司或公司與有限合夥名稱中標明不同業務種類或可資區別之文字者，視爲不相同。

公司所營事業除許可業務應載明於章程外，其餘不受限制。……

第19條

未經設立登記，不得以公司名義經營業務或爲其他法律行爲。

違反前項規定者，行爲人處一年以下有期徒刑、拘役或科或併科新臺幣十五萬元以下罰金，並自負民事責任；行爲人有二人以上者，連帶負民事責任，並由主管機關禁止其使用公司名稱。

Article 20

A company shall, at the end of each fiscal year, submit to its shareholders for their approval or to the shareholders' meeting for ratification the annual business report, the financial statements, and the surplus earnings distribution or loss make-up proposal.

Where a company's equity capital exceeds a certain amount or a company's equity capital does not exceed a certain amount but the company is with a certain scale, the company shall first have its financial statements audited and certified by a certified public accountant. Such certain amount, scale as well as auditing and certification rules shall be prescribed by the central competent authority. ...

Article 23

The responsible person of a company shall have the loyalty and shall exercise the due care of a good administrator in conducting the business operation of the company; and if he / she has acted contrary to this provision, shall be liable for the damages to be sustained by the company there-from.

If the responsible person of a company has, in the course of conducting the business operations, violated any provision of the applicable laws and / or regulations and thus caused damage to any other person, he / she shall be liable, jointly and severally, for the damage to such other person.

In case the responsible person of a company does anything for himself / herself or on behalf of another person in violation of the provisions of Paragraph 1, the meeting of shareholders may, by a resolution, consider the earnings in such an act as earnings of the company unless one year has lapsed since the realization of such earnings.

第20條

公司每屆會計年度終了，應將營業報告書、財務報表及盈餘分派或虧損撥補之議案，提請股東同意或股東常會承認。

公司資本額達一定數額以上或未達一定數額而達一定規模者，其財務報表，應先經會計師查核簽證；其一定數額、規模及簽證之規則，由中央主管機關定之。……

第23條

公司負責人應忠實執行業務並盡善良管理人之注意義務，如有違反致公司受有損害者，負損害賠償責任。

公司負責人對於公司業務之執行，如有違反法令致他人受有損害時，對他人應與公司負連帶賠償之責。

公司負責人對於違反第一項之規定，為自己或他人為該行為時，股東會得以決議，將該行為之所得視為公司之所得。但自所得產生後逾一年者，不在此限。

Article 24

A dissolved company shall be liquidated, unless such dissolution is caused by consolidation or merger, split-up, or bankruptcy.

Article 29

A company may have one or more managerial personnel in accordance with its Articles of Incorporation. Appointment and discharge and the remuneration of the managerial personnel shall be decided in accordance with the following provisions provided, however, that if there are higher standards specified in the Articles of Incorporation, such higher standards shall prevail: ...

Article 31

The sope of duties and power of managerial personnel of a company may, in addition to what are specified in the Articles of Incorporation, also be defined in the employment contract.

A managerial personnel shall be empowered to manage the operation of the company and to sign relevant business documents for the company, subject to the scope of his / her duties and power as specified in the Articles of Incorporation or his / her employment contract.

Article 34

A managerial officer who violates any provision of laws or ordinances, or of Articles of Incorporation, or of the preceding article, thereby causing loss or damage to the company, shall be liable to compensate the company.

第24條

解散之公司除因合併、分割或破產而解散外，應行清算。

第29條

公司得依章程規定置經理人，其委任、解任及報酬，依下列規定定之。但公司章程有較高規定者，從其規定：……

第31條

經理人之職權，除章程規定外，並得依契約之訂定。

經理人在公司章程或契約規定授權範圍內，有為公司管理事務及簽名之權。

第34條

經理人因違反法令、章程或前條之規定，致公司受損害時，對於公司負賠償之責。

Article 36

Any restriction imposed by a company on the duty and power of managerial officers is not valid as defence against a bona fide third person.

Article 129

The promoters of a company limited by shares shall draw up the Articles of Incorporation containing the following particulars and shall affix thereon their respective signatures or personal seals:

1. The name of the company;
2. The scope of business to be operated by the company;
3. For a company issuing par value shares, the total number of shares and the par value of each share certificate; for a company issuing no par value shares, the total number of shares.
4. The location of the company;
5. The number of directors and supervisors, and the term of their respective offices; and
6. The date of establishment of the Articles of Incorporation.

Article 156-4

After its incorporation, for improving its financial structure or resuming its normal operation, the company participating in the special approval of the governmental bailout program may issue and transfer new shares to the government as the consideration for receiving governmental financial help. Such issuing procedure shall not be subject to the restrictions regarding issuance of new shares set forth in this Act and the regulations thereof shall be prescribed by the central competent authority. ...

第36條

公司不得以其所加於經理人職權之限制，對抗善意第三人。

第129條

發起人應以全體之同意訂立章程，載明下列各款事項，並簽名或蓋章：

一、公司名稱。

二、所營事業。

三、採行票面金額股者，股份總數及每股金額；採行無票面金額股者，股份總數。

四、本公司所在地。

五、董事及監察人之人數及任期。

六、訂立章程之年、月、日。

第156-4條

公司設立後，為改善財務結構或回復正常營運，而參與政府專案核定之紓困方案時，得發行新股轉讓於政府，作為接受政府財務上協助之對價；其發行程序不受本法有關發行新股規定之限制，其相關辦法由中央主管機關定之。……

Article 356-1

A close company is a non public offering company whose shares shall be held by not more than 50 persons, and whose Articles of Incorporation shall impose restrictions on transfer of shares of a company. ...

Article 356-3

... Equity capital to be contributed other than cash by the promoters may be in the form of assets required in the business of a close company, technical know-how, or service, provided, however, that equity capital to be contributed by service shall not exceed a certain percentage of the total shares issued by a close company. ...

Article 356-4

A close company shall make no public offering of any of its securities, provided, however, that this provision shall not apply to the crowd-funding portal operated by securities businesses approved by the competent authority in charge of securities affairs. ...

Article 356-5

The restrictions on transfer of shares shall be explicitly described in the Articles of Incorporation of a close company. ...

Article 369-1

The term "affiliated enterprises" as used in this Act shall refer to enterprises which are independent in existence but are interrelated in either of the following relations:

1. Companies having controlling and subordinate relation between them; or

2. Companies having made investment in each other.

第356-1條

閉鎖性股份有限公司,指股東人數不超過五十人,並於章程定有股份轉讓限制之非公開發行股票公司。⋯⋯

第356-3條

⋯⋯發起人之出資除現金外,得以公司事業所需之財產、技術或勞務抵充之。但以勞務抵充之股數,不得超過公司發行股份總數之一定比例。⋯⋯

第356-4條

公司不得公開發行或募集有價證券。但經由證券主管機關許可之證券商經營股權群眾募資平臺募資者,不在此限。⋯⋯

第356-5條

公司股份轉讓之限制,應於章程載明。⋯⋯

第369-1條

本法所稱關係企業,指獨立存在而相互間具有下列關係之企業:

一、有控制與從屬關係之公司。

二、相互投資之公司。

EXERCISES
單元三 練習

Mark the odd word（選意義不同的字）：

acquire – buy – purchase – price

annual report – articles of incorporation – bylaws – memorandum of association

asset – cash – liability – property

acquisition – merger – proxy – takeover

begin – initiate – start – terminate

duty – liability – obligation – right

securities – stocks – shares – shareholder

bid – offer – profit – tender

cease – incorporate – stop – terminate

Find the corresponding noun:

VERB	NOUN
agree	
approve	
associate	
combine	
conflict	
disclose	
dissolve	
exchange	
exist	
form	
inform	
meet	

merge	
oblige	
omit	
register	
require	
state	
terminate	

Find the corresponding noun and person:

VERB	NOUN	PERSON
bid		
control		
distribute		
incorporate		
inspect		
invest		
judge		
liquidate		
manage		
negotiate		
offer		
own		
promote		
protect		
purchase		
regulate		
report		
sell		
transfer		

Find the opposite:

acquiring company	
friendly takeover	
primary market	
voluntary dissolution	

Choose the best answer:

1. A company is a juristic person organized and incorporated for the purpose of making _____ .

   (A) partnership (B) patent (C) profit (D) property

2. No company may be incorporated unless it has _____ with the central competent authority.

   (A) recovered (B) registered (C) regulated (D) restricted

3. Check the memorandum of association to identify the company's

   _____ .

   (A) proxy (B) extraordinary general meeting (C) share capital
   (D) ordinary resolution

4. A company shall, at the end of each fiscal year, submit to its shareholders for their _____ or to the shareholders' meeting for ratification the annual business report, the financial statements, and the surplus earnings distribution or loss make-up proposal.

   (A) administration (B) admission (C) approval (D) audit

5. A dissolved company shall be _____ , unless such dissolution is caused by consolidation or merger, split-up, or bankruptcy.

   (A) liable (B) license (C) liquidated (D) loyal

6. A managerial personnel shall be empowered to manage the operation of the company and to sign relevant business documents for the company, subject to the scope of his/her duties and power as specified in the _____ or his / her employment contract.

(A) articles of confederation   (B) articles of incorporation

(C) accounts   (D) annual report

7. Any restriction imposed by a company on the duty and power of managerial officers is not valid as _____ against a bona fide third person.

(A) donation   (B) degree   (C) defence   (D) declaration

8. A prospectus is an explanatory written statement that an issuer provides to the general public for the purpose of offering or selling

_____ .

(A) signatures   (B) statutes   (C) subsidiaries   (D) securities

9. Any person who _____ , either individually or jointly with other persons, more than ten percent of the total issued shares of a public company shall file a statement with the competent authority within ten days after such acquisition, stating the purpose and the sources of funds for the purchase of shares and any other matters required to be disclosed by the competent authority; such persons shall file timely amendment when there are changes in the matters reported.

(A) acquisition   (B) acquires   (C) acquirer   (D) acquiring

10. Securities issued by an issuer shall not be _____ on the central-ized securities exchange market of a stock exchange without first obtaining the necessary approval for public listing.

    (A) treaty   (B) tort   (C) trust   (D) traded

11. Andy, Ben and Charlie planned to organize a new corporation, ABC, Inc., to manufacture hand-tool in Taiwan. For about four months, Ben has worked on preparations for ABC, Inc., although he had no agreement with Andy and Charlie as to compensation for such work. Last month, Ben entered into a contract, on behalf of ABC, Inc., with China Steel Corporation (CSC), to purchase material. Yesterday, the certificate of incorporation for ABC, Inc., was filed with the Commerce Industrial Service Portal. Which of the following statements is correct? (100年司法官)

    (A) Ben is entitled to the reasonable value of his service as a promoter of ABC, Inc., and the contract he signed with CSC is binding on ABC, Inc.

    (B) Ben is entitled to the reasonable value of his service as a promoter of ABC, Inc., but the contract he signed with CSC is not binding on ABC, Inc.

    (C) Ben is not entitled to the reasonable value of his service as a promoter of ABC, Inc., but the contract he signed with CSC is binding on ABC, Inc.

    (D) Ben is not entitled to the reasonable value of his service as a promoter of ABC, Inc., and the contract he signed with CSC is not binding on ABC, Inc.

12. "Securities Law entitles the purchaser to sue the issuer, underwriter, certified public accountant and lawyer with respect to any material misstatements or omissions in the prospectus. However, except for the issuer, who has absolute liability for any material misstatements or omissions, Securities Law provides an affirmative defense for any other defendant who can demonstrate that he / she met a prescribed standard of diligence with respect to the information contained in the prospectus." Based on the above description, what kind of liability does the issuer have? (100年司法官)

(A) Strict liability　(B) Negligent liability　(C) No liability

(D) Presumption of negligence

13. "Scienter" means a mental state consisting of an intent to deceive, manipulate, or defraud. In this sense, the term is used most often in the context of securities fraud. The court has held that to establish a claim for damages under securities fraud, a plaintiff must prove that the defendant acted with scienter. Based on the above, the word "scienter" can be BEST replaced by the word of _____ . (100年司法官)

(A) knowledge　(B) causation　(C) innocence　(D) action

14. The regulations governing the relationship between the shareholders and directors of a company and required for the establishment of a company are: (100年司法官)

(A) Articles of Incorporation (B) Regulations of Incorporation

(C) Laws of Incorporation　(D) Files of Incorporation

15. The idea behind incorporation is that the rights and liabilities of a corporation are separate and distinct from those of its shareholders. However, creditors of a company can ask a court to "＿＿＿＿," and set aside a company's identity as a juristic person and reach the company owners and shareholders' personal assets. (100年律師)

    (A) pierce the corporate shell　(B) pierce the corporate veil
    (C) cover the corporate shell　(D) cover the corporate veil

16. "A tender offer is an offer to stockholders of a publicly-held corporation to exchange their shares for cash or securities at a price higher than the previous market price. A tender offer is the most common way of carrying out a hostile takeover." Which of the following can NOT be derived from the above description? (100年律師)

    (A) The price offered in a tender offer transaction is often with a premium.
    (B) A tender offer is usually an unfriendly acquisition of the target company.
    (C) The target's shareholders will get cash or shares if they tender their shares.
    (D) An acquirer of a closely-held company can launch a tender offer.

17. Debt security is issued by a company and sold to investors, usually to raise money in order to expand its business. In certain situations, the company's assets may be used as collateral. This debt security is usually called ＿＿＿＿. (100年律師)

    (A) shareholder debt　(B) corporate bond　(C) blank check
    (D) corporate liability

18. The term "capital market" is generally used to refer to those markets

that deal in long-term financial instruments, such as stock, bonds, mortgage, etc., while the term "money market" describes those markets in which short-term debt instruments (typically, having a maturity under one year) are issued and traded. Therefore, which one of the followings is generally NOT considered to be an instrument in the capital market? (100年律師)

(A) Commercial paper　(B) Common share　(C) Preferred share

(D) Government bond

19. What is the term for a for-profit company, organized under the laws of another country, but authorized by the R.O.C. government to transact business in R.O.C.? (101年司法官)

(A) A third party company　(B) A diplomatic company

(C) A foreign company　(D) A certified company

20. Which of the following terms refers to two or more independent enterprises that have made investments between or amongst each other, held by the same major shareholder, or share a controlling / subordinate relationship with each other? (101年司法官)

(A) Major and minor companies　(B) Sister companies

(C) Licensor and licensee　(D) Affiliated enterprises

21. "The laws and rules that govern the securities industry derive from a simple and straightforward concept: all investors, whether large institutions or private individuals, should have access to certain basic facts about an investment prior to buying it, and so long as they hold it." To achieve the above goal, the government authority will most likely require public companies to _____ . (101年司法官)

(A) disclose meaningful information　(B) abstain from trading shares　(C) avoid self-dealing transactions　(D) establish an internal control mechanism

22. "One anti-takeover charter amendment is a provision requiring a supermajority vote – say 80 percent of the common shares instead of the usual bare majority rule – in order to effect a merger or sale of all assets." Which of the following cannot be derived from the above description? (101年司法官)

    (A) The purpose of supermajority vote is to make a takeover somewhat harder and riskier.

    (B) Supermajority vote would not absolutely block a takeover attempt, especially by a bidder willing to buy all the target stock.

    (C) The anti-takeover tactic of supermajority vote requires a charter amendment.

    (D) The anti-takeover tactic of supermajority vote shall be approved by the board of directors.

23. A request that a corporate shareholder authorizes another person to cast the shareholder's vote at a corporate meeting is a _____ . (101年司法官)

    (A) voting trust　(B) proxy solicitation　(C) voting agreement
    (D) sale of control

24. Which of the following is not the duty of a liquidator when a company is in the liquidation process? (101年律師)

    (A) To promote the business of the company.

    (B) To collect all outstanding debts and to pay off all claims.

    (C) To allocate surplus or loss.

    (D) To allocate the residual assets.

25. "A corporation offering and selling its securities to the public has to file a registration statement with the competent authority. The registration statement automatically becomes effective 20 days after it is filed with the competent authority, at which point the issuer is free to sell the registered securities to the public. However, the competent authority has certain powers to delay or suspend the effectiveness of the registration statement if it appears that the statement is on its face incomplete or inaccurate in any material respect." Based on the above description, which of the following is not a part of the securities registration process? (101年律師)

(A) Discuss the terms of the offering with the competent authority.

(B) Prepare the registration statement by the issuer.

(C) File the registration statement with the competent authority.

(D) Wait for a certain period of time before the registration statement becomes effective.

26. During the public offering, issuing, private placement, or trading of securities, there shall be no misrepresentations, frauds, or any other acts which are sufficient to mislead other persons. The word "misrepresentation" can be worst explained by the term of _____. (101年律師)

(A) concealment　(B) false assertion　(C) accurate statement
(D) non-disclosure

27. According to Taiwan Corporation Law, which of the following matters in a company limited by shares does not need to be stipulated in the Articles of Incorporation to take effect? (101年律師)

(A) The number of shares to be issued upon incorporation of the company, if the total authorized numbers of shares are to be issued in installments.

(B) The kind of special shares and the rights and obligations covered by such shares.

(C) The annual business plan.

(D) The cause(s) for dissolution of the company.

28. When a company's shareholders' meeting reaches the unanimous agreement of dissolution, the company will generally cease to carry on business at that time and start the process of _____ before dissolution. (102年司法官)

(A) reincorporation   (B) acquisition   (C) liquidation

(D) consolidation

29. When a corporation earns a profit or surplus, that money can be put to two uses. It can either be re-invested in the business, or it can be paid to the shareholders as _____. (102年司法官)

(A) dividends and bonuses   (B) segments and reserves

(C) divisions and premiums   (D) sections and portions

30. A director of a listed company learns material non-public information regarding the possible huge loss of the company, and prior to the disclosure of such information, the director sells shares of the company. Such an act is a violation of the rule against _____. (102年司法官)

(A) short swing   (B) related party transaction   (C) insider trading

(D) misrepresentation

31. "Short selling is a device whereby the speculator sells stock which he does not own, anticipating that the price will decline and that he will thereby be enabled to make delivery of the stock sold by purchasing it at a lesser price." Based on the above description, if the decline

materializes, what is the short seller's profit? (102年司法官)

(A) The difference between the first purchase price and the second lower sales price.

(B) The difference between the first purchase price and the second lower purchase price.

(C) The difference between the first sales price and the second lower sales price.

(D) The difference between the first sales price and the second lower purchase price.

32. The combination of two or more companies, where the original companies cease to exist, a new company arises instead, and where existing stockholders of the original companies retain a shared interest in the new company, is called a _____ . (102年律師)

(A) merger   (B) acquisition   (C) hostile takeover

(D) asset purchase

33. Where a company that publicly issues shares or corporate bonds suspends its business or there is an expectation that such company will suspend its business due to financial difficulty, but there remains a possibility for such company may be re-constructed or rehabilitated, such company or any of the interested parties may apply to the court for _____ . (102年律師)

(A) liquidation   (B) consolidation   (C) dissolution

(D) reorganization

34. Big Corporation owns 95% of Little Corporation's shares. Little Corporation may be merged into Big Corporation without the approval of the shareholders of either corporation. This type of merger is called

_____. (102年律師)

(A) short-form merger　(B) whale / minnow merger　(C) triangular merger　(D) de facto merger

35. "During 1990, the New York Stock Exchange (NYSE) traded 39.7 billion shares, while the National Association of Securities Dealers Automated Quotations (NASDAQ) traded 33.4 billion shares. NAS-DAQ's phenomenal growth was not envisioned by its founders, who intended it primarily as a quotation system to provide information with respect to securities not considered sufficiently seasoned to list on a securities exchange." The word "seasoned" can be BEST replaced by the word _____. (102年律師)

(A) flavored　(B) experienced　(C) salty　(D) unprofessional

36. In a _____ suit, shareholders are bestowed a right to sue directors on behalf of the corporation to enforce rights of corporation. (103年司法官律師)

(A) direct　(B) deprived　(C) deranged　(D) derivative

37. "Scalping" is a practice in which an investment advisor publicly recommends the purchase of securities without disclosing its practice of purchasing such securities before making recommendation and then selling them at a profit when the price rises after the recommendation is disseminated. Therefore, scalping is a practice attacked by the competent authority as a violation of securities law similar to a _____. (103年司法官律師)

(A) bribery　(B) fraud　(C) mistake　(D) robbery

38. _____ means stock which has been issued as fully paid to stock-

holders and subsequently reacquired by the corporation to be used by it in furtherance of its corporate purpose. (103年司法官律師)

(A) Preferred stock　(B) Treasury stock　(C) Common stock

(D) Special stock

39. In a public company limited by shares, which of the following has the power to elect or remove a director? (104年司法官律師)

(A) directors　(B) supervisors　(C) the shareholders' meeting

(D) president

40. A company, organized by one or more shareholders, with the total capital of the company being divided into shares and each shareholder being liable for the company in an amount equal to the total value of shares subscribed by him, is called: (104年司法官律師)

(A) an unlimited company　(B) a company limited by shares

(C) an unlimited company with limited liability shareholders

(D) a limited company

41. Directors who possess professional knowledge and certain qualifications and may not have any direct or indirect interest in the company are called _____ . (104年司法官律師)

(A) insider directors　(B) independent directors

(C) dummy directors　(D) shadow directors

42. Which of the following is NOT the triggering event of a dissenting shareholder's appraisal right? (104年司法官律師)

(A) merger　(B) sale of substantially all of the company's assets

(C) spin off　(D) share exchange pursuant to Article 156, Paragraph 8 of the Company Law

43. A market manipulation claim can be based on _____ that are entered with the knowledge that sales of substantially the same size, at substantially the same time and price, have been entered by the wrongdoers for the sale of such security. (104年司法官律師)

   (A) wash sales   (B) matched orders   (C) front running
   (D) short sales

44. Under the firm commitment agreement with the issuer, _____ may subscribe to securities before placing them for sale or may reserve certain portion of the securities specified in the agreement for subscription for his own account. (105年司法官律師)

   (A) Broker   (B) Underwriter   (C) Dealer   (D) Trustee

45. Which of the following is NOT required to be contained in the Articles of Incorporation of a corporation limited by shares? (105年司法官律師)

   (A) The names of directors and supervisors, and the term of their respective offices
   (B) The par value of share
   (C) The name of the company
   (D) The date of establishment of the Articles of Incorporation

46. Under Securities Exchange Act, transactions involving securities are subject to registration, mandatory disclosure, and heightened anti-fraud rules. Please identify which of the following is NOT a security in Taiwan. (106年司法官律師)

   (A) A Taiwan depositary receipt   (B) A convertible debenture
   (C) A foreign corporate bond   (D) A commercial paper

47. Under Securities Exchange Act, transactions involving securities are subject to registration, mandatory disclosure, and heightened anti-fraud rules. Please identify which of the following is NOT an equity security in Taiwan. (106年司法官律師)

(A) A convertible corporate bond　(B) A corporate bond with warrants　(C) A debenture　(D) A treasury stock

48. ＿＿＿＿＿ are the rights of shareholders to demand the payment of a fair price for their shares during a merger or other extraordinary corporate event. In this sense, the rights ensure that dissenters receive the benefit of their bargain by preventing corporations involved in mergers from paying less than what the company is worth. (106年司法官律師)

(A) Estimate rights　(B) Appraisal rights　(C) Compelling rights
(D) Forced rights

49. A ＿＿＿＿＿ is a pretended sale made openly in the trading place for the purpose of deceiving other traders. Such manipulative practice is employed to give false appearance and to cause prices to be registered which are not true prices. (106年司法官律師)

(A) Tender Offer　(B) Short Sale　(C) Wash Sale　(D) Short Swing

50. Which of the following statements best describes the function or purpose of securities law? (107年司法官律師)

(A) Helping companies grow by putting various restrictions on them.

(B) Allowing companies to raise money from those whom they do not know much about.

(C) Checking companies' activities ex-ante as well as ex-post to avoid corporate misconduct.

(D) Encouraging investors to take due risk and enjoy economic growth.

51. According to the Close Company chapter of Taiwan's Company Act, which of the following statements is most likely to be incorrect? (107 年司法官律師)

(A) When the number of shareholders exceeds 50, the status of a close company will be lost automatically.

(B) To maintain the status of a close company, using a public channel to raise funds is strictly prohibited with no exception.

(C) To facilitate capital formation, shareholders can use a more flexible way to pay for their shares, such as labor or service.

(D) The corporate charter should stipulate a clear limitation on the free transferability of shares.

ANSWERS
單元四　答案

Mark the odd word（選意義不同的字）：

acquire – buy – purchase – price 價格

annual report – articles of incorporation – bylaws – memorandum of association 年度報告

asset – cash – liability – property 責任

acquisition – merger – proxy – takeover 代理

begin – initiate – start – terminate 終止

duty – liability – obligation – right 權利

securities – stocks – shares – shareholder 股東

bid – offer – profit – tender 利益

cease – incorporate – stop – terminate 使組成公司

Find the corresponding noun:

VERB	NOUN
agree	agreement 協議
approve	approval 批准
associate	association 社團
combine	combination 結合
conflict	conflict 衝突
disclose	disclosure 公開
dissolve	dissolution 解散
exchange	exchange 交換
exist	existence 生存
form	formation 成立
inform	information 資訊
meet	meeting 會議

merge	merger 合併
oblige	obligation 義務
omit	omission 遺漏
register	registration 登記
require	requirement 要求
state	statement 陳述
terminate	termination 終止

Find the corresponding noun and person:

VERB	NOUN	PERSON
bid	bid 投標	bidder
control	control 控制	controller
distribute	distribution 分配	distributer
incorporate	incorporation（使組成）公司	incorporator
inspect	inspection 檢查	inspector
invest	investment 投資	investor
judge	judgment 判決	judge
liquidate	liquidation 清算	liquidator
manage	management 管理	manager
negotiate	negotiation 談判、協商	negotiator
offer	offer 要約	offeror
own	ownership 所有權	owner
promote	promotion 促進	promoter
protect	protection 保護	protector
purchase	purchase 購買	purchaser
regulate	regulation 規章	regulator
report	report 報告	reporter
sell	sale 出售	seller
transfer	transfer 移轉	transferor, transferee

Find the opposite:

acquiring company	acquired company 被合併公司
friendly takeover	hostile takeover 敵意收購
primary market	secondary market 二級市場
voluntary dissolution	involuntary dissolution 強制解散

Choose the best answer:

1. A company is a juristic person organized and incorporated for the purpose of making _____ .

    (A) partnership   (B) patent   (C) profit   (D) property

2. No company may be incorporated unless it has _____ with the central competent authority.

    (A) recovered   (B) registered   (C) regulated   (D) restricted

3. Check the memorandum of association to identify the company's _____

    _____ .

    (A) proxy   (B) extraordinary general meeting   (C) share capital
    (D) ordinary resolution

4. A company shall, at the end of each fiscal year, submit to its shareholders for their _____ or to the shareholders' meeting for ratification the annual business report, the financial statements, and the surplus earnings distribution or loss make-up proposal.

    (A) administration   (B) admission   (C) approval   (D) audit

5. A dissolved company shall be _____ , unless such dissolution is caused by consolidation or merger, split-up, or bankruptcy.

    (A) liable   (B) license   (C) liquidated   (D) loyal

6. A managerial personnel shall be empowered to manage the operation of the company and to sign relevant business documents for the company, subject to the scope of his/her duties and power as specified in the _____ or his / her employment contract.

   (A) articles of confederation   (B) articles of incorporation
   (C) accounts   (D) annual report

7. Any restriction imposed by a company on the duty and power of managerial officers is not valid as _____ against a bona fide third person.

   (A) donation   (B) degree   (C) defence   (D) declaration

8. A prospectus is an explanatory written statement that an issuer provides to the general public for the purpose of offering or selling

   _____ .

   (A) signatures   (B) statutes   (C) subsidiaries   (D) securities

9. Any person who _____, either individually or jointly with other persons, more than ten percent of the total issued shares of a public company shall file a statement with the competent authority within ten days after such acquisition, stating the purpose and the sources of funds for the purchase of shares and any other matters required to be disclosed by the competent authority; such persons shall file timely amendment when there are changes in the matters reported.

   (A) acquisition   (B) acquires   (C) acquirer   (D) acquiring

10. Securities issued by an issuer shall not be _____ on the central-ized securities exchange market of a stock exchange without first ob-taining the necessary approval for public listing.

(A) treaty　(B) tort　(C) trust　(D) traded

11. Andy, Ben and Charlie planned to organize a new corporation, ABC, Inc., to manufacture hand-tool in Taiwan. For about four months, Ben has worked on preparations for ABC, Inc., although he had no agreement with Andy and Charlie as to compensation for such work. Last month, Ben entered into a contract, on behalf of ABC, Inc., with China Steel Corporation (CSC), to purchase material. Yesterday, the certificate of incorporation for ABC, Inc., was filed with the Com-merce Industrial Service Portal. Which of the following statements is correct? (100年司法官)

(A) Ben is entitled to the reasonable value of his service as a promot-er of ABC, Inc., and the contract he signed with CSC is binding on ABC, Inc.

(B) Ben is entitled to the reasonable value of his service as a promoter of ABC, Inc., but the contract he signed with CSC is not binding on ABC, Inc.

(C) Ben is not entitled to the reasonable value of his service as a promoter of ABC, Inc., but the contract he signed with CSC is binding on ABC, Inc.

(D) Ben is not entitled to the reasonable value of his service as a promoter of ABC, Inc., and the contract he signed with CSC is not binding on ABC, Inc.

12. "Securities Law entitles the purchaser to sue the issuer, underwriter, certified public accountant and lawyer with respect to any material misstatements or omissions in the prospectus. However, except for the issuer, who has absolute liability for any material misstatements or omissions, Securities Law provides an affirmative defense for any other defendant who can demonstrate that he / she met a prescribed standard of diligence with respect to the information contained in the prospectus." Based on the above description, what kind of liability does the issuer have? (100年司法官)

(A) Strict liability　(B) Negligent liability　(C) No liability

(D) Presumption of negligence

13. "Scienter" means a mental state consisting of an intent to deceive, manipulate, or defraud. In this sense, the term is used most often in the context of securities fraud. The court has held that to establish a claim for damages under securities fraud, a plaintiff must prove that the defendant acted with scienter. Based on the above, the word "scienter" can be BEST replaced by the word of _____. (100年司法官)

(A) knowledge　(B) causation　(C) innocence　(D) action

14. The regulations governing the relationship between the shareholders and directors of a company and required for the establishment of a company are: (100年司法官)

(A) Articles of Incorporation　(B) Regulations of Incorporation

(C) Laws of Incorporation　(D) Files of Incorporation

15. The idea behind incorporation is that the rights and liabilities of a corporation are separate and distinct from those of its shareholders. However, creditors of a company can ask a court to "_____," and set aside a company's identity as a juristic person and reach the company owners and shareholders' personal assets. (100年律師)

    (A) pierce the corporate shell   (B) pierce the corporate veil
    (C) cover the corporate shell   (D) cover the corporate veil

16. "A tender offer is an offer to stockholders of a publicly-held corporation to exchange their shares for cash or securities at a price higher than the previous market price. A tender offer is the most common way of carrying out a hostile takeover." Which of the following can NOT be derived from the above description? (100年律師)

    (A) The price offered in a tender offer transaction is often with a premium.

    (B) A tender offer is usually an unfriendly acquisition of the target company.

    (C) The target's shareholders will get cash or shares if they tender their shares.

    (D) An acquirer of a closely-held company can launch a tender offer.

17. Debt security is issued by a company and sold to investors, usually to raise money in order to expand its business. In certain situations, the company's assets may be used as collateral. This debt security is usually called _____. (100年律師)

    (A) shareholder debt   (B) corporate bond   (C) blank check
    (D) corporate liability

18. The term "capital market" is generally used to refer to those markets

that deal in long-term financial instruments, such as stock, bonds, mortgage, etc., while the term "money market" describes those markets in which short-term debt instruments (typically, having a maturity under one year) are issued and traded. Therefore, which one of the followings is generally NOT considered to be an instrument in the capital market? (100年律師)

(A) Commercial paper　(B) Common share　(C) Preferred share
(D) Government bond

19. What is the term for a for-profit company, organized under the laws of another country, but authorized by the R.O.C. government to transact business in R.O.C.? (101年司法官)

(A) A third party company　(B) A diplomatic company
(C) A foreign company[1]　(D) A certified company

20. Which of the following terms refers to two or more independent enterprises that have made investments between or amongst each other, held by the same major shareholder, or share a controlling / subordinate relationship with each other? (101年司法官)

(A) Major and minor companies　(B) Sister companies
(C) Licensor and licensee　(D) Affiliated enterprises[2]

21. "The laws and rules that govern the securities industry derive from a simple and straightforward concept: all investors, whether large institutions or private individuals, should have access to certain basic facts about an investment prior to buying it, and so long as they hold

---

1　See Article 4 Company Act.
2　See Article 369-1 Company Act.

it." To achieve the above goal, the government authority will most likely require public companies to _____ . (101年司法官)

(A) disclose meaningful information　(B) abstain from trading shares　(C) avoid self-dealing transactions　(D) establish an internal control mechanism

22. "One anti-takeover charter amendment is a provision requiring a supermajority vote – say 80 percent of the common shares instead of the usual bare majority rule – in order to effect a merger or sale of all assets." Which of the following cannot be derived from the above description? (101年司法官)

(A) The purpose of supermajority vote is to make a takeover some-what harder and riskier.[3]

(B) Supermajority vote would not absolutely block a takeover attempt, especially by a bidder willing to buy all the target stock.

(C) The anti-takeover tactic of supermajority vote requires a charter amendment.

(D) The anti-takeover tactic of supermajority vote shall be approved by the board of directors.

23. A request that a corporate shareholder authorizes another person to cast the shareholder's vote at a corporate meeting is a _____ . (101年司法官)

(A) voting trust　(B) proxy solicitation　(C) voting agreement
(D) sale of control

---

3 See The Free Dictionary, https://financial-dictionary.thefreedictionary.com/supermajority+provision (accessed 10.6.2019), noting that a supermajority provision makes a takeover more difficult.

24. Which of the following is not the duty of a liquidator when a company is in the liquidation process? (101年律師)

(A) To promote the business of the company.

(B) To collect all outstanding debts and to pay off all claims.

(C) To allocate surplus or loss.

(D) To allocate the residual assets.

25. "A corporation offering and selling its securities to the public has to file a registration statement with the competent authority. The registration statement automatically becomes effective 20 days after it is filed with the competent authority, at which point the issuer is free to sell the registered securities to the public. However, the competent authority has certain powers to delay or suspend the effectiveness of the registration statement if it appears that the statement is on its face incomplete or inaccurate in any material respect." Based on the above description, which of the following is not a part of the securities registration process? (101年律師)

(A) Discuss the terms of the offering with the competent authority.

(B) Prepare the registration statement by the issuer.

(C) File the registration statement with the competent authority.

(D) Wait for a certain period of time before the registration statement becomes effective.

26. During the public offering, issuing, private placement, or trading of securities, there shall be no misrepresentations, frauds, or any other acts which are sufficient to mislead other persons. The word "misrepresentation" can be worst explained by the term of _____ . (101年律師)

(A) concealment (B) false assertion (C) accurate statement

(D) non-disclosure

27. According to Taiwan Corporation Law, which of the following matters in a company limited by shares does not need to be stipulated in the Articles of Incorporation to take effect? (101年律師)

(A) The number of shares to be issued upon incorporation of the company, if the total authorized numbers of shares are to be issued in installments.

(B) The kind of special shares and the rights and obligations covered by such shares.

(C) The annual business plan.

(D) The cause(s) for dissolution of the company.

28. When a company's shareholders' meeting reaches the unanimous agreement of dissolution, the company will generally cease to carry on business at that time and start the process of _____ before dissolution. (102年司法官)

(A) reincorporation (B) acquisition (C) liquidation

(D) consolidation

29. When a corporation earns a profit or surplus, that money can be put to two uses. It can either be re-invested in the business, or it can be paid to the shareholders as _____. (102年司法官)

(A) dividends and bonuses (B) segments and reserves

(C) divisions and premiums (D) sections and portions

30. A director of a listed company learns material non-public information regarding the possible huge loss of the company, and prior to the disclosure of such information, the director sells shares of the company. Such an act is a violation of the rule against _____. (102年司法官)

(A) short swing (B) related party transaction (C) insider trading

(D) misrepresentation

31. "Short selling is a device whereby the speculator sells stock which he does not own, anticipating that the price will decline and that he will thereby be enabled to make delivery of the stock sold by purchasing it at a lesser price." Based on the above description, if the decline materializes, what is the short seller's profit? (102年司法官)

(A) The difference between the first purchase price and the second lower sales price.

(B) The difference between the first purchase price and the second lower purchase price.

(C) The difference between the first sales price and the second lower sales price.

(D) The difference between the first sales price and the second lower purchase price.

32. The combination of two or more companies, where the original companies cease to exist, a new company arises instead, and where existing stockholders of the original companies retain a shared interest in the new company, is called a _____ . (102年律師)

(A) merger　(B) acquisition　(C) hostile takeover

(D) asset purchase

33. Where a company that publicly issues shares or corporate bonds suspends its business or there is an expectation that such company will suspend its business due to financial difficulty, but there remains a possibility for such company may be re-constructed or rehabilitated, such company or any of the interested parties may apply to the court for _____ . (102年律師)

(A) liquidation　(B) consolidation　(C) dissolution

(D) reorganization

34. Big Corporation owns 95% of Little Corporation's shares. Little Corporation may be merged into Big Corporation without the approval of the shareholders of either corporation. This type of merger is called _____. (102年律師)

(A) short-form merger　(B) whale / minnow merger　(C) triangular merger　(D) de facto merger

35. "During 1990, the New York Stock Exchange (NYSE) traded 39.7 billion shares, while the National Association of Securities Dealers Automated Quotations (NASDAQ) traded 33.4 billion shares. NASDAQ's phenomenal growth was not envisioned by its founders, who intended it primarily as a quotation system to provide information with respect to securities not considered sufficiently seasoned to list on a securities exchange." The word "seasoned" can be BEST replaced by the word _____. (102年律師)

(A) flavored　(B) experienced　(C) salty　(D) unprofessional

36. In a _____ suit, shareholders are bestowed a right to sue directors on behalf of the corporation to enforce rights of corporation. (103年司法官律師)

(A) direct　(B) deprived　(C) deranged　(D) derivative

37. "Scalping" is a practice in which an investment advisor publicly recommends the purchase of securities without disclosing its practice of purchasing such securities before making recommendation and then selling them at a profit when the price rises after the recommen-

dation is disseminated. Therefore, scalping is a practice attacked by the competent authority as a violation of securities law similar to a _____ . (103年司法官律師)

(A) bribery   (B) fraud   (C) mistake   (D) robbery

38. _____ means stock which has been issued as fully paid to stock-holders and subsequently reacquired by the corporation to be used by it in furtherance of its corporate purpose. (103年司法官律師)

(A) Preferred stock   (B) Treasury stock   (C) Common stock

(D) Special stock

39. In a public company limited by shares, which of the following has the power to elect or remove a director? (104年司法官律師)

(A) directors   (B) supervisors   (C) the shareholders' meeting

(D) president

40. A company, organized by one or more shareholders, with the total capital of the company being divided into shares and each shareholder being liable for the company in an amount equal to the total value of shares subscribed by him, is called: (104年司法官律師)

(A) an unlimited company[4]   (B) a company limited by shares[5]

(C) an unlimited company with limited liability shareholders[6]

(D) a limited company[7]

4　See Article 2 Section 1 Company Act.

5　See Article 2 Section 4 Company Act.

6　See Article 2 Section 3 Company Act.

7　See Article 2 Section 2 Company Act.

41. Directors who possess professional knowledge and certain qualifications and may not have any direct or indirect interest in the company
are called _____. (104年司法官律師)
(A) insider directors (B) independent directors
(C) dummy directors (D) shadow directors

42. Which of the following is NOT the triggering event of a dissenting
shareholder's appraisal right? (104年司法官律師)
(A) merger (B) sale of substantially all of the company's assets
(C) spin off (D) share exchange pursuant to Article 156, Paragraph
8 of the Company Law[8]

43. A market manipulation claim can be based on _____ that are entered with the knowledge that sales of substantially the same size,
at substantially the same time and price, have been entered by the
wrongdoers for the sale of such security. (104年司法官律師)
(A) wash sales (B) matched orders[9] (C) front running
(D) short sales

44. Under the firm commitment agreement with the issuer, _____ may
subscribe to securities before placing them for sale or may reserve
certain portion of the securities specified in the agreement for subscription for his own account. (105年司法官律師)
(A) Broker (B) Underwriter (C) Dealer (D) Trustee

---

8 See now Article 156-4 Company Act.
9 Cf. My Share Investment, ASX share trading blog and articles, posted on 13.2.2008,
https://mysharesinvestment.blogspot.com/2008/02/market-manipulation.html (accessed 8.6.2019).

45. Which of the following is NOT required to be contained in the Articles of Incorporation of a corporation limited by shares? (105年司法官律師)

   (A) The names of directors and supervisors, and the term of their respective offices[10]

   (B) The par value of share

   (C) The name of the company

   (D) The date of establishment of the Articles of Incorporation

46. Under Securities Exchange Act, transactions involving securities are subject to registration, mandatory disclosure, and heightened anti-fraud rules. Please identify which of the following is NOT a security in Taiwan. (106年司法官律師)

   (A) A Taiwan depositary receipt[11]   (B) A convertible debenture

   (C) A foreign corporate bond   (D) A commercial paper[12]

47. Under Securities Exchange Act, transactions involving securities are subject to registration, mandatory disclosure, and heightened anti-fraud rules. Please identify which of the following is NOT an equity security in Taiwan. (106年司法官律師)

   (A) A convertible corporate bond   (B) A corporate bond with warrants   (C) A debenture   (D) A treasury stock

---

10 See Article 129 Company Act.

11 See CTBC Bank, Taiwan Depositary Receipt (TDR), https://ecorp.chinatrust.com.tw/cts/tdr/tdrAction.do?lang=en&method=start (accessed 8.6.2019).

12 See also Investopedia, Commercial Paper, https://www.investopedia.com/terms/c/commercialpaper.asp (updated 18.2.2019, accessed 8.6.2019).

48. _____ are the rights of shareholders to demand the payment of a fair price for their shares during a merger or other extraordinary corporate event. In this sense, the rights ensure that dissenters receive the benefit of their bargain by preventing corporations involved in mergers from paying less than what the company is worth. (106年司法官律師)

(A) Estimate rights　(B) Appraisal rights　(C) Compelling rights
(D) Forced rights

49. A _____ is a pretended sale made openly in the trading place for the purpose of deceiving other traders. Such manipulative practice is employed to give false appearance and to cause prices to be registered which are not true prices. (106年司法官律師)

(A) Tender Offer　(B) Short Sale　(C) Wash Sale　(D) Short Swing

50. Which of the following statements best describes the function or purpose of securities law? (107年司法官律師)

(A) Helping companies grow by putting various restrictions on them.

(B) Allowing companies to raise money from those whom they do not know much about.

(C) Checking companies' activities ex-ante as well as ex-post to avoid corporate misconduct.

(D) Encouraging investors to take due risk and enjoy economic growth.

51. According to the Close Company chapter of Taiwan's Company Act, which of the following statements is most likely to be incorrect? (107年司法官律師)

(A) When the number of shareholders exceeds 50, the status of a close company will be lost automatically.[13]

(B) To maintain the status of a close company, using a public channel to raise funds is strictly prohibited with no exception.[14]

(C) To facilitate capital formation, shareholders can use a more flexible way to pay for their shares, such as labor or service.[15]

(D) The corporate charter should stipulate a clear limitation on the free transferability of shares.[16]

---

13 See Article 356-1 Company Act.
14 See Article 356-4 Company Act.
15 See Article 356-3 Company Act.
16 See Article 356-5 Company Act.

CONSTITUTIONAL LAW
憲法

U.S. CONSTITUTIONAL LAW
單元一　美國憲法

DECLARATION OF INDEPENDENCE (1776)

ARTICLES OF CONFEDERATION (1777)

CONSTITUTION (1787)

Art. I: Legislative > Congress. Necessary and Proper Clause ("Elastic Clause")

Art. II: Executive > President

Art. III: Judiciary > Supreme Court

Art. IV: Full Faith and Credit Clause

Art. VI: Supremacy Clause

> **BILL OF RIGHTS (1789)**
> 1st Amendment: Freedom of religion and expression
> 2nd Amendment: Right to bear arms
> 4th Amendment: Search and seizure
> **5th Amendment: Due process**
> 6th Amendment: Rights of accused in criminal prosecutions
> 7th Amendment: Right to jury in civil trials
> 8th Amendment: Excessive fines
> 9th Amendment: Unenumerated rights
> 10th Amendment: Reserved powers (Reservation Clause)

> **OTHER AMENDMENTS**
> 11th Amendment: State sovereign immunity
> **14th Amendment: Due process**, equality

The Declaration of Independence 獨立宣言

In 1776, the Declaration of Independence proclaimed the separation of 13 American colonies from Great Britain: "When in the Course of human events, it becomes necessary ... to dissolve the political bands ... they should declare the causes which impel them to the separation" (introduction) ... "We hold these truths to be self-evident, that all men are created equal, that they are endowed by their Creator with certain unalienable Rights, that among these are Life, Liberty, and the pursuit of Happiness. That to secure these rights, Governments are instituted among Men, deriving their just powers from the consent of the governed" (preamble) ... "The history of the present King of Great Britain is a history of repeated injuries and usurpations ... To prove this, let Facts be submitted to a candid world" (list of grievances) ... "therefore, the Representatives of the United States of America ... declare, That these United Colonies are ... Free and Independent States" (resolution of independence).

- separation 分開、分離
- colony 殖民地
- cause 原因、理由
- endowed with unalienable rights 天生具有不可剝奪的權利
- life, liberty, happiness 生命、自由、幸福
- grievance 不滿、不平、抱怨
- state 國家、國土、州

The Articles of Confederation 美國十三州邦聯憲法、邦聯條例

The now independent states adopted the Articles of Confederation in 1777, the first constitution of the United States. The sovereign states retained most powers by forming a loose confederation with a weak central government (e.g. without powers of enforcement or printing money). Due to strong divisions among the states, it soon became apparent that a constitutional revision was necessary.

- constitution 憲法
- sovereign 主權的
- central government 中央政府
- division 不一致、分裂
- revision 修正、修訂、修改

The Constitution 憲法

Ten years later, in 1787, a new constitution was introduced to strengthen the federal government: "We the People of the United States, in Order to form a more perfect Union ... establish this Constitution for the United States of America" (preamble).

- strengthen 加強、增強、鞏固
- federal government 聯邦政府

The Constitution is the supreme law of the United States, as expressly stipulated in Article VI of the U.S. Constitution ("Supremacy Clause"): "This Constitution, and the Laws of the United States which shall be made in Pursuance thereof; and all Treaties made ... under the Authority of the United States, shall be the supreme Law of the Land; and the Judges in every State shall be bound thereby; any Thing in the Constitution or Laws of any State to the Contrary notwithstanding". Hence state laws may not contradict the Constitution or federal laws in general.

- supreme law 最高法律
- Supremacy Clause 最高條款、至上條款、至高條款
- contradict 反駁、與……牴觸

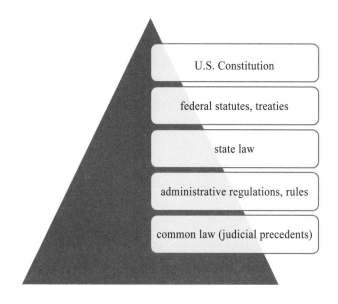

The constitution envisions a separation of powers into three branches (legislative, executive, judiciary), thereby forming a system of mutual checks and balances.

■ separation of powers 權力分立
■ three branches 三個部門／分支
■ legislative, executive, judiciary 立法、行政、 司法
■ system of mutual checks and balances 制衡機制、制約平衡制度

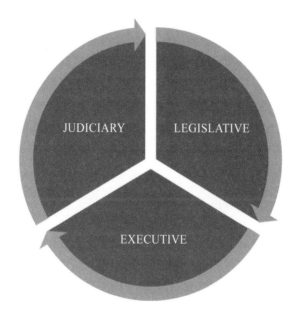

According to Article I of the U.S. Constitution, the legislative power is vested in the Congress, which is divided into a Senate and a House of Representatives: "All legislative Powers herein granted shall be vested in a Congress of the United States, which shall consist of a Senate and House of Representatives" (Section 1). "Every Bill which shall have passed the House of Representatives and the Senate, shall, before it becomes a Law, be presented to the President of the United

States; if he approve he shall sign it" (Section 7).

- legislative power 立法權
- vested 被授予
- Congress 國會
- Senate 參議院
- House of Representatives 眾議院
- bill 法案
- pass 通過

U.S. CONGRESS	
SENATE 參議院 ("upper house")	HOUSE OF REPRESENTATIVES 眾議院 ("lower house")
100 (2 from each state) directly elected for 6 years represent states regardless of population national representation deliberative, long-term policies	435 directly elected for 2 years represent people from "districts" according to population local representation popular, changing policies
advice and consent powers (e.g. ratify treaties, appoint officials)	exclusive power to initiate (e.g. revenue bills, impeachment)

The U.S. Congress has certain expressly enumerated powers (e.g. war and defense, interstate commerce, copyright and patent). In addition, it has implied powers to make all laws which are "necessary and proper" for the execution of its powers: "Congress shall have Power To lay and collect Taxes, ... provide for the common Defence and general Welfare of the United States; ... To regulate Commerce with foreign Nations, and among the several States, ... To make all Laws which shall be necessary and proper for carrying into Execution the foregoing Powers, and all other Powers vested by this Constitution in the Government of the United States" (Article I, Section 8).

- ■ express / implied powers 明示 / 默示權力
- ■ enumerate 列舉
- ■ war and defense 戰爭與國防
- ■ interstate commerce 洲際商業
- ■ copyright and patent 著作權與專利權
- ■ necessary and proper 必要且適當
- ■ execution 實行、執行、履行

The seminal case *McCulloch v. Maryland*, 17 U.S. 316 (1819) clarified that the Necessary and Proper Clause (Art. I, Section 8) of the Constitution does not require "absolute necessity" but gives U.S. Congress broad discretion to choose "appropriate means of exercising any of the powers expressly granted." As a result, the incorporation of national banks and branches is constitutional and must not be impeded by the states: "Among the enumerated powers, we do not find that of establishing a bank or creating a corporation ... yet such power may be exercised ... whenever it becomes an appropriate means of exercising any of the powers expressly granted ... The power of passing all laws necessary and proper to carry into effect the other powers specifically granted ... is a matter of legislative discretion, and those who exercise it, have a wide range of choice in selecting means ... It is sufficient, that it does not ... usurp a new substantive power ... The act incorporating the bank is constitutional; ... the power of establishing a branch in the state of Maryland might be properly exercised by the bank itself ...The power to tax involves the power to destroy ... the states have no power, by taxation or otherwise, to ... burden ... the operations of the constitutional laws enacted by congress to carry into execution the powers vested in the general government. This is ... the unavoidable consequence of that supremacy which the constitution has declared ... the law passed by the legislature of Maryland, imposing a tax on the Bank of the United States, is unconstitutional and void."

- Necessary and Proper Clause 必需與適當條款
- discretion 決定權、判斷力
- appropriate means 適當的手段／方法
- national bank 國家銀行、全國銀行
- branch 分行
- unconstitutional 違反憲法的
- void 無效的

To the extent that powers are not delegated to the Congress, they are generally reserved to the states ("reserved powers"): "The powers not delegated to the United States by the Constitution, nor prohibited by it to the States, are reserved to the States" (Tenth Amendment).

- delegate to 把……委託給
- reserved powers 被保留權力
- prohibit 禁止

Under the federal system of the United States, powers are thus divided between the national government and the individual states:

1. While certain powers are exclusively conferred to the federation ("exclusive federal powers", e.g. coin money, declare war), other powers are exclusively conferred to the states ("exclusive state powers").

2. Sometimes it is possible for states to regulate certain areas to the extent the Congress has not acted ("concurrent federal and state powers", e.g. taxation, bank charters). For instance, where Con-

gress merely sets minimum standards, states may enact similar or additional standards.

3. Certain powers are denied to the federal government and / or the states ("denied powers", e.g. ex post facto law).

- federal system 聯邦制度
- divided 分離的、分裂的、被分割的
- confer 授予
- exclusive federal / state powers 聯邦 / 州專屬權
- concurrent federal and state powers 聯邦與州共同權力
- denied power 禁止（國會 / 各州）行使之權力
- ex post facto law 事後法、有溯及力的法律

FEDERAL POWERS		STATE POWERS
express powers e.g. interstate commerce	**implied powers** "necessary and proper"	**reserved powers** e.g. contracts, corporations
exclusive federal powers e.g. coin money, declare war		**exclusive state powers**
concurrent federal and state powers e.g. taxation, bank charters		
denied powers e.g. ex post facto law		

The executive power is vested in the president of the United States (Article II): "The executive Power shall be vested in a President of the United States of America."

- executive power 行政權
- president 總統

Among others, the president may appoint federal officers with the advice and consent of the Senate. He is also commander-in-chief of the army and has the power to sign international treaties: "The President shall be Commander in Chief of the Army and Navy of the United States ... He shall have Power, by and with the Advice and Consent of the Senate, to make Treaties ... appoint ... Judges of the supreme Court, and all other Officers of the United States, whose Appointments are not herein otherwise provided for" (Article II, Section 2).

- appoint 任命
- officers 公務員、官員、高級職員
- commander-in-chief 統帥、總司令
- army 軍隊
- international treaty 國際條約

The judicial power is vested in the Supreme Court of the United States. It has the ultimate right to interpret the law in certain disputes (Article III): "The judicial Power of the United States, shall be vested in one supreme Court, and in such inferior Courts as the Congress may ... establish ... The judicial Power shall extend to all Cases, in Law and Equity, arising under this Constitution, the Laws of the United States, and Treaties made ... under their Authority; ... Controversies to which the United States shall be a Party; ... Controversies between ... States; ... between Citizens of different States."

- judicial power 司法權
- supreme court 最高法院
- interpret 解釋
- dispute, controversy 爭論、糾紛

The first time the Supreme Court asserted its power of judicial review over legislative and executive acts was in *Marbury v. Madison*, 5 U.S. 137 (1803). In this landmark case, the Supreme Court affirmed that plaintiff had a "vested legal right" but refused to grant the requested remedy since the legal basis for doing so (i.e. the Judiciary Act of 1789) was unconstitutional.

　　■judicial review 司法審查

The judicial power is restricted by various requirements (e.g. plaintiff must have standing to sue; judicial self-restraint in political questions). In particular, federal and state governments enjoy immunity from lawsuits brought by private citizens ("sovereign immunity"). Only with its express consent ("waiver") can a government be sued by an individual: "The Judicial power of the United States shall not ... extend to any suit in law or equity, commenced or prosecuted against one of the United States by Citizens of another State, or by Citizens or Subjects of any Foreign State." (Eleventh Amendment)

　　■standing 當事人適格
　　■sovereign immunity 主權豁免

A valid judgment rendered by a court in one state must be given "full faith and credit" and can therefore be enforced in other states (Article IV): "Full Faith and Credit shall be given in each State to the public Acts, Records, and judicial Proceedings of every other State."

　　■full faith and credit 完全誠意與信任
　　■enforce 實施、執行、強制

The Bill of Rights 人權法案、權利清單

When the U.S. Constitution was ratified in 1788, there was a political understanding that additional amendments should be supplemented to protect the rights of individual persons against the government. Consequently, the first ten amendments to the federal Constitution ("Bill of Rights") stipulating a list of fundamental rights were promptly adopted in 1789.

- ratify 批准
- amendment to the Constitution 憲法增修條文
- list of fundamental rights 基本權利表

The First Amendment guarantees the freedom of religion, expression (speech, press, assembly) and petition: "Congress shall make no law respecting an establishment of religion, or prohibiting the free exercise thereof; or abridging the freedom of speech, ... press, or the right of the people peaceably to assemble, and to petition the Government for a redress of grievances."

- guarantee 保障、保證
- freedom of religion 宗教信仰自由
- freedom of expression (speech, press, assembly) 表達自由（言論、出版、集會）
- petition 請願、請求、申請

The Second Amendment grants people the right to bear arms: "A well regulated Militia, being necessary to the security of a free state, the right of the people to keep and bear Arms, shall not be infringed."

- bear arms 帶武器
- infringe 違反

The Fourth Amendment protects people against illegal searches and seizures: "The right of the people to be secure in their persons, houses ... against unreasonable searches and seizures, shall not be violated, and no Warrants shall issue, but upon probable cause ... particularly describing the place to be searched, and the persons or things to be seized."

- search and seizure 搜索及扣押
- warrant 搜查令、授權令、逮捕狀
- probable cause 合理根據、合理充足理由、可能成立的理由

The Fifth Amendment stipulates certain rights in criminal proceedings (e.g. indictment by grand jury, prohibition of double jeopardy, privilege against self-incrimination). Most importantly, it enshrines the principle of due process of law: "No person shall be held to answer for a capital ... crime ... unless on ... indictment of a Grand Jury ... nor shall any person be subject for the same offense to be twice put in jeopardy of life or limb, nor shall be compelled in any criminal case to be a witness against himself, nor be deprived of life, liberty, or property, without due process of law; nor shall private property be taken for public use without just compensation."

- criminal 刑事
- indictment 控告、起訴
- grand jury 大陪審團
- prohibition of double jeopardy 禁止重複追訴
- self-incrimination 自證有罪
- due process of law 正當法律程序、合法訴訟程序
- deprive 剝奪
- life, liberty, property 生命、自由、財產

The Sixth Amendment lists further safeguards for the accused in criminal prosecutions: "In all criminal prosecutions, the accused shall enjoy the right to a speedy and public trial, by an impartial jury ... and to be informed of the ... cause of the accusation; to be confronted with the witnesses against him ... and to have the assistance of counsel for his defence."

- safeguard 保護、防衛、預防措施
- accused 被告
- criminal prosecution 刑事訴訟
- speedy and public trial 迅速和公開的審判
- impartial jury 公正陪審團
- cause of the accusation 控告的理由
- confronted with the witnesses 與證人進行對質
- assistance of counsel 律師幫助
- defence 辯護

The Seventh Amendment concerns the right to a jury in civil trials: "In Suits at common law, where the value in controversy shall exceed twenty dollars, the right of trial by jury shall be preserved, and no fact tried by a jury shall be otherwise reexamined in any Court of the United States, than according to the rules of the common law."

- civil trial 民事訴訟

The Eighth Amendment prohibits excessive fines and punishments: "Excessive bail shall not be required, nor excessive fines imposed, nor cruel and unusual punishments inflicted."

- excessive fine 過重罰金
- bail 保釋金
- cruel and unusual punishment 殘酷異常之處罰

The Ninth Amendment clarifies that the Bill of Rights is not exhaustive and other fundamental rights exist: "The enumeration in the Constitution of certain rights shall not be construed to deny or disparage others retained by the people."

- ■ exhaustive 徹底的、詳盡的、全面的
- ■ enumeration 列舉

The Fourteenth Amendment 增修條文第十四條

Though originally addressed to the federal government, most of the above mentioned rights have been incorporated under the Fourteenth Amendment due process clause and thus also apply to the states now: "No State shall make or enforce any law which shall abridge the privileges or immunities of citizens of the United States; nor shall any State deprive any person of life, liberty, or property, without due process of law".

- ■ incorporate 納入、適用
- ■ due process clause 正當程序條款

Due process requires not only certain procedural safeguards (e.g. notice, hearing) where a person is deprived of "life, liberty, or property", but from a substantive viewpoint also requires strict scrutiny whenever fundamental rights are restricted (e.g. freedom of religion and expression, right to privacy, right to vote).

- ■ procedural safeguard 程序保障
- ■ notice and hearing 通知與聽審
- ■ substantive 實質的、實體的
- ■ strict scrutiny 嚴格審查標準
- ■ fundamental rights 基本權利

Furthermore, the Fourteenth Amendment includes an equal protection clause: "nor shall any State deprive any person of life, liberty, or property, without due process of law; nor deny to any person within its jurisdiction the equal protection of the laws." Though formally addressed to the states, also the federal government must respect equal protection in light of the Fifth Amendment due process clause.

■ equal protection clause 平等保護條款

One of the most famous cases in this context is *Brown v. Board of Education*, 347 U.S. 483 (1954) concerning class actions filed on behalf of black students who had been denied admission to white public schools in accordance with several state laws. No longer supporting the doctrine of "separate but equal" the U.S. Supreme Court held that: "Segregation of children in public schools solely on the basis of race, even though the physical facilities and other tangible factors may be equal, deprives the children of the minority group of equal educational opportunities, in contravention of the Equal Protection Clause of the Fourteenth Amendment."

■ class action 團體訴訟
■ separate but equal 隔離但平等
■ on the basis of 以……為基礎
■ race 種族
■ contravention 違反、矛盾

Statutes and government actions are evaluated based on three judicial standards of review:

1. A strict scrutiny standard applies to suspect classifications (e.g. race) and restrictions of fundamental rights. Hence a discriminatory measure will be held unconstitutional, unless it is necessary to further a compelling governmental interest.

2. Under the intermediate review standard the government must prove that quasi-suspect classifications (e.g. gender) are substantially related to an important governmental interest.

3. All other classifications (e.g. age, wealth) are only required to have a "rational basis" in accordance with traditional standards of review.

- evaluate 評估
- standard of review 審查標準
- strict scrutiny 嚴格審查標準
- suspect classification 嫌疑分類
- discriminatory measure 歧視性措施
- compelling governmental interest 重大迫切的政府利益
- intermediate review standard 中度審查標準
- quasi-suspect classification (e.g. gender) 準嫌疑分類（例如：性別）
- substantially related to an important governmental interest 與重要之政府利益具有實質關連性
- other classifications (e.g. age, wealth) 其他分類（例如：年齡、財富）
- rational basis 合理基礎

STANDARD	STRICT SCRUTINY	INTERMEDIATE SCRUTINY	TRADITIONAL SCRUTINY
application	suspect classifications (e.g. race) fundamental rights	quasi-suspect classifications (e.g. gender)	all other classifications (e.g. age)
government interest	compelling	important	legitimate
method	necessary	substantially related	rational

References:

1. The U.S. National Archives and Records Administration, America's Founding Documents, https://www.archives.gov/founding-docs (accessed 31.3.2019).

2. The U.S. National Archives and Records Administration, America's Founding Documents, Declaration of Independence: A Transcript, https://www.archives.gov/ founding-docs/declaration-transcript (accessed 1.4.2019).

3. The U.S. National Archives and Records Administration, America's Founding Documents, Constitution of the United States, The Constitution: How Did it Happen? https://www.archives.gov/founding-docs/constitution/how-did-it-happen (accessed 31.3.2019).

4. Library of Congress, Exhibitions, Creating the United States, Road to the Constitution, https://www.loc.gov/exhibits/creating-the-united-states/road-to-the- constitution.html (accessed 31.3.2019).

5. Library of Congress, Exhibitions, Creating the United States, Forging a Federal Government, https://www.loc.gov/exhibits/creating-the-united-states/forging-a- federal-government.html (accessed 31.3.2019).

6. Library of Congress, Exhibitions, Creating the United States, Demand for a Bill of Rights, https://www.loc.gov/exhibits/creating-the-united-states/demand-for-a-bill-of-rights.html (accessed 31.3.2019).

7. Library of Congress, Constitution Annotated, https://www.congress.gov/constitution-annotated/ (accessed 31.3.2019).

8. U.S. Government Publishing Office, Constitution of the United States of America: Analysis and Interpretation (2017), https://www.congress.gov/content/conan/pdf/GPO- CONAN-2017.pdf (accessed 31.3.2019).

9. U.S. Government Printing Office, The Constitution of the United States with Index and The Declaration of Independence, https://www.govinfo.gov/content/pkg/CDOC-105sdoc11/html/CDOC-105sdoc11.htm (accessed 3.4.2019).

10. History, Declaration of Independence, https://www.history.com/topics/american-revolution/declaration-of- independence (accessed 1.4.2019).

11. TheFreeDictionary.com, https://legal-dictionary.thefreedictionary.com/Full+Faith+and+Credit+Clause (accessed 3.4.2019).

12. Legal dictionary, https://legaldictionary.net/enumerated-powers/ (accessed 31.3.2019).

13. Infoplease, Powers of the Government, https://www.infoplease.com/history-and-government/us-government/ powers-government (accessed 10.10.2019).

14. UShistory.org, American Government, http://www.ushistory.org/gov/3a.asp (accessed 3.4.2019).

15. 司法院全球資訊網，The Constitution of the United States of America，美利堅合眾國憲法，https://www.judicial.gov.tw/db/db04/美利堅合眾國憲法.pdf (accessed10.10.2019)。

16. Thomson Reuters, Westlaw.

THE CONSTITUTION OF THE REPUBLIC OF CHINA (TAIWAN)
單元二　中華民國憲法

Constitutional revisions 修憲

The original version of the ROC Constitution was adopted in mainland China in December 1946, promulgated in January 1947 and became effective in December 1947. However, many provisions never applied in practice and were significantly amended during the period 1991-2005 under a new era of government in Taiwan.[1] Following seven rounds of revisions, the constitution now consists of 175 articles and 12 additional articles ("Additional Articles of the Constitution of the Republic of China").[2]

- ◾ promulgate 公布、發表
- ◾ effective 生效
- ◾ amend 修正、修訂、修改
- ◾ Additional Articles of the Constitution of the Republic of China (Taiwan) 中華民國憲法增修條文

General principles 總綱

Chapter I ("General Provisions") of the ROC Constitution proclaims that the nation is a sovereign and democratic republic.

---

1 Wikipedia, Constitution of the Republic of China, https://en.wikipedia.org/wiki/Constitution_of_the_Republic_of_China (accessed 5.4.2019); Wikipedia, Additional Articles of the Constitution of the Republic of China, https://en.wikipedia.org/wiki/Additional_Articles_of_the_Constitution_of_the_Republic_of_China (accessed 5.4.2019).

2 Office of the President, Constitution of the Republic of China (Taiwan), https://english.president.gov.tw/Page/93 (accessed 4.4.2019); 中華民國總統府，中華民國憲法，https://www.president.gov.tw/Default.aspx?tabid=64 (4.4.2019)。

■ sovereign 主權

■ democratic republic 民主共和國

Constitution of the Republic of China (Taiwan) Chapter I General Provisions	中華民國憲法 第一章 總綱
Article 1 The Republic of China, founded on the Three Principles of the People, shall be a **democratic republic** of the people, to be governed by the people and for the people.	第一條 中華民國基於三民主義，為民有民治民享之**民主共和國**。
Article 2 The **sovereignty** of the Republic of China shall reside in the whole body of citizens.	第二條 中華民國之**主權**屬於國民全體。

Fundamental rights 基本權利

Chapter II ("Rights and Duties of the People") of the ROC Constitution enshrines the principle of equality before the law (Article 7) and guarantees certain fundamental freedoms, including personal freedom (Article 8), freedom of residence (Article 10), freedom of speech, teaching, writing and publication (Article 11), privacy of correspondence (Article 12), religious belief (Article 13), right to assembly and association (Article 14), right to own property (Article 15), right of election, initiative and referendum (Article 17).

■ rights and duties of the people 人民之權利義務

■ equality before the law 在法律上一律平等

■ personal freedom 身體之自由

■ freedom of residence 居住之自由

- freedom of speech, teaching, writing and publication 言論、講學、著作及出版之自由
- privacy of correspondence 秘密通訊
- religious belief 信仰宗教
- assembly and association 集會及結社
- right to own property 財產權
- right of election, initiative and referendum 選舉、創制及複決之權

Constitution of the Republic of China (Taiwan) Chapter II Rights and Duties of the People	中華民國憲法 第二章人民之權利義務
Article 7 All citizens of the Republic of China, irrespective of sex, religion, race, class, or party affiliation, shall be **equal before the law**.	第七條 中華民國人民，無分男女、宗教、種族、階級、黨派，在法律上一律平等。
Article 8 **Personal freedom** shall be guaranteed to the people. ... No person shall be arrested or detained otherwise than by a judicial or a police organ in accordance with the procedure prescribed by law. No person shall be tried or punished otherwise than by a law court in accordance with the procedure prescribed by law. ...	第八條 人民身體之自由應予保障。……非經司法或警察機關依法定程序，不得逮捕拘禁。非由法院依法定程序，不得審問處罰。……
Article 10 The people shall have **freedom of residence** and of change of residence.	第十條 人民有居住及遷徙之自由。

Article 11 The people shall have **freedom of speech, teaching, writing and publication**.	第十一條 人民有**言論、講學、著作及出版**之自由。
Article 12 The people shall have freedom of **privacy of correspondence**.	第十二條 人民有**秘密通訊**之自由。
Article 13 The people shall have freedom of **religious belief**.	第十三條 人民有**信仰宗教**之自由。
Article 14 The people shall have **freedom of assembly and association**.	第十四條 人民有**集會及結社**之自由。
Article 15 The right of existence, the right of work, and the **right of property** shall be guaranteed to the people.	第十五條 人民之**生存權、工作權**及**財產權**，應予保障。
Article 17 The people shall have the **right of election, recall, initiative and referendum**.	第十七條 人民有**選舉、罷免、創制及複決**之權。

Division of powers 權限劃分

Chapters IV to IX establish a central government that is composed of five branches (Legislative Yuan, Executive Yuan, Judicial Yuan, Examination Yuan, Control Yuan) under the overall leadership of a president. In addition, Chapter X allocates certain legislative and administrative powers to the central and local governments. Unlike the U.S. Constitution, where powers not delegated to the federation are reserved to the States (Tenth Amendment), the ROC Constitution does not contain a general provision in favour of local governments: "Any matter not enumerated in Articles 107, 108, 109 and 110 shall fall within the jurisdiction of the Central Government, if it is national in nature; of the province, if it is provincial in nature; and of the hsien, if it concerns the hsien. In case of dispute, it shall be settled by the Legislative Yuan" (Article 111).

- five branches 五個分支／部門
- Legislative Yuan 立法院
- Executive Yuan 行政院
- Judicial Yuan 司法院
- Examination Yuan 考試院
- Control Yuan 監察院
- president 總統
- allocate 分配
- central; local 中央；地方

Constitution of the Republic of China (Taiwan) Chapter X Powers of the Central and Local Governments	中華民國憲法 第十章中央與地方之權限
Article 107 In the following matters, the **Central Government shall have the power of legislation and administration**: ...	第一百零七條 左列事項，由中央立法並執行之：……
Article 108 In the following matters, the **Central Government shall have the power of legislation and administration**, but the Central Government may **delegate the power of administration to the provincial and hsien governments**: ...	第一百零八條 左列事項，由中央立法並執行之，或交由省縣執行之：……

Article 109 In the following matters, the **provinces shall have the power of legislation and administration**, but the provinces may **delegate the power of administration to the hsien**: ...	第一百零九條 左列事項，由省立法並執行之，或交由縣執行之：……
Article 110 In the following matters, the **hsien shall have the power of legislation and administration**: ...	第一百十條 左列事項，由縣立法並執行之：……
Article 111 Any matter not enumerated in Articles 107, 108, 109 and 110 shall fall within the jurisdiction of the Central Government, if it is national in nature; of the province, if it is provincial in nature; and of the hsien, if it concerns the hsien. In case of dispute, it shall be settled by the **Legislative Yuan**.	第一百十一條 除第一百零七條，第一百零八條，第一百零九條及第一百十條列舉事項外，如有未列舉事項發生時，其事務有全國一致之性質者屬於中央，有全省一致之性質者屬於省，有一縣之性質者屬於縣。遇有爭議時，由立法院解決之。

Interpretation and enforcement 解釋及施行

Since the Constitution is the supreme law, any conflicting laws and ordinances are void. In this context, Chapter XIV ("Enforcement and Amendment of the Constitution") defines the term "law" and entrusts the interpretation of the Constitution to the Judicial Yuan.

■ conflicting 衝突的

■ ordinance 命令

Constitution of the Republic of China (Taiwan) Chapter XIV Enforcement and Amendment of the Constitution	中華民國憲法 第十四章憲法之施行
Article 170 The term "**law**", as used in this Constitution, shall denote any legislative bill that shall have been passed by the Legislative Yuan and promulgated by the President of the Republic.	第一百七十條 本憲法所稱之**法律**，謂經立法院通過，總統公布之法律。
Article 171 **Laws that are in conflict with the Constitution shall be null and void.** When doubt arises as to whether or not a law is in conflict with the Constitution, interpretation thereon shall be made by the Judicial Yuan.	第一百七十一條 **法律與憲法牴觸者無效。** 法律與憲法有無牴觸發生疑義時，由司法院解釋之。
Article 172 **Ordinances** that are in conflict with the Constitution or with laws shall be null and void.	第一百七十二條 命令與憲法或法律牴觸者無效。
Article 173 The Constitution shall be interpreted by the **Judicial Yuan**.	第一百七十三條 憲法之解釋，由**司法院**為之。

EXERCISES
單元三　練習

Mark the odd word（選意義不同的字）:

highest – supreme – strict – ultimate

Congress – Government – House of Representatives – Senate

amend – modify – pre-empt – revise

federation – limit – restrain – restrict

examination – review – scrutiny – federal

alien – foreigner – noncitizen – suspect

freedom – liberty – privilege – property

compel – concurrent – force – overpower

agreement – clause – convention – treaty

authority – power – sovereignty – standing

branch – division – separation – standard

referendum – poll – power – vote

application – petition – request – religion

defend – political – protect – safeguard

confer – deprive – endow – vest

between – intermediate – middle – rational

as if – fundamental – quasi – resembling

Find the corresponding noun:

VERB	NOUN
amend	
classify	
consent	
discriminate	
divide	
defend	

evaluate	
impeach	
interfere	
live	
vote	

Find the corresponding noun and person:

VERB	NOUN	PERSON
interpret		
legislate		
speak		
suspect		
travel		

Find the corresponding noun and adjective:

VERB	NOUN	ADJECTIVE
constitute		
exclude		
execute		
legislate		
protect		
restrict		

Find the corresponding adjective:

NOUN	ADJECTIVE
commerce	
equality	
democracy	
immunity	
importance	
interest	
legitimacy	
privacy	
procedure	
sovereignty	
substance	

Choose the best answer:

1. According to the 11th Amendment of the U.S. Constitution, a citizen is not entitled to sue the government without the government's consent. This preclusion of jurisdiction is called _____.

   (A) sovereignty   (B) sovereign power   (C) sovereign liability
   (D) sovereign immunity

2. In order to bring a lawsuit before the Supreme Court, the plaintiff must have suffered a real injury. This requirement of plaintiff having a personal stake in the outcome of the case is called _____.

   (A) statute   (B) standing   (C) satisfaction   (D) supremacy

3. The Supreme Court can dismiss a case under the _____ doctrine due to lack of judicially ascertainable standards, so as not to interfere with policies which should be decided by the executive or legislative

branch.

(A) political question　(B) privilege　(C) presumption
(D) publicity

4. Article 11 of the R.O.C. Constitution stipulates that "people shall have freedom of _____, teaching, writing and publication.
(A) army　(B) gender　(C) property　(D) speech

5. According to Article 35 of the R.O.C. Constitution the _____ shall be the head of the State and shall represent the Republic of China in foreign relations.
(A) Grand Justice　(B) Legislative Yuan　(C) Premier
(D) President

6. The task of the Judicial Yuan is to _____ the Constitution.
(A) amend　(B) challenge　(C) interpret　(D) suspend

7. According to Article 170 of the R.O.C. Constitution, the term "law" means any legislative _____ that has been passed by the Legislative Yuan and promulgated by the President of the Republic.
(A) bill　(B) directive　(C) injunction　(D) ordinance

8. According to Article 171 of the R.O.C. Constitution, a law that is in conflict with the Constitution shall be _____.
(A) effective　(B) interpreted　(C) incorporated　(D) null and void

9. Which of the following is not a duty of the people as stated in the R.O.C. Constitution? (100年司法官)
(A) The duty of paying taxes　(B) The duty of performing military

services　(C) The duty of receiving citizen's education　(D) The duty of reporting crimes

10. Which constitutional organ is in charge of matters relating to employment, registration, service rating, scale of salaries, promotion and transfer, security of tenure, retirement, and old age pension? (100年司法官)

(A) The Control Yuan　(B) The Examination Yuan　(C) The Judicial Yuan　(D) The Executive Yuan

11. _____ is the process by which a person acquires nationality after birth and becomes entitled to the privileges of citizenship. (100年律師)
(A) Neutralization　(B) Nationalization　(C) Naturalization
(D) Navigation

12. The _____ is to ensure that an individual may freely exercise the rights and powers to use, derive benefits from, and dispose of any and all of his or her properties depending upon the existing status of such properties, so as to secure the resources of life on which the survival of individuals and the free development of characters rely. (101年司法官)
(A) right to work　(B) right of property　(C) right of existence
(D) freedom of residence

13. Freedom of Press is _____ . (101年司法官)
(A) the right of a journalist to commit libel　(B) the right to place a "legal notice" advertisement　(C) the right to publish ideas and opinions without governmental restriction　(D) a judicial prohibition that forbids broadcast media from televising parts of court trials

14. According to Article 86, Paragraph 2 of the Constitution, the qualifi-
    cations for professional occupations shall be determined on the basis
    of examinations administered by the Examination Yuan. This article
    most likely involves: (101年律師)
    (A) the people's right to work   (B) the people's right of election
    (C) the people's right of property   (D) the people's right to engage
    in public services

15. _____ is the branch of government charged with administering
    and carrying out the law. (101年律師)
    (A) Judicial Branch   (B) Executive Branch   (C) Legislature Branch
    (D) Examination Branch

16. A(n) _____ is a law that retroactively changes the legal conse-
    quences of actions committed or relationship that exists prior to the
    enactment of the law. (102年司法官)
    (A) bill   (B) rule of law   (C) amendment   (D) ex post facto law

17. The _____ of the Republic of China is a branch of government
    exercising the powers of auditing and impeachment. (102年司法官)
    (A) Control Yuan   (B) Executive Yuan   (C) Legislature Yuan
    (D) Examination Yuan

18. Which is the best term for the effect of the court's final judgment
    on the merits that is conclusive as to the rights of the parties on the
    cause of action? (103年司法官律師)
    (A) exclusionary rule   (B) stare decisis   (C) precedent effect
    (D) claim preclusion

19. Pursuant to Article 12 of the (2005) Amendment of the Constitution of the R.O.C., an amendment of the Constitution shall be initiated upon the proposal of one-fourth of the total members of the Legislative Yuan, passed by at least three-fourths of the members present at a meeting attended by at least three-fourths of the total members of the Legislative Yuan, and sanctioned by electors in the free area of the Republic of China at _____ held upon expiration of a six-month period of public announcement of the proposal, wherein the number of valid votes in favor exceeds one-half of the total number of electors; and the provisions of Article 174 of the Constitution (Main Text) shall not apply. (104年司法官律師)

    (A) an election (B) a recall (C) an initiative (D) a referendum

20. John uploaded on his blog some information which contained images of naked women. He was then charged by the prosecutor for disseminating pornographic information to the public according to Article 235 of the R.O.C. Criminal Code. During the trial, John claimed that he was merely exercising his _____ guaranteed by the Constitution. (104年司法官律師)

    (A) freedom of assembly (B) freedom of association

    (C) freedom of expression (D) freedom of movement

21. _____ is a formal revision or addition proposed or made to a statute or Constitution. (105年司法官律師)

    (A) Article (B) Decision (C) Legislature (D) Amendment

22. Article 2 of the Additional Articles of the R.O.C. Constitution states, in part, that the President may by resolution of the Executive Yuan Council, issue _____ and take all necessary measures to avert im-

minent danger affecting the security of the State or of the people or to cope with any serious financial crisis, notwithstanding the restrictions in Article 43 of the R.O.C. Constitution. (106年司法官律師)

(A) discretionary order   (B) emergency orders

(C) restraining order   (D) stop order

23. According to Judicial Yuan Interpretation No. 603, fingerprints are important information of a person, who shall have self-control of such fingerprinting information, which is protected under the ＿＿＿＿. Accordingly, Article 8, Paragraphs 2 and 3 of the Household Registration Act, stating to the effect that the new R.O.C. identity card will not be issued without the applicant being fingerprinted is unconstitutional. (106年司法官律師)

(A) the right of privacy   (B) the right of possession

(C) the right of self-defense   (D) the right to be informed

24. A ＿＿＿＿ is an officer whose duty is to keep records, issue process and the like. (106年司法官律師)

(A) judge   (B) prosecutor   (C) paralegal   (D) court clerk

25. The right to have the assistance of counsel for his or her defense is mainly based upon the theory of ＿＿＿＿. (107年司法官律師)

(A) equality of arms   (B) freedom of speech

(C) warrant requirement   (D) double jeopardy

26. The warning of the ＿＿＿＿ must be accompanied by the explanation that anything said can and will be used against the individual in court. This warning is needed in order to make him aware not only of the privilege, but also of the consequences of forgoing it. (107年司法

官律師)

(A) right to have counsel present　(B) right to object

(C) right to trial by jury　(D) right to remain silent

27. The Supreme Court has repeatedly confirmed that denying a gener-ally available benefit solely on account of religious identity imposes a penalty on the _____ that can be justified only by a state interest of the highest order. (107年司法官律師)

(A) free exercise of religion　(B) freedom of expression

(C) establishment of religion religious　(D) equality

Which of the following answers is NOT correct:

1.　The R.O.C. Constitution protects the _____ .

(A) freedom of privacy　(B) freedom of religion　(C) freedom of assembly　(D) right to jury trial

2.　The U.S. Constitution provides for a separation of powers into the ___

_____ .

(A) control branch　(B) executive branch　(C) judicial branch　(D) legislative branch

3.　The U.S. Constitution includes a _____ .

(A) supremacy clause　(B) due process clause　(C) necessary and proper clause　(D) self-executing clause

4.　Which of the following is not a duty imposed by the Constitution? (102年律師)

(A) The duty of work　(B) The duty of paying tax　(C) The duty of serving in the military　(D) The duty of receiving citizens' education

5. Article 37 of the R.O.C. Constitution provides that "[t]he President shall ... issue mandates with the counter-signature of the president of the Executive Yuan". Which of the following orders is not an exception to such counter-signature requirement pursuant to Article 2 of the Additional Articles of the Constitution? (102年律師)

    (A) To appoint or remove from office the president of the Executive Yuan.　(B) To appoint personnel which is required by the Constitution to be confirmed by the Legislative Yuan.　(C) To confer honors and decorations.　(D) To dissolve the Legislative Yuan.

6. Which of the following statements regarding Control Yuan is INCORRECT? (103年司法官律師)

    (A) Members of the Control Yuan shall be beyond party affiliation and independently exercise their powers and discharge their responsibilities in accordance with the law　(B) No Member of the Control Yuan shall be held responsible outside the Yuan for opinions expressed or votes cast in the Yuan　(C) The Control Yuan may, in the exercise of its powers of control, request the Executive Yuan and its Ministries and Commissions to submit to it for perusal the original orders issued by them and all other relevant documents (D) No Member of the Control Yuan shall concurrently hold a public office or engage in any profession

7. Which one of the followings is NOT protected by the freedom of expression? (105年司法官律師)

    (A) Freedom of speech　(B) Freedom of residence　(C) Freedom of assembly　(D) Freedom of publication

ANSWERS
單元四 答案

Mark the odd word（選意義不同的字）：

highest – supreme – strict – ultimate 嚴格的

Congress – Government – House of Representatives – Senate 政府

amend – modify – pre-empt – revise 先占有

federation – limit – restrain – restrict 聯邦

examination – review – scrutiny – federal 聯邦

alien – foreigner – noncitizen – suspect 嫌疑

freedom – liberty – privilege – property 財產

compel – concurrent – force – overpower 同時

agreement – clause – convention – treaty 條款

authority – power – sovereignty – standing 當事人適格

branch – division – separation – standard 標準

referendum – poll – power – vote 權力

application – petition – request – religion 宗教信仰

defend – political – protect – safeguard 政治的

confer – deprive – endow – vest 剝奪

between – intermediate – middle – rational 合理的

as if – fundamental – quasi – resembling 基本的

Find the corresponding noun:

VERB	NOUN
amend	amendment 修正案
classify	classification 分類
consent	consent 同意
discriminate	discrimination 歧視
divide	division 分開

defend	defense 防禦
evaluate	evaluation 評估
impeach	impeachment 彈劾
interfere	interference 干涉
live	life 生命
vote	vote 選舉、投票、表決

Find the corresponding noun and person:

VERB	NOUN	PERSON
interpret	interpretation 解釋	interpreter
legislate	legislation 立法	legislator
speak	speech 言論	speaker
suspect	suspicion 嫌疑	suspect
travel	travel 遷徙、旅行	traveller / traveler

Find the corresponding noun and adjective:

VERB	NOUN	ADJECTIVE
constitute	constitution 憲法	constitutional
exclude	exclusion 排除	exclusive
execute	execution 執行	executive
legislate	legislation 立法	legislative
protect	protection 保護	protective
restrict	restriction 限制	restrictive

Find the corresponding adjective:

NOUN	ADJECTIVE
commerce 商貿	commercial
equality 平等	equal
democracy 民主	democratic

immunity 豁免	immune
importance 重要	important
interest 利益	interesting
legitimacy 合法	legitimate
privacy 隱私	private
procedure 程序	procedural
sovereignty 主權	sovereign
substance 實體	substantive

Choose the best answer:

1. According to the 11ᵗʰ Amendment of the U.S. Constitution, a citizen is not entitled to sue the government without the government's consent. This preclusion of jurisdiction is called _____.
   (A) sovereignty   (B) sovereign power   (C) sovereign liability
   (D) sovereign immunity

2. In order to bring a lawsuit before the Supreme Court, the plaintiff must have suffered a real injury. This requirement of plaintiff having a personal stake in the outcome of the case is called _____.
   (A) statute   (B) standing   (C) satisfaction   (D) supremacy

3. The Supreme Court can dismiss a case under the _____ doctrine due to lack of judicially ascertainable standards, so as not to interfere with policies which should be decided by the executive or legislative branch.
   (A) political question   (B) privilege   (C) presumption
   (D) publicity

4. Article 11 of the R.O.C. Constitution stipulates that "people shall have freedom of _____, teaching, writing and publication.
   (A) army   (B) gender   (C) property   (D) speech

5. According to Article 35 of the R.O.C. Constitution the _____ shall be the head of the State and shall represent the Republic of China in foreign relations.
   (A) Grand Justice   (B) Legislative Yuan   (C) Premier
   (D) President

6. The task of the Judicial Yuan is to _____ the Constitution.
   (A) amend   (B) challenge   (C) interpret   (D) suspend

7. According to Article 170 of the R.O.C. Constitution, the term "law" means any legislative _____ that has been passed by the Legislative Yuan and promulgated by the President of the Republic.
   (A) bill   (B) directive   (C) injunction   (D) ordinance

8. According to Article 171 of a R.O.C. Constitution, a law that is in conflict with the Constitution shall be _____.
   (A) effective   (B) interpreted   (C) incorporated   (D) null and void

9. Which of the following is not a duty of the people as stated in the R.O.C. Constitution? (100年司法官)
   (A) The duty of paying taxes   (B) The duty of performing military services   (C) The duty of receiving citizen's education   (D) The duty of reporting crimes

10. Which constitutional organ is in charge of matters relating to employment, registration, service rating, scale of salaries, promotion and transfer, security of tenure, retirement, and old age pension? (100年司法官)

(A) The Control Yuan　(B) The Examination Yuan　(C) The Judicial Yuan　(D) The Executive Yuan

11. _____ is the process by which a person acquires nationality after birth and becomes entitled to the privileges of citizenship. (100年律師)

(A) Neutralization　(B) Nationalization　(C) Naturalization
(D) Navigation

12. The _____ is to ensure that an individual may freely exercise the rights and powers to use, derive benefits from, and dispose of any and all of his or her properties depending upon the existing status of such properties, so as to secure the resources of life on which the survival of individuals and the free development of characters rely. (101年司法官)

(A) right to work　(B) right of property　(C) right of existence
(D) freedom of residence

13. Freedom of Press is _____. (101年司法官)

(A) the right of a journalist to commit libel　(B) the right to place a "legal notice" advertisement　(C) the right to publish ideas and opinions without governmental restriction　(D) a judicial prohibition that forbids broadcast media from televising parts of court trials

14. According to Article 86, Paragraph 2 of the Constitution, the qualifications for professional occupations shall be determined on the basis of examinations administered by the Examination Yuan. This article most likely involves: (101年律師)

(A) the people's right to work　(B) the people's right of election
(C) the people's right of property　(D) the people's right to engage in public services

15. _____ is the branch of government charged with administering and carrying out the law. (101年律師)

(A) Judicial Branch　(B) Executive Branch　(C) Legislature Branch
(D) Examination Branch

16. A(n) _____ is a law that retroactively changes the legal consequences of actions committed or relationship that exists prior to the enactment of the law. (102年司法官)

(A) bill　(B) rule of law　(C) amendment　(D) ex post facto law

17. The _____ of the Republic of China is a branch of government exercising the powers of auditing and impeachment. (102年司法官)

(A) Control Yuan　(B) Executive Yuan　(C) Legislature Yuan
(D) Examination Yuan

18. Which is the best term for the effect of the court's final judgment on the merits that is conclusive as to the rights of the parties on the cause of action? (103年司法官律師)

(A) exclusionary rule　(B) stare decisis　(C) precedent effect
(D) claim preclusion

19. Pursuant to Article 12 of the (2005) Amendment of the Constitution of the R.O.C., an amendment of the Constitution shall be initiated upon the proposal of one-fourth of the total members of the Legislative Yuan, passed by at least three-fourths of the members present at a meeting attended by at least three-fourths of the total members of the Legislative Yuan, and sanctioned by electors in the free area of the Republic of China at _____ held upon expiration of a six-month period of public announcement of the proposal, wherein the number of valid votes in favor exceeds one-half of the total number of electors; and the provisions of Article 174 of the Constitution (Main Text) shall not apply. (104年司法官律師)

    (A) an election　(B) a recall　(C) an initiative　(D) a referendum

20. John uploaded on his blog some information which contained images of naked women. He was then charged by the prosecutor for disseminating pornographic information to the public according to Article 235 of the R.O.C. Criminal Code. During the trial, John claimed that he was merely exercising his _____ guaranteed by the Constitution. (104年司法官律師)

    (A) freedom of assembly　(B) freedom of association

    (C) freedom of expression　(D) freedom of movement

21. _____ is a formal revision or addition proposed or made to a statute or Constitution. (105年司法官律師)

    (A) Article　(B) Decision　(C) Legislature　(D) Amendment

22. Article 2 of the Additional Articles of the R.O.C. Constitution states, in part, that the President may by resolution of the Executive Yuan Council, issue _____ and take all necessary measures to avert im-

minent danger affecting the security of the State or of the people or to cope with any serious financial crisis, notwithstanding the restrictions in Article 43 of the R.O.C. Constitution. (106年司法官律師)

(A) discretionary order　(B) emergency orders

(C) restraining order　(D) stop order

23. According to Judicial Yuan Interpretation No. 603, fingerprints are important information of a person, who shall have self-control of such fingerprinting information, which is protected under the ＿＿＿. Accordingly, Article 8, Paragraphs 2 and 3 of the Household Registration Act, stating to the effect that the new R.O.C. identity card will not be issued without the applicant being fingerprinted is unconstitutional. (106年司法官律師)

(A) the right of privacy　(B) the right of possession

(C) the right of self-defense　(D) the right to be informed

24. A ＿＿＿ is an officer whose duty is to keep records, issue process and the like. (106年司法官律師)

(A) judge　(B) prosecutor　(C) paralegal　(D) court clerk

25. The right to have the assistance of counsel for his or her defense is mainly based upon the theory of ＿＿＿. (107年司法官律師)

(A) equality of arms　(B) freedom of speech

(C) warrant requirement　(D) double jeopardy

26. The warning of the ＿＿＿ must be accompanied by the explanation that anything said can and will be used against the individual in court. This warning is needed in order to make him aware not only of the privilege, but also of the consequences of forgoing it. (107年司法

官律師)

(A) right to have counsel present (B) right to object

(C) right to trial by jury (D) right to remain silent

27. The Supreme Court has repeatedly confirmed that denying a generally available benefit solely on account of religious identity imposes a penalty on the _____ that can be justified only by a state interest of the highest order. (107年司法官律師)

(A) free exercise of religion (B) freedom of expression

(C) establishment of religion religious (D) equality

Which of the following answers is NOT correct:

1. The R.O.C. Constitution protects the _____.

(A) freedom of privacy (B) freedom of religion (C) freedom of assembly (D) right to jury trial

2. The U.S. Constitution provides for a separation of powers into the _____.

(A) control branch (B) executive branch (C) judicial branch (D) legislative branch

3. The U.S. Constitution includes a _____.

(A) supremacy clause (B) due process clause (C) necessary and proper clause (D) self-executing clause

4. Which of the following is not a duty imposed by the Constitution? (102年律師)

(A) The duty of work (B) The duty of paying tax (C) The duty of serving in the military   (D) The duty of receiving citizens' education

5. Article 37 of the R.O.C. Constitution provides that "[t]he President shall ... issue mandates with the counter-signature of the president of the Executive Yuan". Which of the following orders is not an exception to such counter-signature requirement pursuant to Article 2 of the Additional Articles of the Constitution? (102年律師)

    (A) To appoint or remove from office the president of the Executive Yuan.   (B) To appoint personnel which required by the Constitution to be confirmed by the Legislative Yuan.   (C) To confer honors and decorations.   (D) To dissolve the Legislative Yuan.

6. Which of the following statements regarding Control Yuan is INCORRECT? (103年司法官律師)

    (A) Members of the Control Yuan shall be beyond party affiliation and independently exercise their powers and discharge their responsibilities in accordance with the law   (B) No Member of the Control Yuan shall be held responsible outside the Yuan for opinions expressed or votes cast in the Yuan   (C) The Control Yuan may, in the exercise of its powers of control, request the Executive Yuan and its Ministries and Commissions to submit to it for perusal the original orders issued by them and all other relevant documents   (D) No Member of the Control Yuan shall concurrently hold a public office or engage in any profession

7. Which one of the followings is NOT protected by the freedom of expression? (105年司法官律師)

    (A) Freedom of speech   (B) Freedom of residence   (C) Freedom of assembly   (D) Freedom of publication

Chapter 5

CRIMINAL LAW & CRIMINAL PROCEDURE
刑法、刑事訴訟法

U.S. CRIMINAL LAW & CRIMINAL PROCEDURE
單元一　美國刑法、刑事訴訟法

Definition of crime 犯罪之定義

A crime is a forbidden conduct that is deemed offensive to society as a whole. Due to the severe nature of punishments including not only monetary fines but also imprisonment and even death, a crime must be clearly defined by law (principle of legality) at the time when it was committed (prohibition of ex post facto laws or retroactive laws).

- crime 犯罪、罪行
- forbidden conduct 被禁止的行為、違法行為
- offensive to society as a whole 冒犯了整體社會、對整體社會有害
- punishment 刑罰、懲罰、處罰
- monetary fine 罰金
- imprisonment 徒刑、監禁
- death 死亡
- clearly defined by law 法律有明確定義、法律有明文規定
- principle of legality 合法性原則
- prohibition of ex post facto laws or retroactive laws 禁止事後法、追溯法令、法律溯及既往、有溯及力的法律

Generally, crimes are divided into two broad categories: Serious crimes, which can be punished with imprisonment exceeding one year or even death, are called felonies (e.g. murder, robbery). Other crimes punishable by imprisonment of up to one year are called misdemeanors.

- felony 重罪
- misdemeanor 輕罪

Elements of crime 犯罪要件

Following elements of crime must be proven before imposing a punishment:

1. Criminal act or omission (actus reus): The defendant must have acted voluntarily or – in the event of an omission – had a legal duty to act (e.g. due to special relationship).
   - criminal act (actus reus) 犯罪行為
   - defendant 被告
   - voluntarily 志願
   - omission 不作為、遺漏
   - legal duty to act 作為義務

2. Guilty mind (mens rea): In addition to the objective requirement of criminal conduct, the defendant must also have been in a certain subjective state of mind (e.g. intent, recklessness, negligence). Exception: Proof of a culpable mental state is not required in cases of strict liability.
   - guilty mind (mens rea) 犯罪心態、犯罪意圖
   - intent; recklessness; negligence 故意；魯莽；過失
   - culpable 有罪
   - mental state 心理狀態、精神狀態

3. Actual and proximate causation of injury: As a result of the defendant's conduct, a harm must have occurred that is reasonably foreseeable.

   ◼ actual causation 事實上因果關係
   ◼ proximate causation 近接因果關係
   ◼ injury, harm 傷害、損傷
   ◼ reasonably foreseeable result 合理可預見的結果

Governing law 管轄法律、適用法律、所依據法律、準據法

The U.S. Constitution stipulates essential safeguards to protect the fundamental rights of criminal defendants and to ensure a fair trial.

   ◼ U.S. Constitution 美國憲法

Article III U.S. Constitution	· jury trial in criminal cases 陪審團審判 · venue at place where crime was committed 審判地點
4th Amendment	· search and seizure 搜索及扣押
5th Amendment	· grand jury indictment 大陪審團之起訴書 · prohibition of double jeopardy 禁止重複追訴 · privilege against self-incrimination 不自證己罪特權 · due process of law 正當法律程序
6th Amendment	· speedy and public trial 迅速暨公開審判 · impartial jury 公正陪審團 · confront accusers / witnesses 與控告者 / 證人進行對質 · right to counsel 律師辯護權
8th Amendment	· excessive bail / fines 過重的保釋金 / 罰金 · cruel and unusual punishment 殘酷和逾常之刑罰
14th Amendment	· due process of law 正當法律程序 · equal protection of law 法律的平等保護

Most criminal offenses are defined in federal statutory laws (federal crimes) and state statutory laws (state crimes). The Model Penal Code published by the American Law Institute in 1962 offers a systematic overview of substantive criminal law. Though it does not have the formal status of a law, it has served as a reference for many state penal codes.

- criminal offense 刑事犯罪
- federal / state statutory law 聯邦 / 州成文法
- Model Penal Code 模範刑法典
- American Law Institute 美國法律學會
- substantive criminal law 實體刑法

The formal proceedings in the courts are governed by federal or state rules (e.g. Federal Rules of Criminal Procedure, Federal Rules of Evidence, Federal Rules of Appellate Procedure).

- court 法院
- federal or state rules 聯邦或州規則
- Federal Rules of Criminal Procedure 聯邦刑事訴訟規則
- Federal Rules of Evidence 聯邦證據規則
- Federal Rules of Appellate Procedure 聯邦上訴程序規則

Preliminary proceedings 準備程序、刑事審判前的程序

All criminal cases are initiated by the government, often in cooperation with law enforcement authorities (e.g. Federal Bureau of Investigation, police). Federal prosecutors working within the Department of Justice are called United States Attorneys. State prosecutors are usually called district attorneys.

- law enforcement authority 執法機關

■ Federal Bureau of Investigation (FBI) 聯邦調查局
■ police 警察
■ federal prosecutor / United States Attorney 聯邦檢察官
■ state prosecutor 州檢察官
■ district attorney 地方檢察官

Based on a written complaint establishing probable cause that an offense has been committed, an arrest warrant or summons is issued. It is possible under certain circumstances to arrest a person even without a warrant (e.g. if a crime was committed in a public space in the presence of a police officer).

■ complaint 起訴書、控告、控訴
■ arrest warrant 逮捕令、逮捕證、拘捕狀
■ summons 傳喚、傳票

Once a suspect is in police custody, he must be informed of his constitutional rights before being interrogated. In particular, the privilege against self-incrimination enshrined in the Fifth Amendment requires that following advice be given ("Miranda warnings"): 1. You have the right to remain silent. 2. Anything you say can be held against you in a court of law. 3. You have the right to have an attorney present during questioning. 4. If you cannot afford an attorney, one will be appointed for you.

■ suspect 犯罪嫌疑人、嫌疑犯
■ custody 拘留
■ interrogate 訊問
■ privilege against self-incrimination 不自證己罪特權
■ Miranda warnings 米蘭達警告
■ right to remain silent 保持緘默的權利

■ right to have an attorney present during questioning 審訊時可要求律師在場

Evidence obtained in violation of the defendant's constitutional rights may not be used against him for purposes of criminal prosecution (exclusionary rule). In addition, further (direct or indirect) information derived from illegal government conduct may not be admitted as evidence in a subsequent criminal trial (fruit of the poisonous tree doctrine).

■ exclusionary rule 非法證據排除法則
■ may not be admitted as evidence 不得採爲證據
■ fruit of the poisonous tree doctrine 毒樹果實理論

Formal accusation 正式指控、控告、控訴

A defendant is formally charged by means of a written statement (bill of information) or indictment of a grand jury in felony cases. In response to the accusations brought against him, a defendant may plead guilty, not guilty, or nolo contendere (= neither contest nor admit that he committed the crime). As a matter of fact, most cases are settled by plea agreements (= plea bargain) between the defendant and the prosecutor.

■ charge 指控、控告
■ bill of information 檢察官之訴訟狀
■ indictment of a grand jury 大陪審團之起訴書
■ plead 作爲答辯提出
■ guilty; not guilty 有罪；無罪
■ nolo contendere (= neither contest nor admit) 不爭執 = 既不否認也不承認

- settle a case 解決／處理案件
- plea agreement (= plea bargain) 控辯協議（＝認罪協商、訴辯交易）

Trial 審判、審理

Criminal trials in the United States are based on an adversarial or accusatory system (as opposed to an inquisitorial system). The defendant is presumed to be innocent and the judge plays a passive role because the prosecutor bears the burden of proving the crime "beyond a reasonable doubt". In the end, it is up to the trial jury to decide in its verdict whether or not a defendant is guilty.

- adversarial system; inquisitorial system 對抗制；審問制
- presumed to be innocent 無罪推定、清白的假設
- burden of proof 舉證責任
- beyond a reasonable doubt 超越合理懷疑
- jury 陪審團
- verdict 裁決

Judgment 判決

If the defendant is acquitted, he may not be tried again for the same offense (prohibition of double jeopardy according to the Fifth Amendment). If the defendant is convicted, the judge will impose a sentence (e.g. fine, probation, imprisonment, death penalty).

- acquit; convict 宣告無罪；宣告有罪
- sentence 判刑、宣判、判決
- fine 罰金
- probation 緩刑
- imprisonment 徒刑、監禁
- death penalty 死刑

Appeal 上訴

Although the U.S. constitution does not guarantee a right of appeal, defendants who have been convicted normally have a chance to appeal the judgment on grounds of reversible errors that affect the outcome of the case (e.g. improper admission of evidence).

■reversible error 可逆轉的錯誤、可撤銷判決的錯誤

References:

1. Administrative Office of the United States Courts, Criminal Cases, https://www.uscourts.gov/about-federal-courts/types-cases/criminal-cases (accessed 2.8.2019).

2. The National Court Rules Committee, Federal Rules of Criminal Procedure, 2019 edition, https://www.federalrulesofcriminalprocedure.org/ (accessed 2.8.2019).

3. American Law Institute, Model Penal Code with commentary (1962), available at https://archive.org/details/ModelPenalCode_ALI (accessed 3.8.2019).

4. Lawshelf Educational Media, National Paralegal College, Basics of Criminal Law, https://lawshelf.com/videocourses/videocourse/basics-of-criminal-law (accessed 3.8.2019).

5. UpCounsel, Criminal Trial: Criminal Law Basics, https://www.upcounsel.com/lectl-criminal-trial-criminal-law-basics (accessed 3.8.2019).

6. US Law Essentials, Criminal law videos, https://uslawessentials.com/crimlawvideo1/ (accessed 4.8.2019).

7. Michael Jay Friedman, Outline of the U.S. Legal System (2004), https://usa.usembassy.de/etexts/gov/outlinelegalsystem.pdf, https://www.americancorner.org.tw/zh/outline-of-us-legal-system/ (ac-

cessed 4.8.2019).

8. Justitia, Criminal appeals, https://www.justia.com/criminal/procedure/criminal-appeals/ (updated April 2018, accessed 7.8.2019).

9. Legal Dictionary, Appeal, https://legaldictionary.net/appeal/ (updated 18.1.2015, accessed 7.8.2019).

10. The Free Dictionary, Probation, https://legal-dictionary.thefreedictionary.com/probation (accessed 7.8.2019).

11. Wikipedia, Criminal law of the United States, https://en.wikipedia.org/wiki/Criminal_law_of_the_United_States (edited 10.7.2019, accessed 4.8.2019).

12. Wikipedia, United States criminal procedure, https://en.wikipedia.org/wiki/United_States_criminal_procedure (edited 5.4.2019, accessed 4.8.2019).

13. Wikipedia, Miranda warning, https://en.wikipedia.org/wiki/Miranda_warning (edited 31.7.2019, accessed 6.8.2019).

14. Cambridge Dictionary, https://dictionary.cambridge.org.

15. 最高檢察署，雙語詞彙對照表，https://www.tps.moj.gov.tw/16314/16462/16482/Lpsimplelist (accessed 6.8.2019)。

16. 國家教育研究院，National Academy for Educational Research, http://terms.naer.edu.tw/detail/3618571/ (accessed 6.8.2019)。

17. 線上翻譯，Web dictionary, https://tw.ichacha.net/district%20attorney.html (accessed 6.8.2019)。

18. 高點法律網，http://lawyer.get.com.tw/Dic/DictionaryDetail.aspx?iDT=76772 (accessed 6.8.2019)。

R.O.C. CRIMINAL LAW

R.O.C. Code of Criminal Law[1]

Chapter 1: Application of the Code

Article 1

A conduct is punishable only when expressly so provided by the law at the time of its commission. ...

Chapter 2: Criminal Responsibility

Article 12

A conduct is not punishable unless committed intentionally or negligently.

A negligent conduct is punishable only if specifically so provided.

Article 13

A conduct is committed intentionally if the actor knowingly and intentionally causes the accomplishment of the elements of an offense. A conduct is considered an intentional commission of an offense if the actor is aware that the act will accomplish the elements of the offense and if such accomplishment is not against his will.

---

1 See Ministry of Justice, Laws & Regulations Database of The Republic of China, https://law.moj.gov.tw/Eng/LawClass/LawAll.aspx?PCode=C0000001 (amended on 19.6.2019, accessed 7.7.2019).

單元二　中華民國刑法

中華民國刑法[2]

第一章：法例

第1條

行為之處罰，以行為時之法律有明文規定者為限。……

第二章：刑事責任

第12條

行為非出於故意或過失者，不罰。

過失行為之處罰，以有特別規定者，為限。

第13條

行為人對於構成犯罪之事實，明知並有意使其發生者，為故意。

行為人對於構成犯罪之事實，預見其發生而其發生並不違背其本意者，以故意論。

2　法務部，全國法規資料庫，https://law.moj.gov.tw/LawClass/LawAll. aspx?pcode=C0000001（7.7.2019，修訂於2019年6月19日）。

Article 14

A conduct is committed negligently if the actor fails, although not intentionally, to exercise his duty of care that he should and could have exercised in the circumstances.

A conduct is considered to have been committed negligently if the actor is aware that his conduct would, but firmly believes it will not, accomplish the element of an offense.

Article 15

A person who has a legal obligation and is able to prevent the results of the occurrence of an offense but has failed to do so shall be equal to have caused the occurrence of the result by his positive act.

If a conduct of a person causes the danger of producing the result of an offense, the person has a legal obligation to prevent the occurrence of the result.

Article 23

A conduct performed by a person in defense of his own rights or the rights of another against immediate unlawful aggression thereof is not punishable. If the force of defense is excessive, punishment may be reduced or remitted.

Chapter 3: Attempt

Article 25

An attempt is a conduct performed in the commission of an offense that is not accomplished.

An attempt is punishable only if specifically so provided and the punishment may be reduced from that for an accomplished offense.

第14條

行為人雖非故意，但按其情節應注意，並能注意，而不注意者，為過失。

行為人對於構成犯罪之事實，雖預見其能發生而確信其不發生者，以過失論。

第15條

對於犯罪結果之發生，法律上有防止之義務，能防止而不防止者，與因積極行為發生結果者同。

因自己行為致有發生犯罪結果之危險者，負防止其發生之義務。

第23條

對於現在不法之侵害，而出於防衛自己或他人權利之行為，不罰。但防衛行為過當者，得減輕或免除其刑。

第三章：未遂犯

第25條

已著手於犯罪行為之實行而不遂者，為未遂犯。

未遂犯之處罰，以有特別規定者為限，並得按既遂犯之刑減輕之。

Chapter 4: Principal Offenders and Joint Offenders

Article 28

Each of the two or more persons acting jointly in the commission of an offense is a principal offender.

Article 29

A person who solicits another to have committed an offense is a solicitor.

A solicitor shall be punished according to the punishment prescribed for the solicited offense.

Article 30

A person who aids another in the commission of a crime is an accessory notwithstanding that the person aided does not know of the assistance.

The punishment prescribed for an accessory may be reduced from that prescribed for the principal offender.

Article 31

A person, who joins, solicits or aids another in an offense established on the basis of personal or other special relationship shall be considered a principal offender or solicitor or accessory but the punishment may be reduced. ...

第四章：正犯與共犯

第28條
二人以上共同實行犯罪之行為者，皆為正犯。

第29條
教唆他人使之實行犯罪行為者，為教唆犯。

教唆犯之處罰，依其所教唆之罪處罰之。

第30條
幫助他人實行犯罪行為者，為幫助犯。雖他人不知幫助之情者，亦同。

幫助犯之處罰，得按正犯之刑減輕之。

第31條
因身分或其他特定關係成立之罪，其共同實行、教唆或幫助者，雖無特定關係，仍以正犯或共犯論。但得減輕其刑。……

Chapter 8: Sentencing

Article 57

Sentencing shall base on the liability of the offender and take into account all the circumstances, and special attention shall be given to the following items:

1. The motive and purpose of the offense.
2. The stimulation perceived at the moment of committing the offense.
3. The means used for the commission of the offense.
4. The offender's living condition.
5. The disposition of the offender.
6. The education and intelligence of the offender.
7. Relationship between the offender and the victim.
8. The seriousness of the offender's obligation violation.
9. The danger or damage caused by the offense.
10. The offender's attitude after committing the offense.

Chapter 11: Offenses Against Public Safety

Article 173

A person who sets fire to and destroys an occupied dwelling house or who sets fire to and destroys an occupied structure ..., shall be sentenced to life imprisonment or imprisonment for not less than seven years. ...

第八章：刑之酌科及加減

第57條
科刑時應以行為人之責任為基礎，並審酌一切情狀，尤應注意下列事項，為科刑輕重之標準：

一、犯罪之動機、目的。

二、犯罪時所受之刺激。

三、犯罪之手段。

四、犯罪行為人之生活狀況。

五、犯罪行為人之品行。

六、犯罪行為人之智識程度。

七、犯罪行為人與被害人之關係。

八、犯罪行為人違反義務之程度。

九、犯罪所生之危險或損害。

十、犯罪後之態度。

第十一章：公共危險罪

第173條
放火燒燬現供人使用之住宅或現有人所在之建築物 ……，處無期徒刑或七年以上有期徒刑。……

Article 174

A person who sets fire to and destroys an unoccupied dwelling house belonging to another or who sets fire to and destroys an unoccupied structure ..., shall be sentenced to imprisonment for not less than three years but not more than ten years. ...

Chapter 15: Offenses of Forging Instruments or Seals

Article 210

A person who forges or alters a private document and causes injury to the public or to another shall be sentenced to imprisonment for not more than five years.

Article 211

A person who forges or alters a public document and causes injury to the public or another shall be sentenced to imprisonment for not less than one year but not more than seven years.

Chapter 22: Offenses of Homicide

Article 271

A person who takes the life of another shall be sentenced to death or life imprisonment or imprisonment for not less than ten years.
An attempt to commit an offense specified in the preceding paragraph is punishable.
A person who prepares to commit an offense specified in paragraph 1 shall be sentenced to imprisonment for not more than two years.

第174條

放火燒燬現非供人使用之他人所有住宅或現未有人所在之他人所
有建築物……，處三年以上十年以下有期徒刑。……

第十五章：偽造文書印文罪

第210條

偽造、變造私文書，足以生損害於公眾或他人者，處五年以下有
期徒刑。

第211條

偽造、變造公文書，足以生損害於公眾或他人者，處一年以上七
年以下有期徒刑。

第二十二章：殺人罪

第271條

殺人者，處死刑、無期徒刑或十年以上有期徒刑。

前項之未遂犯罰之。

預備犯第一項之罪者，處二年以下有期徒刑。

Article 273

Any person who kills others on the scene by righteous indignation shall be sentenced to imprisonment for not more than seven years.

An attempt to commit an offense specified in the preceding paragraph is punishable.

Article 276

A person who negligently causes the death of another shall be sentenced to imprisonment for not more than five years, short-term imprisonment, or a fine of not more than five hundred thousand yuan.

Chapter 23: Offenses of Causing Injury

Article 277

A person who causes injury to another shall be sentenced to imprisonment for not more than five years, short-term imprisonment, or a fine of not more than five hundred thousand yuan.

If death results from the commission of an offense specified in the preceding paragraph, the offender shall be sentenced to life imprisonment or imprisonment for not less than seven years; if serious physical injury results, the offender shall be sentenced to imprisonment for not less than three years but not more than ten years.

Article 278

A person who causes serious physical injury to another shall be sentenced to imprisonment for not less than five years but not more than twelve years.

If death results from the commission of an offense specified in the preceding paragraph, the offender shall be sentenced to life imprisonment or imprisonment for not less than ten years.

第273條

當場激於義憤而殺人者，處七年以下有期徒刑。

前項之未遂犯罰之。

第276條

因過失致人於死者，處五年以下有期徒刑、拘役或五十萬元以下罰金。

第二十三章：傷害罪

第277條

傷害人之身體或健康者，處五年以下有期徒刑、拘役或五十萬元以下罰金。

犯前項之罪因而致人於死者，處無期徒刑或七年以上有期徒刑；致重傷者，處三年以上十年以下有期徒刑。

第278條

使人受重傷者，處五年以上十二年以下有期徒刑。

犯前項之罪因而致人於死者，處無期徒刑或十年以上有期徒刑。

An attempt to commit an offense specified in paragraph 1 is punishable.

Article 284

A person who negligently causes injury to another shall be sentenced to imprisonment for not more than one year, short-term imprisonment, or a fine of not more than one hundred thousand yuan; if serious physical injury results, he shall be sentenced to imprisonment for not more than three years, short-term imprisonment, or a fine of not more than three hundred thousand yuan.

Chapter 26: Offenses Against Freedom

Article 304

A person who by violence or threats causes another to do a thing which he has no obligation to do or who prevents another from doing a thing that he has the right to do shall be sentenced to imprisonment for not more than three years, short-term imprisonment, or a fine or not more than three hundred yuan.

An attempt to commit an offense specified in the preceding paragraph is punishable.

Article 305

A person who threatens to cause injury to the life, body, freedom, reputation, or property of another and thereby endangers his safety shall be sentenced to imprisonment for not more than two years, short-term imprisonment, or a fine of not more than three hundred yuan.

第一項之未遂犯罰之。

第284條
因過失傷害人者，處一年以下有期徒刑、拘役或十萬元以下罰金，致重傷者，處三年以下有期徒刑、拘役或三十萬元以下罰金。

第二十六章：妨害自由罪

第304條
以強暴、脅迫使人行無義務之事或妨害人行使權利者，處三年以下有期徒刑、拘役或三百元以下罰金。
前項之未遂犯罰之。

第305條
以加害生命、身體、自由、名譽、財產之事，恐嚇他人致生危害於安全者，處二年以下有期徒刑、拘役或三百元以下罰金。

Article 306

A person who without reason enters a dwelling house or structure of another, the adjacent or surrounding grounds, ... belonging to another shall be sentenced to imprisonment for not more than one year, short-term imprisonment, or a fine of not more than three hundred yuan. ...

Chapter 27: Offenses Against Reputation and Credit

Article 310

A person who points out or disseminates a fact which will injure the reputation of another for purpose that it be communicated to the public commits the offense of slander and shall be sentenced to imprisonment for not more than one year, short-term imprisonment, or a fine of not more than five hundred yuan. ...

Article 311

A person who makes a statement with bona-fide intent under one of the following circumstances shall not be punished:
1. Self-defense, self-justification, or the protection of legal interest
2. A report made by a public official in his official capacity
3. Fair comment on a fact subject to public criticism
4. Fair report on the proceedings of a national or local assembly, court, or a public meeting

第306條

無故侵入他人住宅、建築物或附連圍繞之土地……，處一年以下有期徒刑、拘役或三百元以下罰金。……

第二十七章：妨害名譽及信用罪

第310條

意圖散布於眾，而指摘或傳述足以毀損他人名譽之事者，為誹謗罪，處一年以下有期徒刑、拘役或五百元以下罰金。……

第311條

以善意發表言論，而有左列情形之一者，不罰：

一、因自衛、自辯或保護合法之利益者。

二、公務員因職務而報告者。

三、對於可受公評之事，而為適當之評論者。

四、對於中央及地方之會議或法院或公眾集會之記事，而為適當之載述者。

Chapter 29: Offenses of Larceny

Article 320

A person who for purpose to exercise unlawful control over other's property for himself or for a third person unlawfully takes movable property of another commits larceny and shall be sentenced to imprisonment for not more than five years, short-term imprisonment, or a fine of not more than five hundred thousand yuan.

A person who for purpose to gain unlawful benefit of himself or of a third person unlawfully occupies the real property of another shall be punished in accordance with provisions of the preceding paragraph.

An attempt to commit an offense specified in one of the two preceding paragraphs is punishable.

Chapter 30: Offenses of Abrupt Taking, Robbery and Piracy

Article 325

A person who for purpose to exercise unlawful control over other's property for himself or for a third person abruptly takes from another his movable property shall be sentenced to imprisonment for not less than six months but not more than five years.

If death results from the commission of the offense, the offender shall be sentenced to life imprisonment or imprisonment for not less than seven years; if aggravated injury results, the offender shall be sentenced to imprisonment for not less than three years but not more than ten years.

An attempt to commit an offense specified in paragraph 1 is punishable.

第二十九章：竊盜罪

第320條

意圖為自己或第三人不法之所有，而竊取他人之動產者，為竊盜罪，處五年以下有期徒刑、拘役或五十萬元以下罰金。

意圖為自己或第三人不法之利益，而竊佔他人之不動產者，依前項之規定處斷。

前二項之未遂犯罰之。

第三十章：搶奪強盜及海盜罪

第325條

意圖為自己或第三人不法之所有，而搶奪他人之動產者，處六月以上五年以下有期徒刑。

因而致人於死者，處無期徒刑或七年以上有期徒刑，致重傷者，處三年以上十年以下有期徒刑。

第一項之未遂犯罰之。

Article 328

A person who uses violence, threats, ... or other means to render resistance impossible and to take away property of another or cause him to deliver it over for purpose to exercise unlawful control over other's property for himself or for a third person commits robbery and shall be sentenced to imprisonment for not less than five years.

A person who by means specified in the preceding paragraph obtains for himself or for a third person an illegal benefit in property shall be subject to same punishment.

If death results from the commission of robbery the offender shall be sentenced to life imprisonment or imprisonment for no less than ten years; if aggravated injury results, the offender shall be sentenced to life imprisonment or imprisonment for not less than seven years.

An attempt to commit an offense specified in paragraph 1 or 2 is punishable.

A person who prepares to commit robbery shall be sentenced to imprisonment for not more than one year, short-term imprisonment, or a fine of not more than three thousand yuan.

Chapter 31: Offenses of Embezzlement

Article 335

A person who has lawful possession of property belonging to another and who takes it for purpose to exercise unlawful control over it for himself or for a third person shall be sentenced to imprisonment for not more than five years or short-term imprisonment; in lieu thereof, or in addition thereto, a fine of not more than one thousand yuan may be imposed.

An attempt to commit an offense specified in the preceding paragraph is punishable.

第328條

意圖為自己或第三人不法之所有，以強暴、脅迫、……或他法，至使不能抗拒，而取他人之物或使其交付者，為強盜罪，處五年以上有期徒刑。

以前項方法得財產上不法之利益或使第三人得之者，亦同。

犯強盜罪因而致人於死者，處死刑、無期徒刑或十年以上有期徒刑；致重傷者，處無期徒刑或七年以上有期徒刑。

第一項及第二項之未遂犯罰之。

預備犯強盜罪者，處一年以下有期徒刑、拘役或三千元以下罰金。

第三十一章：侵占罪

第335條

意圖為自己或第三人不法之所有，而侵占自己持有他人之物者，處五年以下有期徒刑、拘役或科或併科一千元以下罰金。

前項之未遂犯罰之。

Chapter 32: Offenses of Fraudulence, Breach of Trust, Taking, and Usury

Article 339

A person who by fraud causes another to deliver to him property belonging to such other or to a third person for purpose to exercise unlawful control over other's property for himself or for a fourth person shall be sentenced to imprisonment for not more than five years or short-term imprisonment; in lieu thereof, or in addition thereto, a fine of not more than five hundred thousand yuan may be imposed.

A person who by the means specified in the preceding paragraph takes an illegal benefit for himself or for a third person shall be subject to the same punishment.

An attempt to commit an offense specified in one of the two preceding paragraphs is punishable.

第三十二章：詐欺背信及重利罪

第339條
意圖為自己或第三人不法之所有，以詐術使人將本人或第三人之物交付者，處五年以下有期徒刑、拘役或科或併科五十萬元以下罰金。以前項方法得財產上不法之利益或使第三人得之者，亦同。
前二項之未遂犯罰之。

EXERCISES
單元三　練習

Appellate review of state court decision:

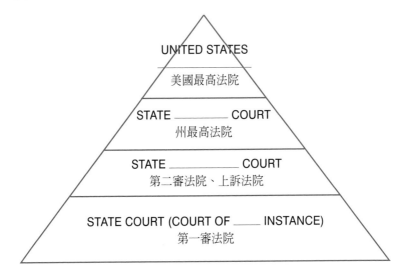

Appellate review of federal court decision:

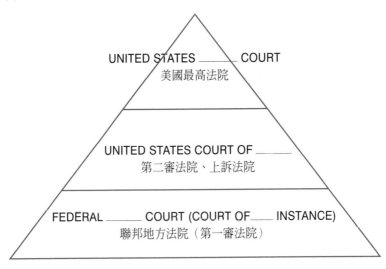

Fill in: accessory before / after the fact, accomplice, attempt, bill of attainder, burglary, conspiracy, ex post facto law, habeas corpus, murder, plea bargain, solicit, theft

	謀殺	unlawful killing of a human being with malice aforethought
	夜盜罪	breaking and entering into the dwelling of another in the nighttime with the intent to commit a felony therein
	偷竊、盜竊罪	larceny, false pretense, embezzlement
	共犯、幫兇	person assisting or participating in the commission of a crime
	事前／事後從犯者	person not present at the scene who helps the principal before / after the crime
	教唆	defendant encourages or requests another to commit a crime
	共謀	two or more people agree to commit a criminal act
	未遂犯	defendant intends to commit a crime and takes a substantial step (beyond mere preparation)
	褫奪公民權法案	legislative act punishing a specified person without trial
	禁止法律溯及既往	prohibition of retroactive / increased punishment; crimes which were not declared as such at the time of the offense
	人身保護令	remedy demanding a court to examine whether a prisoner s detention is lawful
	認罪協商	agreement between prosecutor and defendant whereby defendant admits his guilt in return for a reduced punishment

Mark the odd word（選意義不同的字）：

acquittal – imprisonment – fine – death penalty

fraud – killing – manslaughter – murder

arson – larceny – robbery – theft

conspiracy – intent – negligence – recklessness

search – seizure – solicit – stop and frisk

Find the corresponding noun:

VERB	NOUN
acquit	
admit	
cause	
charge	
complain	
convict	
defend	
detain	
doubt	
exclude	
indict	
injure	
mitigate	
omit	
prove	
punish	
violate	
waive	

Find the corresponding adjective:

NOUN	ADJECTIVE
constitution	
crime	
cruelty	
evidence	
excess	
guilt	
illegality	
intent	
negligence	
poison	
procedure	
recklessness	

Choose the best answer:

1. A conduct is considered _____ commission of an offense if the actor is aware that the act will accomplish the elements of the offense and if such accomplishment is not against his will.

   (A) an intentional   (B) a forceful   (C) a negligent   (D) a strict

2. A conduct performed by a person in _____ of his own rights or the rights of another against immediate unlawful aggression thereof is not punishable.

   (A) default   (B) defense   (C) discovery   (D) discharge

3. An _____ is a conduct performed in the commission of an offense that is not accomplished.

   (A) aggression   (B) appropriation   (C) assault   (D) attempt

4. A person who for purpose to exercise unlawful control over other's property for himself or for a third person unlawfully takes movable property of another commits _____ .

(A) bribe   (B) larceny   (C) rape   (D) robbery

5. Since intent is subjective and, without the cooperation of the accused, cannot be directly and objectively proven, the existence of the required intent may be inferred from surrounding circumstances such as the accused's acts, conduct and words. An intent to kill may be proved by _____ . Therefore, under the proper circumstances, an intent to kill may be inferred from the use of a deadly weapon directed at a vital part of the human body. (100年司法官)

(A) presumptive evidence   (B) circumstantial evidence

(C) corroborating evidence   (D) testimonial evidence

6. Principal offenders were present at the commission of the criminal act. _____ were not present at the commission of the offense but provided assistance to the principal offender either before or after a criminal offense had been committed. (100年司法官)

(A) Young offenders   (B) Habitual offenders   (C) Accessory offenders   (D) Sexual offenders

7. Jae sees Lion about to strike Jae's son Jude. Jae may use reasonable force to prevent Lion from striking Jude based on _____ . (100年司法官)

(A) self-defense   (B) justifiable defense   (C) emergent avoidance (D) defense of others

8. _____ is a privilege which requires the government to prove a

criminal case against the defendant without the aid of the defendant as a witness against himself. (100年律師)

(A) Privilege against self-incrimination   (B) Privileged communications   (C) Privileged debt   (D) Privileged evidence

9. All evidence, obtained by searches and seizures in violation of _____ guaranteeing the right to privacy free from unreasonable government intrusion, is inadmissible in court. (100年律師)

(A) the equal protection principle   (B) the due process principle

(C) the clean slate principle   (D) the protective principle

10. Joe intends to kill George. He buys a gun and hides in the bushes, waiting for George to pass by. Allen, George's twin brother, happens to walk by. Thinking that he is looking at George, Joe aims right at him and fires. Allen is killed instantly. Since Joe only had the intentions to kill George, is he guilty of murder of Allen? (100年律師)

(A) Yes, a case of mistaken identity does not save Joe.

(B) No, a case of mistaken identity does save Joe.

(C) No, because Joe did not have the intentions to kill Allen.

(D) No, because Joe intended to kill George.

11. Objects such as weapons or contraband found in a public place may be seized by the police without a _____ . If there is probable cause to associate the property with criminal activity, the seizure of property in plain view involves no invasion of privacy and is presumptively reasonable. (100年律師)

(A) warrant   (B) waiver   (C) welfare   (D) warfare

12. Austin breaks and enters Britney's home, steals a photograph of

Britney, and publishes it on the magazine to promote the sale of the magazine. Austin is liable to Britney for invasion of _____ . (101 年司法官)

(A) secrecy   (B) privacy   (C) intimacy   (D) expectancy

13. An _____ is defined as an overt act done in pursuance of an intent to do a specific crime, tending to the end but falling short of complete accomplishment of it. In law, the definition must have this further qualification that the overt act must be sufficiently proximate to the intended crime to form one of the natural series of acts which the intent requires for its full execution. (101年司法官)

(A) assault   (B) assent   (C) attaint   (D) attempt

14. A conviction cannot be based on the testimony of an _____ unless such testimony is corroborated by other evidence tending to connect the defendant with the commission of the offense. The corroboration is not sufficient if it merely shows the commission of the offense. (101 年司法官)

(A) accountant   (B) accommodator   (C) accomplishment
(D) accomplice

15. Defendant was not convicted of _____ to commit a crime when the person with whom he conspired feigned agreement and at no time intended to go through with the plan. (101年律師)

(A) conspiracy   (B) constancy   (C) consistency   (D) contingency

16. Which of the following circumstances is not an exception to the search warrant requirement? (101年律師)

(A) The police may conduct a warrantless search incident to a lawful arrest.

(B) The police may conduct a warrantless search if the search is made with the voluntary consent of the person being searched.

(C) Police officers in hot pursuit of a fleeing felon may make a warrantless search.

(D) In order to arrest an accused, police officers may search a dwelling without a search warrant even if there are insufficient facts to justify a conclusion that the accused is therein.

17. Which of the following statements about hearsay is incorrect? (101年律師)

(A) Hearsay is a statement or assertive conduct that was made or occurred out of court, and that is offered in court to prove the truth of the matter asserted.

(B) Hearsay is not admissible, unless it falls within some exceptions to hearsay rule.

(C) Hearsay is admissible, unless it falls within some exceptions to hearsay rule.

(D) Hearsay is not necessarily inadmissible.

18. Which law either makes conduct criminal that was not criminal at the time committed, increases the degree of criminality of conduct beyond what it was at the time it was committed, or increases the maximum permissible punishment for conduct beyond what it was at the time of commission? (102年司法官)

(A) Ex Post Facto Law   (B) Bill of Attainder Law   (C) Loitering Law   (D) Vagueness Law

19. Joe fraudulently converted Johnson's computer, which is lawfully

possessed by Johnson. What crime has Joe committed under Criminal Act? (102年司法官)

(A) Rape (B) False pretenses (C) Embezzlement (D) Larceny

20. A(n) _____ is a law that retroactively changes the legal consequences of actions committed or relationship that exists prior to the enactment of the law. (102年司法官)

(A) bill (B) rule of law (C) amendment (D) ex post facto law

21. Under _____, evidences of crime discovered by a law enforcement officer in making a search without lawful warrant may not be used against the victim of the unlawful search. (102年司法官)

(A) the best evidence rule (B) the exclusionary rule (C) the collateral source rule (D) the adverse interest rule

22. John intentionally burns Mike's house. What crime has John committed under criminal law? (102年律師)

(A) Arson (B) Larceny (C) Perjury (D) Homicide

23. Tory threatens Wang by saying, "Give me $1,000 or I will cut off your ear next week." What crime has Tory committed under criminal law? (102年律師)

(A) Robbery (B) Burglary (C) Extortion (D) Homicide

24. The examination of a witness goes through up to four stages. Which of the following is correct? (102年律師)

(A) The first stage is direct examination, the second stage is redirect examination, the third stage is cross examination, and the fourth stage is recross examination.

(B) The first stage is direct examination, the second stage is cross examination, the third stage is redirect examination, and the fourth stage is recross examination.

(C) The first stage is direct examination, the second stage is recross examination, the third stage is redirect examination, and the fourth stage is cross examination.

(D) The first stage is direct examination, the second stage is cross examination, the third stage is recross examination, and the fourth stage is redirect examination.

25. Before interrogating, an accused shall be informed of a few items under R.O.C. Code of Criminal Procedure. Which of the following is NOT included in such information-giving process? (103年司法官律師)

(A) That the accused is suspected of committing certain offense(s), and all of the offense(s) so charged shall be informed

(B) That the accused may remain silent and does not have to make a statement against his / her own will

(C) That the accused may retain defense attorney(s)

(D) That the accused may make a telephone call to inform his / her family

26. According to Article 1 of the R.O.C. Criminal Code, which one of the following statements is INCORRECT? (103年司法官律師)

(A) Retroactive crime definition is prohibited

(B) A conduct is punishable only when expressly so provided by the law at the time of its commission

(C) No one should be punished for a crime that has not been defined in advance

(D) A conduct is punishable only when expressly so provided by the law at the time of judgment

27. Accessory punishment "deprivation of citizen's rights" under R.O.C. Criminal Code DOES NOT include the deprivation of _____ . (103 年司法官律師)

(A) qualification for being a public official

(B) qualification of becoming a candidate for public office

(C) qualification of exercising citizen's right to vote

(D) qualification of becoming a candidate for a city mayor

28. John uploaded on his blog some information which contained images of naked women, He was then charged by the prosecutor for disseminating pornographic information to the public according to Article 235 of the R.O.C. Criminal Code. During the trial, John claimed that he was merely exercising his _____ guaranteed by the Constitution. (104年司法官律師)

(A) freedom of assembly   (B) freedom of association

(C) freedom of expression   (D) freedom of movement

29. According to Article 319 of the Code of Criminal Procedure, an injured party may file a _____ in the event that he is without legal capacity, or of limited legal capacity, or is dead, it may be filed by his statutory agent, lineal relative or spouse. (104年司法官律師)

(A) public prosecution   (B) private prosecution

(C) public advocate   (D) private offering

30. According to Article 77 of the R.O.C. Criminal Code, anyone who is sentenced to a certain number of years' imprisonment may be considered for _____ after he has served half of his sentence. (104年司法

官律師)

(A) pardon　(B) parole　(C) partition　(D) probation

31. According to Judicial Yuan Interpretation No. 617, which of the following is CORRECT statement regarding Article 235 of the R.O.C. Criminal Code? (105年司法官律師)

(A) A sexually explicit material is per se unprotected by Article 11 of the Constitution due to its lacking of artistic, medical or educational value.

(B) A sexually explicit material will not be classified as "obscene" under Article 235 if, by objective standard, it cannot stimulate or satisfy a prurient interest.

(C) The meaning of the term "obscene" is incomprehensible to the general public or to those who are subject to regulation, and therefore Article 235 is unconstitutional due to its violating the principle of clarity and definiteness of law.

(D) Article 235 imposes excessive restrictions on the expression of sexually explicit material and therefore constitutes an unreasonable restraint on the people's freedom of speech and publication.

32. _____ defines the conduct that society wishes to deter and to punish. (105年司法官律師)

(A) Civil Code　(B) Code of Civil Procedure　(C) Criminal Code
(D) Code of Criminal Procedure

33. In general, the court must be held in public unless under certain circumstances. Which of the following situations is NOT the exception for the public court? (105年司法官律師)

(A) The controversy involves personal privacy.

(B) The controversy involves individual's freedom of speech.

(C) The controversy involves business secret.

(D) Both parties have consented the hearing not be held in public.

34. With regard to interrogating an accused, which of the following is incorrect under R.O.C. Code of Criminal Procedure? (106年司法官律師)

(A) The accused shall be given an opportunity to explain as to the offense of which he / she is suspected.

(B) The accused shall be interrogated in an earnest manner; any improper means involving violence, threat, inducement, fraud, exhausting interrogation or other improper means shall not be used.

(C) A request by the accused for a confrontation shall not be denied, unless it is apparently unnecessary.

(D) The whole proceeding of interrogating the accused shall be consecutively recorded in audio, and also, if necessary, in video with no exceptions.

35. Ned sets a fire to Sarah's house one night, believing that Sarah and her family are in the house. In fact, Sarah and her family are away on vacation. The house is soon completely engulfed in flames. Ned will be convicted of _____. (106年司法官律師)

(A) murder   (B) extortion   (C) attempted arson   (D) attempted murder

36. With respect to evidence in criminal procedure, which of the following is not correct under R.O.C. Code of Criminal Procedure? (106年司法官律師)

(A) Where confession of an accused shall not be used as the sole basis leading to the conviction of offense(s), necessary evidence other than the confession shall nonetheless be investigated to see if the confession is consistent with facts found.

(B) Where a witness fails to sign an affidavit committing him/her to tell the truth as required by law, his / her testimony so made shall still be admitted as evidence.

(C) Unless otherwise provided by law, the admissibility of the evidence obtained unlawfully by an official in execution of criminal procedure shall be determined by balancing the protection of individual rights and the preservation of public interests.

(D) Unless otherwise provided by law, any oral or written statements made out of court by a person other than the accused shall not be admitted as evidence.

ANSWERS
單元四　答案

Appellate review of state court decision:

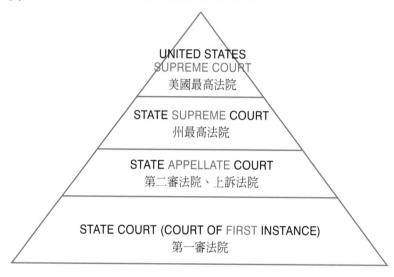

UNITED STATES
SUPREME COURT
美國最高法院

STATE SUPREME COURT
州最高法院

STATE APPELLATE COURT
第二審法院、上訴法院

STATE COURT (COURT OF FIRST INSTANCE)
第一審法院

Appellate review of federal court decision:

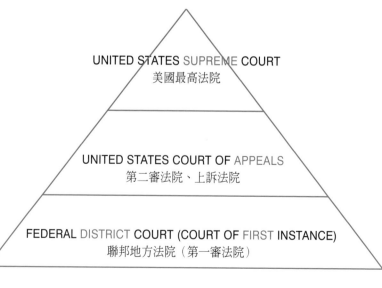

UNITED STATES SUPREME COURT
美國最高法院

UNITED STATES COURT OF APPEALS
第二審法院、上訴法院

FEDERAL DISTRICT COURT (COURT OF FIRST INSTANCE)
聯邦地方法院（第一審法院）

Fill in:

murder	謀殺	unlawful killing of a human being with malice aforethought
burglary	夜盜罪	breaking and entering into the dwelling of another in the nighttime with the intent to commit a felony therein
theft	偷竊、盜竊罪	larceny, false pretense, embezzlement
accomplice	共犯、幫兇	person assisting or participating in the commission of a crime
accessory before / after the fact	事前／事後從犯者	person not present at the scene who helps the principal before / after the crime
solicit	教唆	defendant encourages or requests
conspiracy	共謀	two or more people agree to commit a criminal act
attempt	未遂犯	defendant intends to commit a crime and takes a substantial step (beyond mere preparation)
bill of attainder	褫奪公民權法案	legislative act punishing a specified person without trial
prohibition of ex post facto law	禁止法律溯及既往	prohibition of retroactive / increased punishment; crimes which were not declared as such at the time of the offense
habeas corpus	人身保護令	remedy demanding a court to examine whether a prisoner's detention is lawful
plea bargain	認罪協商	agreement between prosecutor and defendant whereby defendant admits his guilt in return for a reduced punishment

Mark the odd word（選意義不同的字）：

acquittal – imprisonment – fine – death penalty 宣告無罪

fraud – killing – manslaughter – murder 詐欺

arson – larceny – robbery – theft 縱火罪

conspiracy – intent – negligence – recklessness 共謀

search – seizure – solicit – stop and frisk 教唆

Find the corresponding noun:

VERB	NOUN
acquit	acquittal 宣告無罪
admit	admission 自白
cause	cause、causation 因果關係
charge	charge 控告
complain	complaint 起訴狀
convict	conviction 有罪判決
defend	defense 辯護
detain	detention 羈押、拘留
doubt	doubt 懷疑
exclude	exclusion 排除
indict	indictment 起訴書
injure	injury 侵害
mitigate	mitigation 減輕
omit	omission 懈怠、不作為
prove	proof 證據
punish	punishment 刑罰、懲罰、處罰
violate	violation 違反
waive	waiver 放棄權利

Find the corresponding adjective:

NOUN	ADJECTIVE
constitution	constitutional 合憲的
crime	criminal 刑事犯罪的
cruelty	cruel 殘忍的

evidence	evident 明顯的
excess	excessive 過分的
guilt	guilty 有罪的
illegality	illegal 非法的
intent	intentional 故意的
negligence	negligent 過失的
poison	poisonous 有毒的
procedure	procedural 程序的
recklessness	reckless 魯莽的

Choose the best answer:

1. A conduct is considered _____ commission of an offense if the actor is aware that the act will accomplish the elements of the offense and if such accomplishment is not against his will.

   (A) an intentional   (B) a forceful   (C) a negligent   (D) a strict

2. A conduct performed by a person in _____ of his own rights or the rights of another against immediate unlawful aggression thereof is not punishable.

   (A) default   (B) defense   (C) discovery   (D) discharge

3. An _____ is a conduct performed in the commission of an offense that is not accomplished.

   (A) aggression   (B) appropriation   (C) assault   (D) attempt

4. A person who for purpose to exercise unlawful control over other's property for himself or for a third person unlawfully takes movable property of another commits _____.

   (A) bribe   (B) larceny   (C) rape   (D) robbery

5. Since intent is subjective and, without the cooperation of the accused, cannot be directly and objectively proven, the existence of the required intent may be inferred from surrounding circumstances such as the accused's acts, conduct and words. An intent to kill may be proved by _____. Therefore, under the proper circumstances, an intent to kill may be inferred from the use of a deadly weapon directed at a vital part of the human body. (100年司法官)

(A) presumptive evidence　(B) circumstantial evidence
(C) corroborating evidence　(D) testimonial evidence

6. Principal offenders were present at the commission of the criminal act. _____ were not present at the commission of the offense but provided assistance to the principal offender either before or after a criminal offense had been committed. (100年司法官)

(A) Young offenders　(B) Habitual offenders　(C) Accessory offenders　(D) Sexual offenders

7. Jae sees Lion about to strike Jae's son Jude. Jae may use reasonable force to prevent Lion from striking Jude based on _____. (100年司法官)

(A) self-defense　(B) justifiable defense　(C) emergent avoidance
(D) defense of others

8. _____ is a privilege which requires the government to prove a criminal case against the defendant without the aid of the defendant as a witness against himself. (100年律師)

(A) Privilege against self-incrimination　(B) Privileged communications　(C) Privileged debt　(D) Privileged evidence

9. All evidence, obtained by searches and seizures in violation of _____ guaranteeing the right to privacy free from unreasonable government intrusion, is inadmissible in court. (100年律師)
    (A) the equal protection principle   (B) the due process principle
    (C) the clean slate principle   (D) the protective principle

10. Joe intends to kill George. He buys a gun and hides in the bushes, waiting for George to pass by. Allen, George's twin brother, happens to walk by. Thinking that he is looking at George, Joe aims right at him and fires. Allen is killed instantly. Since Joe only had the intentions to kill George, is he guilty of murder of Allen? (100年律師)
    (A) Yes, a case of mistaken identity does not save Joe.
    (B) No, a case of mistaken identity does save Joe.
    (C) No, because Joe did not have the intentions to kill Allen.
    (D) No, because Joe intended to kill George.

11. Objects such as weapons or contraband found in a public place may be seized by the police without a _____ . If there is probable cause to associate the property with criminal activity, the seizure of property in plain view involves no invasion of privacy and is presumptively reasonable. (100年律師)
    (A) warrant   (B) waiver   (C) welfare   (D) warfare

12. Austin breaks and enters Britney's home, steals a photograph of Britney, and publishes it on the magazine to promote the sale of the magazine. Austin is liable to Britney for invasion of _____ . (101年司法官)
    (A) secrecy   (B) privacy   (C) intimacy   (D) expectancy

13. An _____ is defined as an overt act done in pursuance of an intent to do a specific crime, tending to the end but falling short of complete accomplishment of it. In law, the definition must have this further qualification that the overt act must be sufficiently proximate to the intended crime to form one of the natural series of acts which the intent requires for its full execution. (101年司法官)

(A) assault (B) assent (C) attaint (D) attempt

14. A conviction cannot be based on the testimony of an _____ unless such testimony is corroborated by other evidence tending to connect the defendant with the commission of the offense. The corroboration is not sufficient if it merely shows the commission of the offense. (101年司法官)

(A) accountant (B) accommodator (C) accomplishment

(D) accomplice

15. Defendant was not convicted of _____ to commit a crime when the person with whom he conspired feigned agreement and at no time intended to go through with the plan. (101年律師)

(A) conspiracy (B) constancy (C) consistency (D) contingency

16. Which of the following circumstances is not an exception to the search warrant requirement? (101年律師)

(A) The police may conduct a warrantless search incident to a lawful arrest.

(B) The police may conduct a warrantless search if the search is made with the voluntary consent of the person being searched.

(C) Police officers in hot pursuit of a fleeing felon may make a warrantless search.

(D) In order to arrest an accused, police officers may search a dwelling without a search warrant even if there are insufficient facts to justify a conclusion that the accused is therein.

17. Which of the following statements about hearsay is incorrect? (101年律師)

(A) Hearsay is a statement or assertive conduct that was made or occurred out of court, and that is offered in court to prove the truth of the matter asserted.

(B) Hearsay is not admissible, unless it falls within some exceptions to hearsay rule.

(C) Hearsay is admissible, unless it falls within some exceptions to hearsay rule.

(D) Hearsay is not necessarily inadmissible.

18. Which law either makes conduct criminal that was not criminal at the time committed, increases the degree of criminality of conduct beyond what it was at the time it was committed, or increases the maximum permissible punishment for conduct beyond what it was at the time of commission? (102年司法官)

(A) Ex Post Facto Law   (B) Bill of Attainder Law   (C) Loitering Law   (D) Vagueness Law

19. Joe fraudulently converted Johnson's computer, which is lawfully possessed by Johnson. What crime has Joe committed under Criminal Act? (102年司法官)

(A) Rape   (B) False pretenses   (C) Embezzlement   (D) Larceny

20. A(n) _____ is a law that retroactively changes the legal conse-

quences of actions committed or relationship that exists prior to the enactment of the law. (102年司法官)

(A) bill　(B) rule of law　(C) amendment　(D) ex post facto law

21. Under _____, evidences of crime discovered by a law enforcement officer in making a search without lawful warrant may not be used against the victim of the unlawful search. (102年司法官)

(A) the best evidence rule　(B) the exclusionary rule　(C) the collateral source rule　(D) the adverse interest rule

22. John intentionally burns Mike's house. What crime has John committed under criminal law? (102年律師)

(A) Arson　(B) Larceny　(C) Perjury　(D) Homicide

23. Tory threatens Wang by saying, "Give me $1,000 or I will cut off your ear next week." What crime has Tory committed under criminal law? (102年律師)

(A) Robbery　(B) Burglary　(C) Extortion　(D) Homicide

24. The examination of a witness goes through up to four stages. Which of the following is correct? (102年律師)

(A) The first stage is direct examination, the second stage is redirect examination, the third stage is cross examination, and the fourth stage is recross examination.

(B) The first stage is direct examination, the second stage is cross examination, the third stage is redirect examination, and the fourth stage is recross examination.

(C) The first stage is direct examination, the second stage is recross examination, the third stage is redirect examination, and the fourth stage is cross examination.

(D) The first stage is direct examination, the second stage is cross examination, the third stage is recross examination, and the fourth stage is redirect examination.

25. Before interrogating, an accused shall be informed of a few items under R.O.C. Code of Criminal Procedure. Which of the following is NOT included in such information-giving process? (103年司法官律師)

(A) That the accused is suspected of committing certain offense(s), and all of the offense(s) so charged shall be informed

(B) That the accused may remain silent and does not have to make a statement against his / her own will

(C) That the accused may retain defense attorney(s)

(D) That the accused may make a telephone call to inform his / her family

26. According to Article 1 of the R.O.C. Criminal Code, which one of the following statements is INCORRECT? (103年司法官律師)

(A) Retroactive crime definition is prohibited

(B) A conduct is punishable only when expressly so provided by the law at the time of its commission

(C) No one should be punished for a crime that has not been defined in advance

(D) A conduct is punishable only when expressly so provided by the law at the time of judgment

27. Accessory punishment "deprivation of citizen's rights" under R.O.C. Criminal Code DOES NOT include the deprivation of _____ . (103年司法官律師)

(A) qualification for being a public official

(B) qualification of becoming a candidate for public office

(C) qualification of exercising citizen's right to vote

(D) qualification of becoming a candidate for a city mayor

28. John uploaded on his blog some information which contained images of naked women, He was then charged by the prosecutor for disseminating pornographic information to the public according to Article 235 of the R.O.C. Criminal Code. During the trial, John claimed that he was merely exercising his _____ guaranteed by the Constitution. (104年司法官律師)

(A) freedom of assembly   (B) freedom of association

(C) freedom of expression   (D) freedom of movement

29. According to Article 319 of the Code of Criminal Procedure, an injured party may file a _____ in the event that he is without legal capacity, or of limited legal capacity, or is dead, it may be filed by his statutory agent, lineal relative or spouse. (104年司法官律師)

(A) public prosecution   (B) private prosecution

(C) public advocate   (D) private offering

30. According to Article 77 of the R.O.C. Criminal Code, anyone who is sentenced to a certain number of years' imprisonment may be considered for _____ after he has served half of his sentence. (104年司法官律師)

(A) pardon   (B) parole   (C) partition   (D) probation

31. According to Judicial Yuan Interpretation No. 617, which of the following is CORRECT statement regarding Article 235 of the R.O.C.

Criminal Code? (105年司法官律師)

(A) A sexually explicit material is per se unprotected by Article 11 of the Constitution due to its lacking of artistic, medical or educational value.

(B) A sexually explicit material will not be classified as "obscene" under Article 235 if, by objective standard, it cannot stimulate or satisfy a prurient interest.

(C) The meaning of the term "obscene" is incomprehensible to the general public or to those who are subject to regulation, and therefore Article 235 is unconstitutional due to its violating the principle of clarity and definiteness of law.

(D) Article 235 imposes excessive restrictions on the expression of sexually explicit material and therefore constitutes an unreasonable restraint on the people's freedom of speech and publication.

32. _____ defines the conduct that society wishes to deter and to punish. (105年司法官律師)

(A) Civil Code　(B) Code of Civil Procedure　(C) Criminal Code

(D) Code of Criminal Procedure

33. In general, the court must be held in public unless under certain circumstances. Which of the following situations is NOT the exception for the public court? (105年司法官律師)

(A) The controversy involves personal privacy.

(B) The controversy involves individual's freedom of speech.

(C) The controversy involves business secret.

(D) Both parties have consented the hearing not be held in public.

34. With regard to interrogating an accused, which of the following is incorrect under R.O.C. Code of Criminal Procedure? (106年司法官律師)

   (A) The accused shall be given an opportunity to explain as to the offense of which he / she is suspected.

   (B) The accused shall be interrogated in an earnest manner; any improper means involving violence, threat, inducement, fraud, exhausting interrogation or other improper means shall not be used.

   (C) A request by the accused for a confrontation shall not be denied, unless it is apparently unnecessary.

   (D) The whole proceeding of interrogating the accused shall be consecutively recorded in audio, and also, if necessary, in video with no exceptions.

35. Ned sets a fire to Sarah's house one night, believing that Sarah and her family are in the house. In fact, Sarah and her family are away on vacation. The house is soon completely engulfed in flames. Ned will be convicted of _____ . (106年司法官律師)

   (A) murder   (B) extortion   (C) attempted arson   (D) attempted murder

36. With respect to evidence in criminal procedure, which of the following is not correct under R.O.C. Code of Criminal Procedure? (106年司法官律師)

   (A) Where confession of an accused shall not be used as the sole basis leading to the conviction of offense(s), necessary evidence other than the confession shall nonetheless be investigated to see if the confession is consistent with facts found.

   (B) Where a witness fails to sign an affidavit committing him/her to tell the truth as required by law, his / her testimony so made shall still be admitted as evidence.

(C) Unless otherwise provided by law, the admissibility of the evidence obtained unlawfully by an official in execution of criminal procedure shall be determined by balancing the protection of individual rights and the preservation of public interests.

(D) Unless otherwise provided by law, any oral or written statements made out of court by a person other than the accused shall not be admitted as evidence.

CIVIL PROCEDURE LAW
民事訴訟法

U.S. CIVIL PROCEDURE LAW
單元一　美國民事訴訟法

Dual court system 二元法院體系

The United States has a dual court system that is composed of federal courts and state courts.

- federal court 聯邦法院
- state court 州法院

Federal courts are divided into three levels: At the bottom, there are 94 district courts or trial courts. At the intermediate level, 11 circuit courts, the Court of Appeals for the District of Columbia Circuit and the Court of Appeals for the Federal Circuit together form a total of 13 appellate courts. At the top level, the Supreme Court of the United States located in Washington D.C. is the court of last resort. The Supreme Court is authorized by Congress to prescribe rules of procedure for federal courts (e.g. Federal Rules of Civil Procedure, Federal Rules of Appellate Procedure), which may be further specified or supplemented by local court rules and practices.

- three levels 三級
- district court 地方法院
- trial court 初審法院、一審法院

- circuit 巡迴、（司法管轄）地區
- appellate court / appeals court / court of appeals 上訴法院
- Supreme Court of the United States 美國最高法院
- court of last resort 終審法院、終審法庭、最高上訴法院
- Federal Rules of Civil Procedure (FRCP) 聯邦民事訴訟規則
- Federal Rules of Appellate Procedure 聯邦上訴程序規則

A similar structure with trial courts in the first instance, appellate courts in the second instance and a supreme court can be found in the states, even though official court designations may differ. Besides, a number of courts are specialized in certain matters (e.g. family court). States and local courts have their own rules of civil procedure.

- first / second instance 第一審 / 第二審
- family court 家事法庭

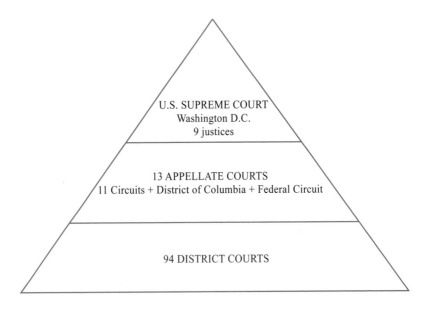

Personal jurisdiction 對人管轄權

When filing a lawsuit, it must first be ensured that the court has personal jurisdiction. This means that the court must have power over the parties for whom the decision will be binding and enforceable. The exercise of such judicial authority must be in accordance with constitutional requirements of due process (Fourteenth Amendment). From a substantive viewpoint (substantive due process), a sufficient connection must exist with the forum state (e.g. defendant is present or has domicile, property, business, other minimum contact). The defendant must also receive notice and an opportunity to be heard (procedural due process).

- jurisdiction 管轄權
- party 當事人
- (substantive / procedural) due process （實質上的 / 程序上的）正當程序
- forum state 管轄法院之州、法院地國、法院所在國
- minimum contact 最低限度聯繫、最低接觸

Personal jurisdiction was thus affirmed in *Burnham v. Superior Court of California*, 495 U.S. 604 (1990). The case arose when a husband residing in New Jersey made a short business trip to California. On this occasion, husband's wife, who had moved to California together with their children, filed for divorce in a California court. The Supreme Court held: "Service of process confers state-court jurisdiction over a physically present nonresident, regardless of whether he was only briefly in the State." In addition, it was argued that "(t)he transient jurisdiction rule will generally satisfy due process requirements ... by visiting the forum State, a transient defendant actually avails himself of significant benefits provided by the State: police, fire, and emergency services, the freedom to travel its roads and waterways, the enjoyment of the fruits of its economy, the protection of its laws, and the right of access to its courts. Without transient jurisdiction, the latter right would create an asymmetry, since a transient would have the full benefit of the power of the State's courts as a plaintiff while retaining immunity from their authority as a defendant. Furthermore, the potential burdens on a transient defendant are slight in light of modern transportation and communications methods, and any burdens that do arise can be ameliorated by a variety of procedural devices."

- service of process 訴訟書狀送達
- physically present 身體所在
- nonresident 非居民
- transient jurisdiction 短暫過境管轄權

Subject matter jurisdiction 主旨管轄權、事物管轄權

In addition to personal jurisdiction, courts must also have the power to deal with the particular issue or subject matter. While state trial courts generally hear all kinds of cases, federal courts have a limited subject matter jurisdiction, notably for (1) suits involving a federal question (arising under the Constitution, laws, or treaties of the United States); (2) suits between citizens of different states ("diversity jurisdiction") if the amount in controversy exceeds $75,000. *Example*: Defendant is a citizen of State A. While driving his car, defendant collides with plaintiff, who is a citizen of State B. Plaintiff can bring a lawsuit against defendant in federal court, if the damages exceed $75,000. Note: Lack of subject matter jurisdiction has the consequence that the case can be dismissed any time! This can happen even after the case has been tried in first instance and on appeal before the Supreme Court.

- issue 問題、爭論、爭議
- subject matter 主題事件、訴訟標的
- federal question 聯邦問題
- citizen 公民
- diversity jurisdiction 多元管轄權
- dismissed any time 隨時被駁回

Federal Rules of Civil Procedure (FRCP)

Rule 12(h)(3) Lack of Subject-Matter Jurisdiction.
If the court determines at any time that it lacks subject-matter jurisdiction, the court must dismiss the action.

Venue 審判地點

After having established jurisdiction over the parties and over the subject matter, the proper venue or geographic location of the court has to be chosen. In which judicial district can the suit be filed? Usually, venue is determined by the defendant's residence or the place where the events giving rise to the dispute occurred. But if it would be more convenient to try the case at another place, defendant can ask the court to dismiss / transfer the case ("forum non conveniens").

- geographic location 地理位置
- judicial district 司法區、法院轄區
- doctrine of forum non conveniens 不便利法庭原則

Pleadings 訴狀、當事人書狀

1. The complaint is filed by the plaintiff to commence an action. It contains three essential elements: Relevant facts (including statements on the grounds of jurisdiction), legal claim (cause of action) and specific relief (e.g. request for damages, injunction). Note that the case must concern an actual controversy in which the plaintiff has a personal stake (standing requirement).
   - complaint 起訴狀
   - actual controversy 事實上的爭議、眞正的爭議
   - personal stake 個人利害關係
   - standing 當事人適格

2. The answer is the defendant's response to plaintiff's complaint. It can include admissions, denials, affirmative defenses (e.g. fraud, illegality, res judicata, statute of limitations) or counterclaims.
   - answer to complaint 答辯狀
   - admission 承認
   - denial 否認
   - affirmative defense 肯定性答辯、積極抗辯
   - counterclaim 反訴、反請求

3. The plaintiff must serve a reply, if the answer contains a counterclaim.
   - reply 回覆狀、反訴答辯

Discovery 證據發現程序、事證開示程序、調查證據、披露程序

Discovery is a stage of great practical significance in the United States in which non-privileged evidence that is relevant to a party's claim or defense can be obtained from the opposing party.

- ▪ evidence 證據
- ▪ obtain 得到、獲得、取得
- ▪ opposing party 對方當事人

1. Automatic disclosure: Even without request a party must disclose all witnesses, documents and tangible things that the party plans to use in its case, including details of expert testimony. If the party does not perform the automatic mandatory disclosure, that information may not be used as evidence, unless the failure to disclose was substantially justified or harmless.

- ▪ automatic disclosure 自動披露
- ▪ without request 不待要求
- ▪ witnesses 證人
- ▪ documents 文件、文書
- ▪ tangible 有形的
- ▪ expert testimony 專家證詞、鑑定

2. Depositions are (transcripts of) oral testimonies taken out of court from any person (e.g. distant witnesses).

- ▪ deposition 宣誓證言
- ▪ transcript 文字記錄
- ▪ oral testimony 口頭證言

3. Interrogatories are written questions, which are addressed to a party and must be answered in writing.

- ▪ interrogatory 書面質問
- ▪ written questions 書面提問

4. A request to inspect documents or property may concern not only tangible things, but also electronically stored information and permission to enter designated land.

■ request to inspect 請求檢查／勘驗
■ permission to enter 允許進入

5. A request for physical or mental examination requires a motion, a court order and good cause. *Example*: While driving his car, defendant hits and injures plaintiff. Plaintiff sues defendant for negligence. If plaintiff claims that the accident was caused because of defendant's impaired eyesight, there is good cause to request a physical examination. If plaintiff's theory is that the brakes of the car were defective, there is no good cause for physical examination.

■ physical／mental examination 身體／精神檢查
■ motion 動議、請求、申請
■ court order 法庭命令
■ good cause 正當理由

6. Requests for admission require a party to admit or deny the truth of certain facts or the genuineness of certain documents.

■ admission 承認
■ truth 眞理

Burden of proof 舉證責任

Burden of producing evidence: A party must produce some evidence that a fact exists, otherwise the judge will find that the fact does not exist.

■ burden of producing evidence 提出證據責任

Burden of persuasion: If it cannot be decided whether or not a fact exists, the judge will find that the fact does not exist.

■ burden of persuasion 說服責任

Preponderance of evidence ("more likely than not") is the standard proof in civil actions. A higher standard is the requirement of "clear and convincing proof" (e.g. often applied in equity proceedings). The highest standard applies in criminal procedures, where the prosecutor is required to prove the elements of a crime "beyond a reasonable doubt".

■ preponderance of evidence 證據優勢
■ more likely than not 可能之機率大於不可能之機率、可能多於不可能
■ civil action 民事訴訟
■ clear and convincing proof 清楚且令人信服的證據
■ beyond a reasonable doubt 超越合理的懷疑

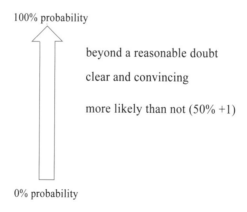

Judgment 判決

If a party fails to take action (e.g. by not appearing in court), a default judgment may be entered against that party (FRCP 55).

■ default judgment 缺席判決、缺席裁判

If in the course of pretrial discovery the evidence shows that material facts are not disputed, the court shall grant a summary judgment (FRCP 56).

■ summary judgment 簡易判決、即決判決

After a party has been heard during trial and there is insufficient evidence for that party, the court can grant a motion for judgment as a matter of law without involving a jury (FRCP 50).

■ judgment as a matter of law 依據法律問題的判決、依據法律自為判決

Appeal 上訴

The party who loses a trial generally has the right to appeal the adverse judgment within a certain time (usually 30 days in civil cases). An appeal must be based on grounds of certain errors. It must be evident from the court records that the party has made an "objection" during trial and stated her grounds for that objection.

■ lose a trial 敗訴

■ right to appeal 上訴權

■ adverse judgment 不利的判決

■ error 錯誤、失誤、瑕疵

■ objection 異議

Appellate courts typically decide questions of law without deference to the trial court's ruling. But appeals courts are extremely limited in their ability to reverse for fact-finding errors ("clearly erroneous").

▪ question of law 法律問題

Federal Rules of Civil Procedure (FRCP)

Rule 52(a)(6) Setting Aside the Findings.
Findings of fact, whether based on oral or other evidence, must not be set aside unless clearly erroneous, and the reviewing court must give due regard to the trial court's opportunity to judge the witnesses' credibility.

Res judicata 一事不再理、既決事項

Once a final judgment can no longer be appealed, it becomes binding and enforceable. According to the doctrine of res judicata, the same case or underlying events can not be litigated again by the same parties.

▪ final judgment 終局判決、終審判決
▪ binding 有約束力的、必須遵守的

Moreover, the Full Faith and Credit Clause (Article IV of the U.S. Constitution) requires each state to give to the judgment of any other state the same binding effect that judgment would have in the state which rendered it. *Example*: plaintiff wins a judgment against defendant in State 1, but defendant has property only in State 2. Plaintiff may collect in State 2 by bringing a suit based on the judgment rendered in State 1. The court in State 2 must accept the judgment (not reconsider any issues) and enforce it.

▪ Full Faith and Credit Clause 完全誠意與信任條款、充分互信條款

References:

1. Administrative Office of the United States Courts, https://www.us-courts.gov/ (accessed 30.7.2019).

2. U.S. Government Publishing Office, Federal Rules of Civil Procedure (2018), available at https://www.uscourts.gov/sites/default/files/cv_rules_eff._dec._1_2018_0.pdf (accessed 13.10.2019).

3. The National Court Rules Committee, Federal Rules of Civil Procedure, 2019 edition, https://www.federalrulesofcivilprocedure.org/ (accessed 28.7.2019).

4. Cornell Law School, Legal Information Institute, Civil Procedure, https://www.law.cornell.edu/wex/civil_procedure (accessed 27.7.2019).

5. Lawshelf Educational Media, National Paralegal College, Basics of Civil Litigation, https://lawshelf.com/videocourses/videocourse/basics-of-civil-litigation (accessed 29.7.2019).

6. Steven L. Emanuel, Law Outlines: Civil Procedure, Wolters Kluwer, 26th edition (2018).

7. USLawEssentials, What is the difference between judgment as a matter of law and summary judgment?, https://uslawessentials.com/difference-judgment-matter-law-summary-judgment/ (accessed 29.7.2019).

8. The White House, The Judicial Branch, https://www.whitehouse.gov/1600/judicial-branch (accessed 30.7.2019).

9. Difference Between.Com, Difference Between Judgement and Verdict, https://www.differencebetween.com/difference-between-judgement-and-vs-verdict/ (posted 10.2.2015, accessed 29.7.2019).

10. The Free Dictionary, res judicata, https://legal-dictionary.thefreedictionary.com/res+judicata (accessed 29.7.2019).

11. Wikipedia, Res judicata, https://en.wikipedia.org/wiki/Res_judicata (edited 15.4.2019, accessed 29.7.2019).

12. 維基百科，自由的百科全書，美國法院，https://zh.wikipedia.org/zh-tw/美國法院 (accessed 30.7.2019)。

13. 國家教育研究院 National Academy for Educational Research, http://lawyer.get.com.tw/Dic/DictionaryDetail.aspx?iDT=76689 (accessed 30.7.2019)。

14. 高點法律網，http://lawyer.get.com.tw/Dic/DictionaryDetail.aspx?iDT=64460 (accessed 30.7.2019)。

15. 線上翻譯 Web dictionary, https://tw.ichacha.net/forum%20state.html (accessed 30.7.2019)。

16. 司法院，雙語詞彙，https://www.judicial.gov.tw/blg/bilingual.asp?show=all (accessed 30.7.2019)。

17. Thomson Reuters, Westlaw.

TAIWAN CODE OF CIVIL PROCEDURE

Code of Civil Procedure[1]

CHAPTER I: THE COURT
Section 1: Jurisdiction

Article 1

A defendant may be sued in the court for the place of the defendant's domicile or, when that court cannot exercise jurisdiction, in the court for the place of defendant's residence. A defendant may also be sued in the court for the place of defendant's residence for a claim arising from transactions or occurrences taking place within the jurisdiction of that court. ...

Article 10

In matters relating to rights in rem, partition, or demarcation of real property, exclusive jurisdiction resides in court for the place where the real property is located. ...

Article 24

Parties may, by agreement, designate a court of first instance to exercise jurisdiction, provided that such agreement relates to a particular legal relation. ...

---

1 See Ministry of Justice, Laws & Regulations Database of The Republic of China, https://law.moj.gov.tw/ENG/LawClass/LawAll.aspx?pcode=B0010001 (amended on 28.11.2018, accessed 31.7.2019).

單元二 臺灣民事訴訟法

民事訴訟法[2]

第一章 法院
第一節 管轄

第1條
訴訟，由被告住所地之法院管轄。被告住所地之法院不能行使職權者，由其居所地之法院管轄。訴之原因事實發生於被告居所地者，亦得由其居所地之法院管轄。……

第10條
因不動產之物權或其分割或經界涉訟者，專屬不動產所在地之法院管轄。……

第24條
當事人得以合意定第一審管轄法院。但以關於由一定法律關係而生之訴訟為限。……

---

2 法務部，全國法規資料庫，https://law.moj.gov.tw/LawClass/LawAll.aspx?PCode=B0010001（31.7.2019，修訂於2018年11月28日）。

Article 25

A court obtains jurisdiction over an action where the defendant proceeds orally on the merits without contesting lack of jurisdiction.

Article 28

A court, upon determining a lack of jurisdiction over the action in whole or in part, will transfer the action to a court with jurisdiction either by ruling on the plaintiff's motion or on its own initiative. ...

CHAPTER II: PARTIES
Section 1: Capacity to be Parties and Capacity to Litigate

Article 40

Any person who has legal capacity has the capacity to be a party. ...

Article 45

Any person who has the capacity to undertake obligations through independent juridical acts has the capacity to litigate.

CHAPTER IV: LITIGATION PROCEEDINGS
Section 1: Pleadings

Article 116

Except as otherwise provided, a pleading submitted by a party shall indicate the following matters:

1. The full name and domicile or residence of the parties; in the case of a juridical person, an unincorporated association or agency, then its name and principal office, office or place of business.

第25條
被告不抗辯法院無管轄權,而爲本案之言詞辯論者,以其法院爲有管轄權之法院。

第28條
訴訟之全部或一部,法院認爲無管轄權者,依原告聲請或依職權以裁定移送於其管轄法院。……

第二章　當事人
第一節　當事人能力及訴訟能力

第40條
有權利能力者,有當事人能力。……

第45條
能獨立以法律行爲負義務者,有訴訟能力。

第四章　訴訟程序
第一節　當事人書狀

第116條
當事人書狀,除別有規定外,應記載下列各款事項:
一、當事人姓名及住所或居所;當事人爲法人、其他團體或機關者,其名稱及公務所、事務所或營業所。

2. The full name and domicile or residence of such party's statutory agent and advocate, if any, and the relationship between such party and the statutory agent;

3. The subject matter of the action;

4. Any motion or statement required to be made in the pleading;

5. The evidence necessary to prove the fact or to make a preliminary showing; ...

Section 6: Decision

Article 220

Except for decisions to be rendered in the form of a judgment as provided by this Code, all decisions shall be made in the form of a ruling.

PART II: PROCEDURE IN THE FIRST INSTANCE
CHAPTER I: ORDINARY PROCEEDING
Section 1: Initiation of an Action

Article 244

To initiate an action, a complaint shall be submitted to the court and indicate the following matters:

1. The parties and their statutory agents;

2. The claim and the transaction or occurrence giving rise to such claim; and

3. The demand for judgment for the relief sought.

It is advisable to indicate in the complaint all matters necessary for determining the competent court to exercise jurisdiction and the applicable proceeding. ...

二、有法定代理人、訴訟代理人者，其姓名、住所或居所，及法
　　定代理人與當事人之關係。

三、訴訟事件。

四、應為之聲明或陳述。

五、供證明或釋明用之證據。……

第六節　裁判

第220條
裁判，除依本法應用判決者外，以裁定行之。

第二編　第一審程序
第一章　通常程序
第一節　起訴

第244條
起訴，應以訴狀表明下列各款事項，提出於法院為之：

一、當事人及法定代理人。

二、訴訟標的及其原因事實。

三、應受判決事項之聲明。

訴狀內宜記載因定法院管轄及其適用程序所必要之事項。……

Article 249

In case of any of the following, the court shall dismiss the plaintiff's action by a ruling, but where the defect is rectifiable, the presiding judge shall order rectification within a designated period of time:

1. Where the civil court does not have subject matter jurisdiction over the action;

2. Where the court in which the action is pending does not have territorial jurisdiction over the action and cannot issue a ruling provided in Article 28;

3. Where the plaintiff or defendant lacks the capacity to be a party;

4. Where the plaintiff or defendant lacks the capacity to litigate and is not legally represented by his/her statutory agent; ...

Article 259

The defendant may, prior to the conclusion of the oral argument, raise a counterclaim against the plaintiff and the persons with regard to whom the counterclaim shall be adjudicated jointly in the court where the plaintiff's claim is pending.

Section 3: Evidence

Article 277

A party bears the burden of proof with regard to the facts which he / she alleges in his / her favor, except either where the law provides otherwise or where the circumstances render it manifestly unfair.

第249條

原告之訴，有下列各款情形之一，法院應以裁定駁回之。但其情形可以補正者，審判長應定期間先命補正：

一、訴訟事件不屬普通法院之權限，不能依第三十一條之二第二項規定移送者。

二、訴訟事件不屬受訴法院管轄而不能為第二十八條之裁定者。

三、原告或被告無當事人能力者。

四、原告或被告無訴訟能力，未由法定代理人合法代理者。……

第259條

被告於言詞辯論終結前，得在本訴繫屬之法院，對於原告及就訴訟標的必須合一確定之人提起反訴。

第三節　證據

第277條

當事人主張有利於己之事實者，就其事實有舉證之責任。但法律別有規定，或依其情形顯失公平者，不在此限。

Article 279

A fact need not be proved if it is alleged by a party and admitted by the opposing party in the preparatory pleadings, in the oral-argument sessions, or before the commissioned judge or the assigned judge. ...

Item 2: Examination of Witnesses

Article 302

Except as otherwise provided by the laws, every person is under a general duty to testify in an action between others.

Article 307

A witness may refuse to testify in case of any of the following:

1. Where the witness is the spouse, former spouse, or the betrothed, or the witness is or was a relative by blood within the fourth degree or a relative by marriage within the third degree to a party; ...

Item 3: Expert Testimony

Article 328

The person who has special knowledge or experience needed for giving expert testimony or who has been commissioned by a government agency to perform the function of giving expert opinion is under a duty to give expert testimony in an action between others.

第279條
當事人主張之事實，經他造於準備書狀內或言詞辯論時或在受命法官、受託法官前自認者，無庸舉證。……

第二目 人證

第302條
除法律別有規定外，不問何人，於他人之訴訟，有為證人之義務。

第307條
證人有下列各款情形之一者，得拒絕證言：
一、證人為當事人之配偶、前配偶、未婚配偶或四親等內之血親、三親等內之姻親或曾有此親屬關係者。……

第三目 鑑定

第328條
具有鑑定所需之特別學識經驗，或經機關委任有鑑定職務者，於他人之訴訟，有為鑑定人之義務。

Item 4: Documentary Evidence

Article 341

A document must be produced when it is identified to be introduced as documentary evidence.

Article 344

A party has the duty to produce the following documents:

1. Documents to which such party has made reference in the course of the litigation proceeding;

2. Documents which the opposing party may require the delivery or an inspection thereof pursuant to the applicable laws; ...

Where the content of a document provided in the fifth subparagraph of the preceding paragraph involves the privacy or business secret of a party or a third person and the resulting disclosure may result in material harm to such party or third person, the party may refuse to produce such document. Notwithstanding, in order to determine whether the party has a justifiable reason to refuse the production of the document, the court, if necessary, may order the party to produce the document and examine it in private.

Article 357

Except in the case where the opposing party does not dispute the authenticity of the document, the party who introduces a private document shall prove its authenticity.

第四目　書證

第341條
聲明書證，應提出文書爲之。

第344條
下列各款文書，當事人有提出之義務：

一、該當事人於訴訟程序中曾經引用者。

二、他造依法律規定，得請求交付或閱覽者。……

前項第五款之文書內容，涉及當事人或第三人之隱私或業務秘密，如予公開，有致該當事人或第三人受重大損害之虞者，當事人得拒絕提出。但法院爲判斷其有無拒絕提出之正當理由，必要時，得命其提出，並以不公開之方式行之。

第357條
私文書應由舉證人證其眞正。但他造於其眞正無爭執者，不在此限。

Item 5: Inspection

Article 366
Where necessary, the inspection shall be represented in drawings or pictures which shall be annexed to the transcript; tapes, videotapes, or other relevant objects in connection with the inspection may be annexed to the dossier.

Item 5-1: Examination of Parties

Article 367-1
The court may examine the parties on its own initiative when it considers it necessary. ...

Section 5: Judgments

Article 381
Where an action is mature for decision, the court shall enter a final judgment. ...

Article 385
Where one of the parties fails to appear at the oral-argument session, the court may, on the appearing party's motion, enter a default judgment based on the appearing party's arguments; where the party who fails to appear is summoned and fails to appear again, the court may also on its own initiative enter a default judgment based on the appearing party's arguments. ...

第五目　勘驗

第366條

勘驗，於必要時，應以圖畫或照片附於筆錄；並得以錄音、錄影或其他有關物件附於卷宗。

第五目之一　當事人訊問

第367-1條

法院認為必要時，得依職權訊問當事人。……

第五節　判決

第381條

訴訟達於可為裁判之程度者，法院應為終局判決。……

第385條

言詞辯論期日，當事人之一造不到場者，得依到場當事人之聲請，由其一造辯論而為判決；不到場之當事人，經再次通知而仍不到場者，並得依職權由一造辯論而為判決。……

Article 398

A final judgment becomes binding upon the expiration of the period of time for taking an appeal from a judgment. Notwithstanding, a timely appeal taken from a final judgment in conformity with the law shall prevent that judgment from becoming binding.

A final judgment from which no appeal may be taken becomes binding upon its announcement, or, if it is not announced, upon its publication.

Article 400

Except as otherwise provided, res judicata exists as to a claim adjudicated in a final judgment with binding effect. ...

PART III: APPELLATE PROCEDURE
CHAPTER I: PROCEDURE IN THE SECOND INSTANCE

Article 437

Except as otherwise provided, an appeal may be taken from the final judgment entered in the first instance to the court of second instance having jurisdiction.

Article 440

An appeal from a judgment entered in the first instance must be filed within the peremptory period of twenty days following the service of such judgment. ...

Article 441

An appeal must be filed with a notice of appeal, which notice shall specify the following matters and be submitted to the original court of first instance:

第398條

判決，於上訴期間屆滿時確定。但於上訴期間內有合法之上訴者，阻其確定。

不得上訴之判決，於宣示時確定；不宣示者，於公告時確定。

第400條

除別有規定外，確定之終局判決就經裁判之訴訟標的，有既判力。……

第三編　上訴審程序

第一章　第二審程序

第437條

對於第一審之終局判決，除別有規定外，得上訴於管轄第二審之法院。

第440條

提起上訴，應於第一審判決送達後二十日之不變期間內為之。……

第441條

提起上訴，應以上訴狀表明下列各款事項，提出於原第一審法院為之：

1. The parties and their statutory agents;
2. The judgment entered in the first instance ...
3. The extent of appeal and the demand how such judgment should be reversed or amended; and
4. The basis for the appeal.

The basis for the appeal shall specify the following matters:
1. The reasons why the original judgment should be reversed or amended;
2. Facts and evidence in support of the basis provided in the preceding subparagraph.

Article 451

In case of a material defect in the litigation proceeding of the first instance, the court of second instance may reverse the original judgment and remand the case to the original court, provided that such action is considered necessary for purposes of maintaining the system of court instances. ...

CHAPTER II: PROCEDURE IN THE THIRD INSTANCE

Article 466

No appeal may be taken from the judgment of a court of second instance on an action arising from proprietary rights when the value of the interests in such appeal is not more than NTD 1,000,000. ...

Article 467

No appeal may be taken to the court of third instance except on the ground that the original judgment is in contravention of the laws and regulations.

一、當事人及法定代理人。

二、第一審判決……。

三、對於第一審判決不服之程度，及應如何廢棄或變更之聲明。

四、上訴理由。

上訴理由應表明下列各款事項：

一、應廢棄或變更原判決之理由。

二、關於前款理由之事實及證據。

第451條

第一審之訴訟程序有重大之瑕疵者，第二審法院得廢棄原判決，而將該事件發回原法院。但以因維持審級制度認為必要時為限。……

第二章　第三審程序

第466條

對於財產權訴訟之第二審判決，如因上訴所得受之利益，不逾新臺幣一百萬元者，不得上訴。……

第467條

上訴第三審法院，非以原判決違背法令為理由，不得為之。

Article 469

A judgment shall be automatically held in contravention of the laws and regulations in the following situations:

1. Where the court is not organized in conformity with the laws;

2. Where a judge who should have disqualified himself / herself by operation of law or by decision has participated in making the decision;

3. Where the court lacks the subject matter jurisdiction or acts in violation of exclusive jurisdiction;

4. Where the parties are not legally represented in the action;

5. Where the court violates the provision that the oral argument should be open to the public;

6. Where the judgment does not provide reasons or provides contradictory reasons.

Article 469-1

A court of third instance must permit an appeal taken to a court of third instance on grounds other than those provided in the preceding article.

The permission provided in the preceding paragraph shall be granted only when such an appeal is necessary for the continued development of the laws, or to ensure coherence of decisions, or when other legal opinions involved are significant in principle.

第469條

有下列各款情形之一者，其判決當然為違背法令：

一、判決法院之組織不合法者。

二、依法律或裁判應迴避之法官參與裁判者。

三、法院於權限之有無辨別不當或違背專屬管轄之規定者。

四、當事人於訴訟未經合法代理者。

五、違背言詞辯論公開之規定者。

六、判決不備理由或理由矛盾者。

第469-1條

以前條所列各款外之事由提起第三審上訴者，須經第三審法院之許可。

前項許可，以從事法之續造、確保裁判之一致性或其他所涉及之法律見解具有原則上重要性者為限。

EXERCISES
單元三　練習

Mark the odd word（選意義不同的字）：

residence – domicile – address – venue

absence – lack – shortage – trial

evidence – jury – testimony – witness

attorney – advocate – expert – lawyer

argument –　ground – reason – verdict

adjudication – judgment – jurisdiction – ruling

Fill in (choose from the following types of courts): appellate court (court of appeals, appeals court);　juvenile court; lower court (court of first instance); moot court; tribunal

	一級法院	trial court, where a case is heard for the first time
	少年法庭	court where minors are tried
	法院，法庭，審理團	specialized court
	模擬法庭，實習法庭	court where hypothetical cases are simulated
	上訴法院	court reviewing a case from a lower court

The court system:

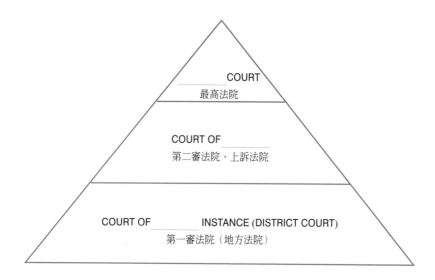

Fill in (choose from the following persons in court): advocate; appellant; bailiff; clerk; defendant / respondent; judge; jury; plaintiff / petitioner; prosecutor; reasonably prudent person; (expert) witness

	法官	public official who has the authority to hear and decide cases
	原告	party starting a lawsuit
	被告	party being sued
	上訴人	party appealing to a higher court
	辯護人，律師	lawyer, attorney
	檢察官	government attorney who institutes criminal proceedings
	陪審團	group of persons sworn in to determine the facts of a case
	（鑑定人）證人	person providing testimony (in form of professional opinion)
	書記官	court employee

	法警	court officer responsible for maintaining order during trial
	合理謹慎的人	hypothetical person exercising ordinary care and skill

Fill in (choose from the following documents and phrases): affidavit; answer; complaint; injunction; motion; notice; pleading; writ; to draft a document; to file a document with an authority; to issue a document; to serve a document on someone (or to serve someone with a document); to submit a document to an authority

	起訴狀	plaintiff's first pleading, which initiates a lawsuit
	答辯	defendant's written response to a complaint
	訴狀	formal written statement
	宣誓書，口供書	written statement made under oath
	通知書	formal notification
	令狀	formal written order of a sovereign authority
	動議	application for a court order
	強制令、禁止令	court order compelling a party to do or refrain from doing a specified act
	起草一份文件	to prepare an outline
	發布一份資料	to publish officially
	提出，提交	to present a document for approval
	送達	to officially deliver a document to a party

Fill in (choose from the following principles): due process; good faith; statute of limitations; burden of proof; beyond a reasonable doubt; clear and convincing evidence; preponderance of evidence

	正當程序	formal proceedings carried out regularly, fairly, and in accordance with established rules and principles
	誠信，善意	in accordance with standards of honesty, trust, sincerity; opposite of bad faith
	訴訟時效法規	a statute defining the period within which legal action may be taken
	舉證責任	responsibility of producing sufficient evidence in support of a fact or issue
	優勢證據	more likely than not
	清楚且令人信服的證據	evidence showing a high probability of truth of the factual matter at issue
	超越合理的懷疑（適用於刑訴）	no plausible reason to believe otherwise (typically applies in criminal proceedings)

Find the corresponding noun:

VERB	NOUN
admit	
answer	
complain	
deny	
determine	
disclose	
discover	
dismiss	

doubt	
evidence	
examine	
hear	
lack	
prevent	
prove	
reside	
request	
question	
sue	
summarize	

Find the corresponding adjective:

NOUN	ADJECTIVE
constitution	
controversy	
convince	
effect	
error	
illegality	
procedure	
relevance	

Find the corresponding noun and adjective:

VERB	NOUN	ADJECTIVE
affirm		
differ		
dispute		

exceed		
exist		
persuade		

Find the corresponding noun and person:

VERB	NOUN	PERSON
appeal		
claim		
defend		
judge		
litigate		
produce		
prosecute		
receive		
respond		

Choose the best answer:

1. To initiate an action, a _____ shall be submitted to the court.

   (A) counterclaim   (B) complaint   (C) collateral

   (D) commencement

2. A party bears the burden of _____ with regard to the facts which he/she alleges in his/her favor, except either where the law provides otherwise or where the circumstances render it manifestly unfair.

   (A) presumption   (B) precedent   (C) proof   (D) privilege

3. Where an action is mature for decision, the court shall enter a final

   _____.

   (A) juvenile   (B) judgment   (C) jurisdiction   (D) jury

4. Regarding the settlement proceeding under R.O.C. Code of Civil Procedure, which one of the following is incorrect? (100年司法官)

(A) When both parties are close to agreeing on a settlement, they may ask the court to provide a settlement proposal within the scope specified by the parties.

(B) Where settlement is reached, a settlement transcript shall be made in writing.

(C) The court may seek settlement at any time irrespective of the phase of the proceeding reached.

(D) A final settlement shall not have the same effect as a final judgment, which means the settlement has no binding effect.

5. _____ means power and authority of a court to hear and determine a judicial proceeding, and power to render particular judgment in question. (100年司法官)

(A) Territoriality   (B) Jurisdiction   (C) Administration
(D) Petition

6. Morgan has been sued in a competent court in a civil case. It means that he has the obligation to _____ before the court. (100年律師)
(A) reach   (B) approach   (C) arrive   (D) appear

7. Pursuant to Article 1 of R.O.C. Code of Civil Procedure, "A defendant may be sued in the court for the place of the defendant's domicile or, when that court cannot exercise _____, in the court for the place of defendant's residence." (101年司法官)

(A) sovereignty   (B) judgment   (C) immunity   (D) jurisdiction

8. Which of the following is the correct description of "Civil Proce-

dure"? (102年司法官)

(A) Annual examination that must be taken by many who wish to become government employees.

(B) The rules applicable to constitutional civil rights claims, such as an alleged denial of due process of law.

(C) The rules applicable to civil litigation.

(D) Court-enforced rules of civility, especially as they may apply to trial lawyers.

9. Pursuant to Article 116 of R.O.C. Code of Civil Procedure, "Parties may submit to the court by telefax or by any other technological devices, and _____ so submitted shall take full effect as if they were submitted in the original copy." (102年律師)

(A) application form　(B) pleadings　(C) transcriptions

(D) verdicts

10. Jonathan negligently breaks two valuable vases of Evelyn in front of her. Three years later, Evelyn asks Jonathan to compensate her for her loss for the first time. Under Article 197 of R.O.C. Civil Code, Jonathan may assert _____ defense and refuse to pay. (106年司法官律師)

(A) statute of limitations　(B) statute of expiration　(C) expiration of effectiveness　(D) expiration of time

ANSWERS
單元四　答案

Mark the odd word（選意義不同的字）：

residence – domicile – address – venue 審判地點

absence – lack – shortage – trial 審判

evidence – jury – testimony – witness 陪審團

attorney – advocate – expert – lawyer 鑑定人

argument – ground – reason – verdict 判決

adjudication – judgment – jurisdiction – ruling 管轄權

Types of courts

lower court (court of first instance)	一級法院	trial court, where a case is heard for the first time
juvenile court	少年法庭	court where minors are tried
tribunal	法院，法庭，審理團	specialized court
moot court	模擬法庭，實習法庭	court where hypothetical cases are simulated
appellate court (court of appeals, appeals court)	上訴法院	court reviewing a case from a lower court

The court system:

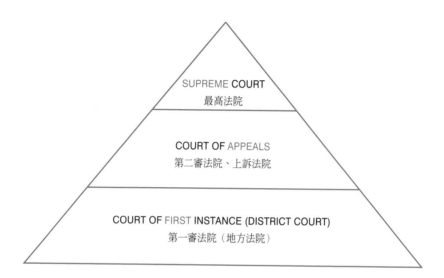

SUPREME COURT
最高法院

COURT OF APPEALS
第二審法院、上訴法院

COURT OF FIRST INSTANCE (DISTRICT COURT)
第一審法院（地方法院）

Persons in court

judge	法官	public official who has the authority to hear and decide cases
plaintiff / petitioner	原告	party starting a lawsuit
defendant / respondent	被告	party being sued
appellant	上訴人	party appealing to a higher court
advocate	辯護人，律師	lawyer, attorney
prosecutor	檢察官	government attorney who institutes criminal proceedings
jury	陪審團	group of persons sworn in to determine the facts of a case
(expert) witness	（鑑定人）證人	person providing testimony (in form of professional opinion)
clerk	書記官	court employee

| bailiff | 法警 | court officer responsible for maintaining order during trial |
| reasonably prudent person | 合理謹慎的人 | hypothetical person exercising ordinary care and skill |

Documents in court

complaint	起訴狀	plaintiff's first pleading, which initiates a lawsuit
answer	答辯	defendant's written response to a complaint
pleading	訴狀	formal written statement
affidavit	宣誓書，口供書	written statement made under oath
notice	通知書	formal notification
writ	令狀	formal written order of a sovereign authority
motion	動議	application for a court order
injunction	強制令、禁止令	court order compelling a party to do or refrain from doing a specified act
to draft a document	起草一份文件	to prepare an outline
to issue a document	發布一份資料	to publish officially
to submit a document to an authority	提出，提交	to present a document for approval
to serve a document on someone (or to serve someone with a document)	送達	to officially deliver a document to a party

Principles

due process	正當程序	formal proceedings carried out regularly, fairly, and in accordance with established rules and principles
good faith	誠信，善意	in accordance with standards of honesty, trust, sincerity; opposite of bad faith
statute of limitations	訴訟時效法規	a statute defining the period within which legal action may be taken
burden of proof	舉證責任	responsibility of producing sufficient evidence in support of a fact or issue
preponderance of evidence	優勢證據	more likely than not
clear and convincing evidence	清楚且令人信服的證據	evidence showing a high probability of truth of the factual matter at issue
beyond a reasonable doubt	超越合理的懷疑（適用於刑訴）	no plausible reason to believe otherwise (typically applies in criminal proceedings)

Find the corresponding noun:

VERB	NOUN
admit	admission 承認
answer	answer 答辯狀
complain	complaint 起訴狀
deny	denial 否認
determine	determination 確定
disclose	disclosure 公開
discover	discovery 發現
dismiss	dismissal 駁回

doubt	doubt 懷疑
evidence	evidence 證據
examine	examination 檢查
hear	hearing 聽審
lack	lack 缺乏
prevent	prevention 防止
prove	proof 證據
reside	residence 居所
request	request 請求
question	question 詢問
sue	suit 訴訟
summarize	summary 摘要

Find the corresponding adjective:

NOUN	ADJECTIVE
constitution	constitutional 合憲的
controversy	controversial 有爭議的
convince	convincing 令人信服的
effect	effective 有效的
error	erroneous 錯誤的
illegality	illegal 非法的
procedure	procedural 程序的
relevance	relevant 相關的

Find the corresponding noun and adjective:

VERB	NOUN	ADJECTIVE
affirm	affirmation 肯定	affirmative 肯定的
differ	difference 差別	different 不同的
dispute	dispute 爭議	disputed 有爭議的
exceed	excess 超額	excessive 超額的
exist	existence 生存	existing 現存的
persuade	persuasion 說服	persuasive 有說服力的

Find the corresponding noun and person:

VERB	NOUN	PERSON
appeal	appeal 上訴	appellant 上訴人
claim	claim 主張	claimant 主張者
defend	defense 防衛	defendant 被告
judge	judgment 判決	judge 法官
litigate	litigation 訴訟	litigant 訴訟當事人
produce	production 生產	producer 生產者
prosecute	prosecution 起訴	prosecutor 檢察官
receive	receipt 收據	recipient 受領人
respond	response 答辯	respondent 被告

Choose the best answer:

1. To initiate an action, a _____ shall be submitted to the court
   (A) counterclaim (B) complaint (C) collateral
   (D) commencement

2. A party bears the burden of _____ with regard to the facts which he/she alleges in his/her favor, except either where the law provides otherwise or where the circumstances render it manifestly unfair.

(A) presumption (B) precedent (C) proof (D) privilege

3. Where an action is mature for decision, the court shall enter a final _____.

(A) juvenile (B) judgment (C) jurisdiction (D) jury

4. Regarding the settlement proceeding under R.O.C. Code of Civil Procedure, which one of the following is incorrect? (100年司法官)

(A) When both parties are close to agreeing on a settlement, they may ask the court to provide a settlement proposal within the scope specified by the parties.

(B) Where settlement is reached, a settlement transcript shall be made in writing.

(C) The court may seek settlement at any time irrespective of the phase of the proceeding reached.

(D) A final settlement shall not have the same effect as a final judgment, which means the settlement has no binding effect.

5. _____ means power and authority of a court to hear and determine a judicial proceeding, and power to render particular judgment in question. (100年司法官)

(A) Territoriality (B) Jurisdiction (C) Administration
(D) Petition

6. Morgan has been sued in a competent court in a civil case. It means that he has the obligation to _____ before the court. (100年律師)
   (A) reach (B) approach (C) arrive (D) appear

7. Pursuant to Article 1 of R.O.C. Code of Civil Procedure, "A defendant may be sued in the court for the place of the defendant's domicile or, when that court cannot exercise _____, in the court for the place of defendant's residence." (101年司法官)
   (A) sovereignty (B) judgment (C) immunity (D) jurisdiction

8. Which of the following is the correct description of "Civil Procedure"? (102年司法官)
   (A) Annual examination that must be taken by many who wish to become government employees.
   (B) The rules applicable to constitutional civil rights claims, such as an alleged denial of due process of law.
   (C) The rules applicable to civil litigation.
   (D) Court-enforced rules of civility, especially as they may apply to trial lawyers.

9. Pursuant to Article 116 of R.O.C. Code of Civil Procedure, "Parties may submit to the court by telefax or by any other technological devices, and _____ so submitted shall take full effect as if they were submitted in the original copy." (102年律師)
   (A) application form (B) pleadings (C) transcriptions
   (D) verdicts

10. Jonathan negligently breaks two valuable vases of Evelyn in front of her. Three years later, Evelyn asks Jonathan to compensate her for her loss for the first time. Under Article 197 of R.O.C. Civil Code, Jonathan may assert _____ defense and refuse to pay. (106年司法官律師)

(A) statute of limitations　(B) statute of expiration　(C) expiration of effectiveness　(D) expiration of time

圖書館出版品預行編目資料

學英文／邱彥琳著. －－三版.－－臺
北市：五南圖書出版股份有限公司，
2019.11
面； 公分
3N 978-957-763-657-7（平裝）

法學英語   2.讀本

5.18   108015205

1QJ5

法學英文

作　　　者 ─ 邱彥琳(150.7)

發 行 人 ─ 楊榮川

總 經 理 ─ 楊士清

總 編 輯 ─ 楊秀麗

副總編輯 ─ 劉靜芬

責任編輯 ─ 林佳瑩、呂伊真

封面設計 ─ 王麗娟

出 版 者 ─ 五南圖書出版股份有限公司

地　　　址：106台北市大安區和平東路二段339號4樓

電　　　話：(02)2705-5066　　傳　　　真：(02)2706-6100

網　　　址：https://www.wunan.com.tw

電子郵件：wunan@wunan.com.tw

劃撥帳號：01068953

戶　　　名：五南圖書出版股份有限公司

法律顧問　林勝安律師

出版日期　2012年 8 月初版一刷
　　　　　2015年 9 月二版一刷（共二刷）
　　　　　2019年11月三版一刷
　　　　　2024年 6 月三版五刷

定　　　價　新臺幣520元

經典永恆・名著常在

五十週年的獻禮——經典名著文庫

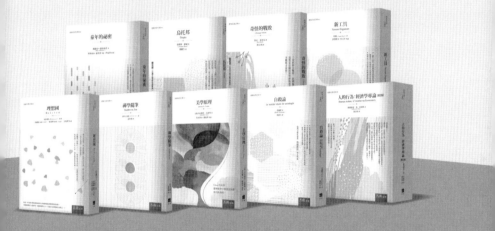

五南，五十年了，半個世紀，人生旅程的一大半，走過來了。

思索著，邁向百年的未來歷程，能為知識界、文化學術界作些什麼？

在速食文化的生態下，有什麼值得讓人雋永品味的？

歷代經典・當今名著，經過時間的洗禮，千錘百鍊，流傳至今，光芒耀人；

不僅使我們能領悟前人的智慧，同時也增深加廣我們思考的深度與視野。

我們決心投入巨資，有計畫的系統梳選，成立「經典名著文庫」，

希望收入古今中外思想性的、充滿睿智與獨見的經典、名著。

這是一項理想性的、永續性的巨大出版工程。

不在意讀者的眾寡，只考慮它的學術價值，力求完整展現先哲思想的軌跡；

為知識界開啟一片智慧之窗，營造一座百花綻放的世界文明公園，

任君遨遊、取菁吸蜜、嘉惠學子！